HERO AND THE TERROR

MICHAEL BLODGETT

HERO
AND THE
TERROR

HARMONY BOOKS / NEW YORK

Published by Harmony Books, a division of Crown Publishers, Inc.,
One Park Avenue, New York, New York 10016 and simultaneously
in Canada by General Publishing Company Limited

HARMONY BOOKS and colophon are trademarks of Crown Publishers, Inc.
Manufactured in the United States of America

Library of Congress Cataloging in Publication Data

Blodgett, Michael.
Hero and the terror.
I. Title.
PS3552.L6355H4   813′.54   82-6212
                                AACR2

ISBN: 0-517-54692-2

Designed by Ken Sansone
Typed by Roy Wallenstein, Starlight. Los Angeles.

10 9 8 7 6 5 4 3 2 1
First Edition

For Esther Mitgang, who believes,

and for Lanetta

Herrera Fiddleman
Poetry II B
UCLA Extension
Tues. Thurs. Eve.

To Feel

To feel to feel is unreal
unreal
You're not real with your spiel
you're not real
At the meal you can't conceal
you're a heel a heel
It's too late for your fate too late
But your mate thinks you're great
great as eight
Trouble is he knows ten twelve
and twenty
This you know and it plagues you
and plenty
So you go to extremes with your
schemes with your schemes
And cry long and hard for
your dreams
Under it all ho ho ho
it's beginning to show to grow to blow
cause it's never as good as it seems
But you starch up your lace
just to cover your face
and meet all your foes with a whim
The trouble is that your art
is not playing the part
and your heart has but truth
just for him.

BOOK ONE

C

ome on, Simon, join the party, have some fun. It's Merry Christmas time."

The legal secretary they called Slam puckered her lips and kissed the air in Simon Moon's direction. Simon thought that Slam had a sexy mouth, pouty, good enough to stick your dick into, even though she often said that her lips were too full. But that wasn't what was on his mind.

It was her soft-skinned throat and fear for his own safety if he did what he was capable of doing. He had never considered a female like Slam, a female with a personality. Not that he gave a damn or thought that it mattered. They're all no good, he figured. In one way or another.

Simon Moon always went for the innocuous ones. The indecisive, lost, gutless ones. The sick women that didn't know love or if they knew it, withheld it. But it had been years, the summer of 1979, since he'd laid a hand on one of them.

Simon had tried to be good. He'd tried to be a family man,

to practice law, to defend those dope-dealer scum and lowlife pimps and make a buck. He maintained an obsequious, even kiss-ass posture and somehow avoided staring at the women around him who should be taught a lesson. But now his loathing was back.

It had returned by degrees—like an activated, gnawing, low-grade virus—ever present, creeping, eager to consume. Simon had tried desperately to hold onto sensible, level-headed thinking, but his faculty for pretense, for keeping his secret, was gone. And in a certain way, like peeling a scab, it felt good.

Standing there now, gaping at Slam and smiling pointlessly, perspiring and about ready to shake to pieces, he realized that the moment was upon him. That there was probably no saving himself from himself, from his insanity, any longer.

Turning, Slam bumped into Simon's open office door, spilling most of her glass of champagne onto the dark-brown carpet. Laughing, she shook her shiny auburn curls and rubbed at the wetness with her foot. She paused to become transfixed by it.

He despised her. His anger twisted him into a hunch. He tried to stand straight. He was going to scream it at her if she didn't leave. But he yelled it in his head. You fucking tramp . . . get out of here before. . . .

"Well," she said, looking up with a sigh, "that's why they call me Slam. Come on, Simon, let's find the mistletoe." She wiggled her bottom, looked at it herself admiringly and said, "I've waited all year. Come on, big and sexy, tomorrow is Christmas Eve."

Then she did something he had never seen her do before. She looked directly at his crotch. "Come on," she added in an urgent tone. His prostate tingled. He felt dizzy.

Simon quickly understood that she was a fraud. That she was being nice for Christmas. His armpits and the nape of his neck were soaked. His hands ached. He fought for propriety.

"All right, in a minute, Slam . . ." His mouth was cotton. "Let me clean off my desk. Go ahead, I'll be right there."

"I'll be waiting," she said with a beckoning smile, and off she went down the long dark office hallway. She said something to the others when she joined them. About me, Simon told himself with a shudder. He watched them all laugh together cliquishly and look his way.

"Cocksuckers," Simon mumbled. He closed his office door. He held it shut and leaned against it with his strong shoulder and all his weight. He stopped breathing and cocked his head to listen. They were laughing at him again. Then the whole universe began to laugh and he wished he could die. He held himself and rocked. He gritted his teeth and bit his tongue until he swallowed the taste of blood, which alleviated his thinking. He moved along the door to hang against the wall. He listened. The laughing stopped. Breathing a long sigh of relief, he felt better.

Observing himself, his reflection in the darkening windows across his wood-paneled office, Simon moved from foot to foot to make his burly shoulders roll. His shadow appeared on the wall, a shifting range of mountains.

Simon had built his upper-body strength to its maximum. But it was more of an awkward than a graceful build. The kind of brutish development that a lame man might possess. He could dead lift a horse and had never been beaten arm wrestling.

A red beacon flashed in the dusky evening sky, way out past his reflected image. A sudden anxious chill came over him and he watched himself tremble before walking over to the window. Standing next to the cool glass, Simon looked down over Westwood Village.

Traffic was bad as it always was in the evening. He thought that the last-minute Christmas shoppers were adding even more confusion to the scene. Red-and-white automobile lights snaked along through the black. Bustling pedestrians jammed the street corners, waiting. Simon watched them chitter until white-gloved policemen let them crowd into the intersections and cross.

Amidst the bright neon lights along Westwood Boulevard he found the black roof of the Westwood Crown movie theater. He stepped aside for a better view but the more he examined it, the more vague, shifting and incomprehensible it became. His stomach felt queasy.

Looking up to observe the red beacon throbbing off in the distance, Simon stared at the reflection of his face. It was a double image. He blinked his eyes and wondered if he were sick, delirious.

Then there was a shrill manic laugh in the office and Simon had to admit he'd been the best pick in the firm, the one best suited to play Santa Claus. He'd have picked himself if given the choice.

Simon put on the pillow, rouge and the red suit, and handed out the gifts. He watched the pile of presents and saw to it that Mr. Dirkson, his boss, *the* boss, was given his gifts with appropriate timing, pomp and ceremony.

Dirkson said that Simon was a "good man" and a "great Santa Claus," and slapped him so hard on the back that one of Simon's suspenders popped, causing Santa to have a lopsided belly. Simon felt self-conscious and guilty about being singled out and touched that way by the top lawyer in the corporation who, on this holiday occasion, seemed a reconcilable man. A man who the rest of the year was a dislikable, recalcitrant old shyster prick.

After the gifts were distributed, Simon felt uncomfortable and silly in the ill-fitting red suit and finally became humiliated and depressed over being there at all. He knew that the women were staring, snickering. It's a cinch, he told himself, I'm never going back to that fucking bunch. Suzanne, Betty, Sylvia and Mary Ann would still be there. Women he'd watched.

He tried to picture them but couldn't. They were all the same. Fish, he told himself beginning to perspire again. Gaping-mouthed, vacant-eyed, numbskulls, swimming exactly where they were told. Yes-ing and no-ing, serving, imitating the men in their lives—their bosses.

A sudden surge of anger rushed over him and he could have gone for them right then but he shook his head back and forth to dispel that kind of thinking.

Standing at his desk, Simon popped open the alligator watch box, his Christmas gift from the firm. Removing his own watch he tried the new one on and didn't like it. He didn't like his own watch either and put them both into his top desk drawer next to the small green velvet ring box that was Carol's Christmas present. He shut the drawer.

He opened and closed his hand to regain circulation in his wrist. The terrible aching came as it always did and Simon held his huge hands up like a doctor who was ready for rubber gloves and surgery.

Back at the window, he rested his forehead against the cool plate glass and closed his eyes. He remembered that his wife had asked his mother and father for Christmas.

The thought of his parents made Simon nauseous. He despised them to the point of exasperation and would have disposed of them both long ago were it not for the feeling of impotence that came when he was alone with them.

He jammed his forehead against the glass and concentrated until the hum of the big office building was all he could hear. The sound helped to soothe him.

The telephone rang. He glanced distractedly at the jangling thing, at the last white light, his private line. That will be Carol, he thought. It's her time. It will be my wife urging me on, wanting me to be right. To be like all the rest of the men in Westwood on Christmas. To be responsive, cheerful and normal.

When he answered she said "Hello, darling" in a tone that somehow always seemed syrupy sick to him. As if he were a child. Carol said "Hello, darling" in her thick salutary tone and Simon thought, but she means it, she loves me, treasures me, or something like that, so it seems.

Carol said, "Merry Christmas to Simon," and Simon said, "Yes, sweetheart . . . Merry Christmas to you."

And she said, "You are so sweet."

Simon guessed that he was sweet but that Carol didn't understand. He thought that she might go through the motions of trying but she seemed to see only one of him. She'd announce, "I like strong men." She'd say it supportively as though he were one, and Simon would sulk away, aching and feeling ill, wondering, how in the fuck do I integrate my selves?

Simon held the beige telephone receiver away from his ear but continued to listen. Carol talked about the holidays and all she had planned, about his mother and father. Simon perspired and trembled. He wanted to tell her, to insist again, not to invite them, but it was no use.

She spoke lovingly and Simon pictured her at home standing against the kitchen counter, the lovely dark woman he knew her to be, and he said to himself, I love Carol. Carol is the right one. She is the best one. She is a perfect love. If there ever was a good woman, it is Carol.

"I want to take you to bed," he said. After an appropriately shy pause to gather her thoughts on the subject, Carol came back with what he considered her completely *right,* totally accommodating disposition.

"Oh, you do, do you? Does that mean you'll give it the powerful Simon Moon twist . . . ?"

"Yes," he said, and he felt himself flush with the feeling of sex. But he knew that she might just as easily have said, "Oh, you do, do you? That's sweet . . . let's talk about it later." Simon figured, with it being Christmas and all, she would give him a little verbal incentive. It worked too. It made him think of her fragrance and what kept him in line.

Carol's sexy conversations were prompted by her observations, her calculations about him and what it took to keep him moving onward and upward through life. He figured that she manipulated him. "Is it time to talk sexy? Hmmm. Let's see. It's been Tuesday, Wednesday, Thursday . . . How about it, Mother? 'Tis Friday. 'Tis sure enough Friday and time to say, 'Come on Sweet Simon, let's talk about that big old Simon twist. Let's talk about a reward. Let's talk about . . . my wet pussy.'"

And from the cage in the back of his mind, Simon would howl, oweee Mama, yeah . . . yes, yes owee Carol Mama, hot pussy yeah. It makes me good, if you know what I mean. It makes me keep these twisted paws off of dem sweet necks.

Simon hung his tongue out like a horny dog and looked to see his reflection in the dark office window. The red beacon pounded into the shadowy overcast sky at the Santa Monica Airport. He watched himself pant.

8

The office door flew open and Slam barged in. "Simon . . . Come on, we . . . Oops, sorry . . . I didn't know you were on the phone."

She slammed the door behind her when she went out.

Simon said, "Yes, yes, I'm listening, sweetheart," and was suddenly reminded of what his friend Andy called "a woman's job." Andy was a smartass lawyer with good sense. Simon liked him despite the fact that many others found him offensive. Andy always laughed when he spoke. But he was positive about what he thought. You could tell by the self-determined look in his dark eyes.

"What do you think, Simon? Don't be a dumb goy. Don't be a schmuck. Christ almighty, man, they've got a job. Look at it like that, man, a job. They're born and raised for it, to get that dick hard and keep it that way . . . all the way to the bank. Nothing . . . nothing means nothing to them, Simon . . . but security, getting the guy to come through, to provide for them. That's the name of the game. You might think you've got a sure thing, then some guy with a lot of bread comes along and boom, she's gone . . . gone-o."

Simon would listen to Andy and laugh and not be afraid to bullshit with him in an open braggadocious way. "Not with me they don't gone-o, pal. Not the way I leave them, lying there, fucked good in the mornings with their eyes rolled up into their head saying, 'Oh baby, you know what I like . . .'"

And Andy would laugh as though Simon were still a kid talking baby talk and say, "Aw man, bullshit. Sex ain't that much to them. Grow up, man, it's security. Don't be a schmuck all of your life. Besides, some of those guys with dough fuck okay too—did you know that, Simon? I'll bet you never thought of that. And if it's not too hot who cares? They sure don't. They've got their security and a memory or two of some stud, maybe even a real live stud on the side if they've got the guts. Or they've got their imagination and a vibrator. You see what I mean, Simon—I mean wise up before you get your ass in a sling."

Simon never understood what it was that Andy wanted him

to wise up to, but figured that Andy liked to talk or maybe needed to talk, and Simon considered himself enough of a friend to listen.

Sometimes Simon suspected that Andy might be right. He couldn't ever tell though because the women Simon asked, his clients, hookers or Carol, said that it was a theory based on nonsense. Then they would lay you back and take charge of your body and your mind and you'd forget that there ever was a theory, or an Andy.

Simon interrupted Carol's Christmas dialogue by asking, "Do you control me with your tongue?"

Carol laughed a good loud one at the other end and said, "Aren't you sweet."

Carol said that Charlotte, their baby, missed him.

Although it seemed that he'd seen little Charlotte that very morning, he couldn't remember what she looked like. How do you suppose you could have forgotten that? he asked himself. You must be crazy. Simon wondered how a three-year-old could miss anything but food and sleep anyway. But he guessed that Carol was right and it pleased him to be missed by the little girl.

Carol stopped talking. The phone was quiet. Finally she said something and Simon answered. Carol spoke again and Simon responded. It all seemed like nonsense, every word. He hung up the phone, put his face onto the backs of his hands and began to weep. It was a frustrated, enraged weeping, without tears.

Suddenly, with a scream, he bolted to his office door. Leaving his office, Simon raced down the long, dark paneled hallway to the emergency exit. The abrasive party sounds clashed in his ears. He thought he heard his name called but wouldn't look back.

Down the concrete stairs he ran. Down and down, leaping, pursued by the voracious milieu. He didn't stop to think until he had dashed the fourteen flights to the street.

Waiting with the mob at the corner to cross, Simon overheard two women concurring that it didn't seem like Christmas without snow. Their smugness brought a resentment that made his face burn.

His hands hurt and his knees felt suddenly weak as he stood in the ticket line of the Westwood Crown theater.

He steadied himself on the person in front of him who turned to look questioningly and ask, "Are you okay?"

Simon sat in the front row of the theater and easily lost track of the blurred images before him. Images that appeared now as hallucinogenic blobs of flowing color. The loud indistinguishable sound track made his inner ears pain, the bottoms of his feet tingle.

"Where's my Coca-Cola?" he asked.

Looking around, he couldn't remember whether or not he had bought a treat. He had absolutely no recollection of being at the candy counter and had to laugh because the next thing he knew he was digging the wax off the bottom of an empty popcorn carton with his fingernails.

Upstairs, Simon paced the flamingo pink hallway. He walked from the men's room past the ladies' room, down the soft carpeted hallway and back again. He kept at it until the coast was clear.

He moved one of the heavy standing ashtrays directly beneath a ventilating duct built into the wall five or six feet above his head. He leaned against the pink concrete wall to wait for a woman and her child to use the ladies' room and go back down the stairs. The corridor was still.

With his heart pounding, Simon stood up onto the round metal rim of the ashtray. Surprisingly sturdy, the thing held him easily. Like a ten-by-ten.

Standing up high above it all, he was made to think of the permanent corner posts, the ten-by-tens on his father's Kansas farm. A person could feel secure standing up on one of those, surveying the countryside.

Simon quickly reached up and removed the protective mesh grillwork from the opening of the air duct. He laid the lightweight metal shield back into and against the inside of the narrow tunnel.

He tossed his shoes in and on the second try, tearing the arms out of his suit coat as he made the effort, he easily pulled himself up into the shadowy receptacle. He breathed carefully

11

at first but the place wasn't as dusty as it might have been.

Turning quickly around, he craned his neck to peek out into the hallway below. There was no one in sight. Using both aching hands, he lined the grillwork cover up and pulled it back into place.

The air in the vent moved ever so slightly past him. On all fours, giggling and feeling exhilarated, he crawled to the rear of the ventilating shaft where the air moved over him with slightly more force. Stopping just short of the caged rotating fan at the end of the passageway, he turned left and crawled out into the black theater attic.

He put his nose into the sensation of vastness that surrounded him. The air felt heavy and stagnant. Moving a bit farther, unable to see even his own trembling hands in front of him, Simon felt suddenly swallowed up by the darkness. It brought him a chill but after a moment he stood, and by shuffling along in his stocking feet, ventured into the place.

Grinding his teeth to contain his excitement, careful not to step directly onto the theater's plaster ceiling, Simon tottered along, spread-eagled as he straddled the narrow rafters. Guessing at his position and approximating the number of rafters that ran parallel beneath him, it wasn't long before he found the spot he was searching for.

Kneeling, he felt under the insulation. His temples pounded. The bottles and cans were still there and after a moment, he found the newspapers, the candles and paperback novels. He felt intoxicated. He wanted to scream.

He touched the glossy cover of his all-time favorite fuck magazine. Smiling, he rubbed at his penis which stiffened while he recalled the picture that he loved the most.

She was a bleached blonde with shining black pubic hair. She wore red, spiked high heels. She stood in two pools of blood on a man's chest. Her knees were turned outward, her body hunched into a half squat. She fingered her labia which hung unusually long, brown and glistening from between her legs. Simon could tell by her expression that it was more than just a paid photo session for her. He was sure she really loved it.

He eased himself down to sit between the rafters with his legs outstretched. He held the glossy-covered sex magazine over his lap and sat perfectly still. He rubbed the magazine against his hard penis. It sent shivers through him.

He listened to the distant booming of the movie's sound track. He removed his torn suit coat and vest from his perspiring upper body and placed them at his side.

Simon scrounged under the insulation until he found an old *Los Angeles Times* Sunday newspaper and two cloth objects he knew to be women's blouses. Hoping, he smelled them but they had lost their scent.

Using his jacket, vest, the blouses and the fat old newspaper, Simon fashioned a pillow and after wiggling around in the soft insulation to adjust himself, relaxed and felt comfortable. He put the sex magazine over his breastbone and folded his hands there too. Closing his eyes, he tried to clear his mind and had to say, "Shoo . . . shoo" to the guilt that came from feeling so good.

Soon he heard nothing but his own heartbeat and breathing. The darkness that surrounded him in the theater attic matched exactly what he found under his closed eyelids.

He became drowsy, and with a peculiar sort of awareness, slept. His dream was primitive and made little sense.

Naked, brown jungle females danced on the faces of their men who lay beneath them masturbating furiously. The women were Ubangi-lipped, and after straining to see, Simon finally was able to observe their genitalia that hung down between their legs, leathery and cracked like elephants' ears. He said, "Jeeesus," out into the jungle blackness, and fumbled to get his hand into his fly. The ground shook. The bottoms of his feet tingled.

A flock of very ordinary sparrows fluttered in to land all around him. Acting as though they had something to hide, they wouldn't match stares with him. He was frightened of them.

One particularly intelligent-appearing bird lighted upon his knee. She was a red-breasted robin. Then they were all robins, with full, pendulous, red-nippled, human female breasts. The bird had a kind, understanding look in her eye but Simon wasn't duped. She winked at him in a slow, wise way, as an owl might. Her yellow beak parted into a sly smile.

Simon smiled back and reached to pet the creature on her soft crown. But the bird moved aside, cooed and said, "Birdie with the yellow bill . . . hopped upon your windowsill . . . cocked her shining eye and said . . . come with me, Simon . . . come and see." He didn't want to go but they brandished long, red stylish talons.

Backing away, he fell into a tiny green-walled room. The chamber was close and filled with the sweet odor of cyanide. It was a room he'd seen before in other dreams. He saw the thick leather straps on the arms of the heavy terrible chair. His throat closed. His hair stood on end.

But the females were there and wouldn't let him go, and he saw that they would never, ever try to understand. So, before he screamed himself awake, he went a little crazy and tore off all their heads.

Simon awoke in a fit of depression, the kind that made him whine. He groped for an image of Carol and pretended to be on top of her. He watched himself pound her and saw her infuriatingly calm expression. Straining to watch her eyelids flutter, Simon thought he observed an almost imperceptible sensualistic deliberation that betrayed her aloofness, that demonstrated her enthusiasm for the fucking she was getting.

Then she told him he was sweet and he felt a surge of anger so intense that he began to strangle her. Strangle her good, too, with both thumbs dug in deep.

But he let up and she bolted from their king-size bed to run gasping into the bathroom. She locked the door and stayed there without making a sound.

Simon paced the hall outside the bathroom for hours until he lost touch and threw himself against the door. It went down with a crash. His imagination had the room empty, Carol disappeared, but she was there, in the corner, cowering.

Grabbing her by the shoulders, he shook her hard until her head flew awkwardly, disjointedly around and around, snapping from front to back. Carol's head flopped and Simon screamed, "Leave me alone . . . goddamn it . . . leave me alone."

Carol suddenly stopped her head from moving. She held it strong and straight and with a smirk said, "You broke in here to tell me that? To leave you alone?"

She laughed with her head thrown back until she went to her knees to make him hard.

Simon screamed, "But . . . but . . . but. . . ."

And she sucked on him awfully good while he raged and cried in his sleep in the attic.

TWO

Betsy Weighgood hated school. She hated the homework and the teachers, but most of all she hated the boys. They were a cruel bunch, every last one.

Betsy had tried to lose weight. She had tried everything you could think of: buying clothing the size that she soon hoped to be, taking diet pills that made her ears ring, not eating for what seemed like weeks at a time, and especially praying.

But she obeyed her father, the reverend, and prayed and prayed. But nothing worked. She stayed fat and looked at the floor whenever anyone addressed her, especially a boy.

Betsy had no friends and her mother had died long ago from tuberculosis. Her father, the Reverend Weighgood of television fame, didn't understand her, and she hated living alone with him in the same house.

But she did what he said, and he said he was sick and tired of listening to her cry about her weight. He said that she must take "action." "Get a job after school and on weekends, Betsy. Develop some self-esteem."

Betsy tried to find a job. She searched the want ads and made herself available for interviews when asked.

Job hunting, she wore her pink cotton blouse with the ruffles in front. The blouse that kept them looking at her large bust, away from her fat behind.

With school recessed for the Christmas holidays, Betsy watched the television soap operas until late afternoon. She washed her pink blouse and ironed the ruffles special. Then she took the bus to Westwood Village.

As she walked from the bus stop to the theater, she thought that job hunting was depressing. She really didn't know how to perform any task in particular. She had no skills. She thought that it was a big drag to walk from a bank to a beauty shop to a hamburger stand and not know what to say, how to explain herself. How to say that it wasn't the job that she needed but to be wanted, to feel a part of things, to be loved.

She wished she knew how to ask her father for attention, but he was always too busy with his televised church broadcasts and the people that needed him. Besides, with what was coming in from tithes and offerings, a bigger and better, all-glass church was soon to be constructed.

The theater's manager, the one that did the hiring, had gone to another theater in the chain to cover for a no-show employee, but would be back to close up. Betsy watched the movie twice, walked around Westwood Village aimlessly and went back to see the movie again.

When Mr. Brooks, the manager, returned, he didn't apologize, but treated Betsy to a giant Coke while he locked up. Then he made her wait some more in his office.

Betsy felt exhausted and hated herself after drinking the Coke, for the slow, easy yet insecure way the sugar made her feel. The liquid ran through her. Unable to hold it any longer, she went to use the toilet. She hoped the theater manager wouldn't be upset if he had to wait.

As she walked the silent, upstairs flamingo pink hallway, Betsy thought that if coincidences had anything to do with getting jobs, she would surely get this one. Even though it was only selling movie tickets. Her blouse was the same exact color as the hallway. Getting up close, she touched her shoulder to the wall and said, "Exactly the same pink color."

She sat on the toilet and when she finished urinating, said, "Darn . . ." to the empty toilet paper dispenser.

While looking around the tiled floor beneath her for a loose, perhaps clean sheet of toilet tissue, Betsy suddenly caught her breath and stared. She put her trembling hand to her heart. Two large, black stocking feet were sticking under, protruding into her stall. She tried to speak but squeaked instead.

After a deep breath to regain her composure, she was able to ask, "Mister Brooks . . . Is . . . is that you?"

The stall's door swung open. A man stood before her whom she didn't know. A huge-shouldered man who stepped into the stall, filling it up.

Betsy wanted to scream but when she saw his eyes, her throat went dry. She felt paralyzed. Her mind flashed to her father, the reverend, and how he described the ungodly, fiendish eyes of the Devil; afflicted, yet compelling. She stared. She felt numb. Her jaw hung.

Then he used his incredibly strong hands. He did it to her and her head swam. Her arms flopped at her sides. She was a rag doll. She felt lightweight at last and loved it. Then blackness stopped her thinking.

THREE

Hero said, "Nineteen, eigh-
teen, Doc," and bounced the racquetball at his feet. He stalled
and bounced the ball to regain his poise. Then, just as he knew
the Doc was about to scream at him to hurry up, he served.

Switching from his low hard serve, Hero sent the ball easily
along the left wall into the rear left corner of the court. He loved
the slow serve when it worked; when the ball bounced back out
along the wall. You could bust a racquet against the wall trying
for the shot.

But the serve stunk. It bounced wrong and out into the court
to the Doc's backhand. Watching over his shoulder, Hero
mumbled "Shit" between clenched teeth and steeled himself
for the return.

The Doc picked the ball off and slammed it fast and low into
the front wall. Hero was only able to save the kill by diving. On
one scorched knee, he got his racquet under the ball and shot it
around the walls. He scrambled for center court.

After the ball hit two walls, with Hero out of position, the

Doc cut it off and hit a perfect overhanded kill shot. The ball rolled back out and the Doc ran to retrieve it.

Grinning, the Doc said, "Eighteen, nineteen, Hero," and moved quickly into the box to serve.

Keeping his back to the ophthalmologist from San Diego, Hero used a towel to wipe the perspiration from his eyes.

"Come on, Hero, three more points. Eighteen, nineteen— three more points and . . ."

"I know the fucking score, Doc," Hero blurted, his chest thrown out and heaving.

Hero threw the towel back into the corner, turned and said coldly, "So, serve, Doc, I'm waiting." The Doc looked into Hero's eyes and Hero smiled like a gentleman while he thought, serve the ball, sucker. I'm going to smash it up your ophthalmological ass.

When the Doc drew his arm back to serve, an amplified female voice squawked onto the small court. "Hero Fiddleman- . . . telephone . . . an important call for Chief Fiddleman."

For a moment, neither of them moved. They hung there with their arms crooked, muscles tensed, suspended in that close white-walled room. Finally, Hero said, "Sheeeit," and let up on his grip, a grip that if squeezed any tighter, might have oozed the racquet handle out from between his white fingers.

Hero hated the look that came over the Doc's face. It frustrated him to no end. Sort of a "just as I had your ass in a sling, you get called away" look. Hero swung his racquet through the air as hard as he could, saying, "Aw, the hell with it." He let himself out of the court's small door and ran for the telephone.

He thought about the sign on the gate outside Frank Sinatra's home up on Mulholland Drive: "If you haven't called or been invited, you'd better have a goddamned good reason for ringing this bell." Hero had gone up to the house as a rookie years before, on a prowling call. There was no prowler but the memory of the sign stayed with him. Thinking about the Doc pacing the court, waiting, he said it to himself now as he ran: "Whoever is on that phone better have a goddamned good reason for ringing my bell . . . a good goddamned reason."

Hero knew who would be on the phone, or at least he had a pretty good idea. Kay and Dwight were the only two people that knew for sure where he was. And then there was the precinct. The club phone number was on his card down at the station. But they wouldn't call him while he was on Christmas holiday. Hell, he thought, they don't even know I'm back.

The air in the club felt too cold against his wet skin. He grabbed a towel from a stack as he ran and wrapped it around his neck.

He hoped it wasn't Kay. She was down at the houseboat putting their vacation stuff away, and adding her own things to his. Jesus, he flashed uneasily, today's the day. She's moving in with me today; or rather, we're moving in together. Good grief, what have I done? Stretch's intuition better be right. He laughed. Still, Kay wouldn't call me from a game unless she had fallen or hurt herself or unless Stretch had been run over; or unless she'd gotten into another fight with Clyde over the laundry machines. "And she *knows,*" Hero huffed, "that I'm playing the Doc today."

Jumping over the locker-room desk, slowing to avoid an elderly man backing out of the sun room, Hero sprang at the members' wall phone. The receptionist made the connection. It was Dwight.

"Chief, is that you? Sorry to bother you when you're playing. I know how darned aggravating it can be. You've done it to me, right?"

"Right, Dwight. What do you need? I'm playing the Doc. He's up from San Diego. I've got him nineteen, eighteen. I'm on vacation, remember?"

"The Doc? Oh, that's good. Well, I thought you'd like to know, I know how you feel about Calhoun and all and I think we've got him cornered."

It was as though Dwight had said magical words. The thought of the Doc from San Diego and the racquetball game began to slip from Hero's preoccupation. He gulped a breath and eagerly said, "Calhoun? Oh, yeah?"

Aside from a disaster involving family or friends, there were only two things that would tear Hero away from racquetball.

There were two open police files that could make him forget everything else. Calhoun the freak—Calhoun the sleek freak who would surely bite off a chicken's head. Calhoun the sleek geek freak, the filthy perverted son of a bitch—and The Terror. Hero took both cases personally.

Hero called Calhoun the movie star. Calhoun called Hero Jewboy. Whenever Hero envisioned sweating, fat, sleek, blue-black Calhoun, it was with his feet up, manicuring his nails, smiling arrogantly, saying, "Don't fuck with me, Jewboy. I ain't doing nothing wrong. Just leave me alone and go sell some bonds for Israel, or I'll call me a cop... a real cop... or my lawyer." And he would laugh with a nelly "tee hee hee."

Calhoun liked kids. Young ones, preferably pretty and blond, of either sex. He liked to take them off the street when they were desperate and bring them to his Venice lair; a storefront space on Lincoln Boulevard converted into a plush studio.

Calhoun loved the strays, the young runaways. He loved to wipe away their tears with his fat, well-kept paws and dispel their misgivings with candy, drugs, fireworks or any other amusement that would hold their attention as he did things to them; horrible, sordid, murderous things.

Calhoun would roll around on top of the young, always white children, crushing them with his three hundred pounds of sweaty blackness while he made them mouth his inconsequential genitals.

He would play his sex scenes in front of a motion-picture camera. He would wallow in the children's sexual wetness and when things were most calm, when they were most relaxed, he would strike.

The audiences could never see Calhoun's face in the snuff films. Only his giant blue-black body and well-manicured hands.

"It could be any large black man's body," Calhoun's lawyers would say, and Calhoun would jiggle in his fatness with a "tee hee hee."

Word on the street from dependable snitches had it that Calhoun's films were available to certain wealthy sickies for twenty-five thousand a pop. Only two films had fallen into the hands of the police and Hero had seen them both.

Hero had been to war in Asia and the cities but swore he'd never seen anything like it before.

After viewing Calhoun's movies he said he'd seen it all, in short, the bottom of the shithole.

Hero had watched the black flesh carefully: the chest, the belly, the buttocks, the genitals. He strained to see the shoulders and arms, the wrists, the hands, the nails, the cuticles, the wrinkles in the fingers. He searched for scars or scabs, idiosyncratic gestures, anything to identify the black butcher, but any hope of that had been edited out. They had to catch him at it.

Calhoun had been arrested thirty-three times for sexual offenses against children and had done two stretches in prison for the same crime. His last prison job was as projectionist in the Soledad prison theater. It was at this occupation that he learned to make movies.

Just the thought of Calhoun galled Hero and would click his heart up a beat. He wanted him in the worst way.

As chief of detectives in Venice, California, Hero had used all his influence to no avail. He pushed the thing until he was catching it from Calhoun's screaming big-shot friends and the American Civil Liberties Union who said Hero was way out of line. There was no actual proof against Calhoun, but Hero kept after him.

On the Fourth of July, a year ago, after a tip, they had taken Calhoun's studio. There were no cameras or films of any kind to be found and only a small amount of drugs. Hero ended up busting Calhoun for illegal possession of fireworks. Boxes and boxes of powerful, dangerous explosives that he was giving to the kids. Chickenshit, but it was all he had.

Calhoun had laughed and squealed and called Hero a paranoid sheeny while they were taking him away. He was back on the street in three hours and Hero was upset about it for the rest of the Fourth of July holiday. That was the weekend he'd met Kay for the first time.

Hero caught his breath and listened to Dwight. "You know, Chief, the fat black guy, the movie star?"

"Shit, Dwight, of course I know. I couldn't forget him in a lifetime, let alone a two-week vacation. What have you got?"

"The Harper girl, that little blond farm girl, the one with the white hair from South Dakota? She was in the report that I sent over."

"Okay, I read it. Go on."

"Well, she's sitting on the corner of Calhoun's roof in the sun, stoned out of her head on something. I doubt that Calhoun knows she's up there. It's possible he's not even home. One of the uniform guys already tried to talk her down. She's stark naked, crying like a baby and going to jump."

"How far is it? Two stories?"

"Yeah, two stories. It's his studio place. You remember, we—"

"Yeah, I remember."

"I thought that you would want to know about this one, Chief. I mean, she's only fourteen years old."

Hero imagined catching Calhoun at it with a fourteen-year-old. He felt the adrenaline rush through him. It was a different more powerfully intoxicating sensation than what came to him on a racquetball court or even under fire in Vietnam.

When civilians were within earshot, his fellow officers called the phenomenon "copper adrenaline," to identify the exhilarating surge. Because of the expression, the feeling always made Hero imagine a sparkling golden amphetamine gushing into his veins.

Once the stuff begins pumping, you can't keep a cop away from the scene of a crime in progress, no matter how hard you try. It's a problem to police administrators everywhere. An emergency call goes out and three hundred officers fly to the adventure from all over the city, their adrenaline coursing. Cops are addicted to the sensation. It either burns them out or keeps them on the force forever.

"Are you there, Chief?"

"Yeah, sure. Fill me in."

Dwight explained that although Calhoun himself had not been observed, his studio was more or less surrounded by uniformed men from the Venice Division. Dwight was in the phone booth directly across the street from the mouth of the alley that ran east and west along the south side of the studio.

As Dwight spoke he could see the girl shivering and holding herself at the rear southwest corner of the studio roof. Every once in a while she would wobble and lean out over the alleyway.

"How do you know she's the Harper girl, the runaway?"

"Oh, she'll say her name. She told the black-and-white. That's how we got the call, why I'm here. She's on the sheet. It's her all right. No question about it, Chief. I've got her picture right here in my hand. I'm looking at both of them right now. It's her, positively. Bonnie Harper, Sioux Falls, South Dakota."

Hero was aware of his heart jolting hard in his chest. He let his eyes dart around from locker to locker, thinking the thing through. His drying perspiration was a cold astringent over his body. "All right, Dwight, pull the uniforms back a block. Get the cars out of sight. Get some of our plainclothes guys out there to replace the uniforms—now, before anything else. If Calhoun comes, let him go in. Let him do whatever he wants. Unless he tries to leave, with or without the girl—stop him and hold him. Hold anyone that comes out. Call the fire boys and fill them in. Get a jump net ready to come up the alley, fast, if we need it for the kid. Get them close and on the ball but out of the way—if you can. What else?"

"Have you got a gun?"

"Always."

"Then you've got it covered, Chief. What are you going to do?"

"I'm coming. Hold the fort."

Hero told Dwight to stay close to the phone booth just in case, and memorized the number. Slamming the phone down, he bolted for his locker. He decided not to change. Moving quickly, he pinned his gold detective shield to the breast of his soggy shirt, which caused it to hang. To make sure his snub-nosed .38 special was loaded, he pointed it at his face to observe the lead slugs neatly in place in the revolver's cylinder. Into his shoulder holster went the pistol; over his shoulder and around his rib cage went the holster straps. Locking his racquet and everything else into his locker, with his wallet and keys in his hand, Hero ran for the door to the outside.

Stopping in the middle of the lobby, he ran back to the receptionist, who was asmile over him, and asked her to open the intercom into Court One. He picked up the microphone. "Sorry, Doc, police business . . . gotta go. I'll drive down to San Diego soon, and we'll finish it. Please accept my apology."

Hero ran from the club thinking that the Doc would figure him for a chicken, which irked him plenty. He promised himself that no matter what, he would never let the Doc beat him the next time they played. I absolutely must, he told himself, kick his ass good.

The day was hot and smoggy. He shielded his eyes with his hand while he ran. Hero called his 1967 black Porsche speedster convert The Tub. The Tub's top was down and Hero leaped into the driver's seat without using the door. The leather was hot, as were the frames of his sunglasses. The Porsche started with the first try. "Christmas week," he mumbled, roaring up to the end of the parking lot. "No snow, but lots of other shit in the air. What a drag." He wouldn't breathe deeply.

He paused for two men to pass in front of him in the crosswalk. "Hey, Hero, good to see you, man," they said, waving and making a fuss. Hero didn't know them; probably club members, but it didn't matter. Lots of people knew Hero. He was famous. But he didn't want to be, and disliked the press for trying to make him a star.

Squealing out of the parking lot, he headed for Lincoln Boulevard in Venice, and for Calhoun the crime, the slime.

Herrera Fiddleman was born September 26, 1946, in Coney Island, New York. His mother, Theresa, was Puerto Rican. His father, Hyman, was a Jew. The memory everyone seemed to have of young Herrera was that he carried himself with his chest thrown out like a star. His four younger sisters teasingly said it made him look like a penguin. His mother would laugh and say it was as though his thumbs were hooked around make-believe suspenders. It made Hyman think his boy would grow up to be an athlete. A Brooklyn Dodger in the World Series.

When his mother wasn't available, the neighborhood women would be watching out for him. From the beginning he gave people the impression that he could be trusted, that he was serious and responsible. With his shining black hair and dark smokey eyes that could stare you down in a minute and make you question yourself, Herrera was intensely handsome. What's more, people seemed to like him. Hyman's friends said he was a mensch.

But his name, everybody, including his father, had trouble pronouncing his name properly. "Herrera . . . Hera . . . Hero." So Theresa gave in and Hero became the name he was known by.

Many people thought he was special and that was all right with him. It could be handled, but Hero was fed up with reporters making him into a big deal. It aggravated him even before he realized that most news, especially television, was slanted, sensationalistic, product-serving entertainment.

He was nearly killed looking out for a *Newsweek* reporter in Vietnam only to have the picture taken of him in action win the Pulitzer Prize. They always were around when you didn't need them. Pushing and shoving. "We're the free press, step aside." Flak jackets and all.

They were there when he found Tania and damn near blew it, damn near forced him into taking her in L.A. rather than letting the Feds get the credit up north. Then they did the big *L.A. Times* story anyway. Giving Hero all the credit. Drawing more attention to him, making him feel scrutinized. Sometimes he thought they specifically followed his career.

It was the Billy Barnes photo for the *Herald Examiner* that started his police notoriety. During Hero's eleventh day on the force, Barnes got a shot of him in downtown Los Angeles evacuating a Mexican family from their blazing seventh-floor hovel. Barnes caught Hero going hand over hand across a power line to the next building with a seventy-two-year-old woman on his back. He was only doing his job, but somehow it was a big deal.

When he was in Narcotics in West Los Angeles, drug dealing to school kids virtually stopped. He had admittedly been tenacious about it. A reporter heard a rumor on the street and asked Hero about it point-blank in front of a live Channel 7 minicam. "I've heard you actually killed a couple of dealers to get your point across. Is that true?"

Hero stared at the reporter in a way that made the man look down, but answered. "All talk," he said. "I don't do that sort of thing." But the public, using their imagination, loved him and wanted more.

Under his leadership, Venice Missing Persons had a find rate unequaled by any other major police force in America. Hero had found Ninja Rockefeller, Sandy McDaniel, Judy Paulsen, Thomas Reeves, M.D., Princess Toomey and Paddy Kaufman, all alive. Abused perhaps, but alive. Plus dozens of other less-publicized cases. Hero pursued them all with the same scrupulous vigor but he was not a zealot. "A person of conscience," he called himself. "Someone has to do it, so it might as well be done right." And he had a special talent for the close, aggressive yet friendly supervision of his men. They would do anything for him because they knew he would do anything for them.

Hero raced south down Sepulveda Boulevard past Veterans Cemetery, thinking about Calhoun. He realized he was grinding his molars and stopped. When he squealed off Pico Boulevard to head south down Lincoln, he had to pause almost immediately for a red light. As he did, he saw her. A ravishingly tanned blonde in a white halter top and shorts coming his way.

She was a beauty of a girl, big-busted with hard nipples. At the side of his car she tried to lean in by resting her forearm above the windshield, but the metal was too hot. She modeled instead with her chest out, her hands on her hips.

"Going to the beach?" she asked with a wild glint in her eye.

"No, ah, I'm going the other way, south. The beach is behind me, north and west. You'll always know it, that's where the sun goes down." He laughed good-naturedly.

"Oh, well," she said, "is there anything fun to do down that way, down south?"

Hero turned his badge toward her. "I'm on business. Maybe some other time."

She saw his gun too and, acting astonished, said, "Jesus, what a darling cop. I've never—"

Hero waved and sped on through the green light. He watched her wave to him in the rearview. Putting his hand up in a friendly gesture, he felt a surge of disappointment and regret. Why not? he asked himself. At least get her number for another time. In case this thing with Kay. . . But he shook his head and said, "Bullshit."

You've got a girl, he told himself. The neatest, straightest, prettiest, most together girl you've ever known, and you don't need to fuck it up. You don't need to spend any more time deep in anyone else's eyes. Accidents do happen.

Besides, what would happen if things were reversed? What is trust? Jesus, Kay is so damned gorgeous she could have anybody. But she's true to you, so it seems, and your Christmas trip was perfect, and she's moving into the boathouse right this minute, probably rearranging all of your things. A powder puff at home full time. "Woe be and Jesus, it scares the shit out of me." But it made him feel super too, sort of tingly and proud.

Hero had known lots of women. Dwight said they stood in line for him. It had always been that way. But the last six months with Kay had been astoundingly, comfortably special and the feelings kept on. Even now, right this second, thinking about her made him feel anxious and horny. "You've played around long enough, so? So, marry her. Quit fucking around. She's the one. Yeah? Well, we'll see."

Perhaps it was being in his mid-thirties, or maybe it was his idea that a man has only so many emotional experiences in him before he flames out and ends up with nothing . . . alone. Or probably it was Kay, that special girl at last, but Hero quickly forgot the California blonde. For the first time in his life, he was beginning to truly understand temptation . . . the rancorous male ego. And when it arose, to deal with it using the big head instead of the little one. To stay out of trouble. To stay feeling good about yourself.

Hero passed two black-and-white units parked behind each other in an alley and saw Dwight. He stood on Lincoln Boulevard out in front of the phone booth flailing his long arms. Hero hadn't seen him for a couple of weeks and thought that he looked nice and neat. His curly blond hair held the sun.

Screeching to a stop next to Dwight, Hero looked over to Calhoun's studio and found it unchanged, large plate-glass windows painted out with flat charcoal black. He quickly checked the area. Mexican restaurants and a bar. Dirty unlit neon, a quiet corner car wash down the street, and flat, two-story, expressionless facades. Artists, manufacturers, God knows what else. There was no one out on the street.

Dwight was talking fast. "He's back, he's inside, Chief. He got back as soon as we hung up."

"Where's the girl?" Hero asked.

"Still on the roof. Hasn't moved. If you come over here, you can see."

"No, no. Where is your car?"

"Right there, behind that big Coppertone sign." Dwight gestured to the south.

"Go use your car phone and call up the troops. Let's take this guy. I'll wait for you in front."

Hero and Dwight moved simultaneously and fast. Hero parked The Tub illegally against the red curb. Leaving his dark glasses on the dash, the keys in the ignition, he set the hand brake tight and jumped from the car. He watched himself move agilely in a storefront plate-glass window. The Tub was left bouncing on its springs.

Hero considered the possibility that Calhoun's storefront might be one-way glass and that he might be inside watching it all. When he saw Dwight, he yelled, "Cross at the corner," which, after waiting for a bus to pass, Dwight did with the efficiency of a gazelle. Natural ability, Hero mused. God-given talent.

Anxious as he was to move on Calhoun, he watched Dwight come running and was made to think of their runs together through UCLA, up around Westwood past the cemetery when, loping along like a deer, Dwight would ask, "Can't we go any faster? Are you going to run the whole thing this slow?"

Hero, who ran three miles in nineteen minutes, would hold back a gag and say, "Ah, yeah, I feel like taking it easy today."

To play handball with Dwight was downright discouraging. As good, as competitive, as flat-out tough as Hero could be on the court, he wouldn't play handball with Dwight anymore. Racquetball, yes, but not handball. Hero was lucky to get ten points off Dwight in handball.

Dwight had two absolutely perfect hands. Total and complete God-given ambidexterity. He had been the national collegiate handball champ and currently held the national police title. He was considered by many the most physically gifted player in the game. Dwight could also play "A" tennis with either hand. Switching the racquet from hand to hand without his game dropping was an astonishing feat to observe. His natural talent kept him up there with the best of them in several sports, but his easygoing disposition and his thirty-seven years prevented him from remaining the top guy. Except with his gun.

Dwight was the American national, free-fire, sharpshooting pistol champion. He had owned the title for years and it was with a continuing, gossiping incredulity among his opponents that he competed and won on odd years with his left hand, on even years with his right.

On the job, Dwight carried a long-barreled, nickel-plated Smith and Wesson .44 Magnum under his left arm that he called his cannon. It took a near calamity for him to bring it out but when it happened, the long shining weapon, in either of Dwight's hands, meant deadly accurate business.

Hero watched him come, rolling on the outsides of his oxfords, his beige slacks doing nice things over his long runner's legs; his tasteful, muted plaid sport coat unbuttoned and flying. His "cannon" holstered along his ribs. Looking serious, Dwight jumped the curb in some sort of smooth talented-appearing way and Hero felt a brotherly love for him that easily smothered the tinge of jealousy he could feel. The envy he perceived when they were in their stocking feet in the gym, and Hero found himself looking up at Dwight to talk.

And there was a sadness in his feeling for Dwight. A melancholic, paternal sense of protectiveness that he had for the big blond galoot. As though the gifted man knew nothing about taking care of himself. Dwight loved God and went beyond the rules that bind us, to be fair. He gave them all, every shitheel, the benefit of the doubt.

Dwight came near and was smiling. Smiling that wonderful friendly smile of his that said he was glad to see Hero back from vacation, happy because it was the two of them together again, heading into the underworld . . . partners.

"Hero, gosh darn it's good to see you. I like your outfit."

Hero reached inside Dwight's open sport coat, slapped him on the ribs and said, "Come on, partner, let's get this kid. Is there a net out there?"

"Now there is, right under her. Of course she'll see the men, the uniforms will be down there again. I called them all up." As they spoke, Lincoln Boulevard was being cordoned off a block away in each direction. Hero was pleased with how fast his colleagues worked.

"What if she jumps?" Hero asked.

"They'll catch her. More than likely they'll get her. There are some good men back there. Tom Bisher and that bunch, firemen rescue, athletes. They'll talk to her too, if she'll talk. They're good guys."

Hero said, "Good, come on," and went for Calhoun's front door. It was locked tight. Going past his inclination to bust the place right off, Hero pounded loudly on the smoked-glass door. Two unmarked Plymouth police cars screeched to a stop behind them in the street. Hero pounded again while three plainclothes detectives and one uniformed sergeant joined them at the door, their service revolvers drawn. They waited, listening patiently until Hero broke the silence. "I don't hear anything—do you guys hear anything?"

"Naw, shit, Calhoun won't answer even if he hears us. He never answers unless it's kids, and he's expecting. He's extra careful."

"Yeah," Hero said. "Well, with the kid in there we've got cause. I say we break the place, yes?"

Everyone agreed. Hero nodded at the sergeant to break the plate-glass door with his nightstick. They all stepped back. The sergeant aimed and threw his club at the door. Missing the mark, the hickory stick bounced off the door frame and out into the street.

Before Hero could finish a sigh and shake his head in disbelief, Dwight had the stick. Showing off, he threw it underhanded into the exact dead center of the door with a crash. Plate glass splashed onto the sidewalk. Hero laughed and with his gun drawn, was the first one to jump through the broken door into the place.

FOUR

T he bright day came in with him to help illuminate an anteroom of a kind, another heavy wall and door. "Something new," Hero mumbled, putting his ear to the door. He heard music. Though muffled, he could tell it was being played loudly. The Commodores, he thought. It sounds like "Flying High" by the Commodores. A good song.

"Feel the door, Dwight, what do you think?"

Stepping over broken glass like a cat, Dwight felt around and whispered, "Heavy. . . thick."

"Like my joint, Dwight." Hero laughed. "You don't have to whisper. If breaking that door didn't roust them, talking won't." Hero thought for a moment before changing his attitude and saying, "All right," in a determined, positive way. He wanted in the place bad and was done fooling around. "One of you people go out back and tell the guys there what we're doing. And keep an eye on the kid. I'll be right back."

Hero ran to his car and quickly returned brandishing a tire iron. "All at once—I'll rip it, you guys hit it with your shoulders. Here, you, stand here. Dwight here." Hero arranged his men as he wanted them, with their shoulders to the door. "On three, give it all you've got. One . . ."

On the count of "Two," Hero forced the tip of the tire iron deep into the lock mechanism and on "Three," wrenched it while his men hit the door hard. The door flew completely off its hinges and down with a slam into a large dark room.

Hero had been right. The song was an oldie but a goodie by the Commodores, "Flying High." It was loud. Cool air conditioning engulfed them and a smell that made Hero think of the perfume counter at Bullocks Westwood, where Kay liked to go. They stepped quickly into the large room, onto thick purple carpeting, and let their eyes adjust.

The studio had been redone in chrome and glass and dark violet shades: mauves, heliotropes, purples. A tree grew tall and healthy up toward a muted skylight in the ceiling. Because of indirect lighting, the ceilings were dark, probably black or deep purple. The bare walls were plum-colored and gleamed with high-gloss enamel. A stack of large colorful oil paintings leaned against a partition in the middle of the room.

Hero ran to the room divider which was a sturdy chrome-and-glass partition separating the main front room from Calhoun's living quarters in the rear. From where he stood, Hero could easily see the chromium ladder that scaled the south wall up to a hatch opened to the roof. The bright day flooded in. Motioning for his men to stay behind him, Hero peeked around the corner into the back room.

The music blasted. A large flocked-white Christmas tree stood in the corner without lights. A fancy hot tub was there steaming, a gleaming modern kitchen and finally, raised up into the room under a four-poster canopy, a huge king-size bed. On it, oblivious to the invasion, were fat black Calhoun and two emaciated blond white boys; all of them lying nude on the light purple sheets.

Hero's heart jumped into his throat. His adrenaline surged. He watched the two boys sit and share a cigarette while Calhoun lay out on his back between them. Whatever they had been doing, probably giving Calhoun a double head job, they had finished. A pink towel was over Calhoun's huge stomach, tucked into the crook of his buttocks, covering his genitals.

In the heavily air-conditioned room, a powerful urge to sneeze came over Hero. He let it happen. Calhoun and the two boys froze, then slowly turned and stared. Hero, motioning his men to follow behind him, stepped into the room. He shouted, "Find out who the kids are, Dwight. How old, where they're from. Keep them all right where they are, and turn the music off."

Hero ran to the chromium ladder, jumped on it and began climbing for the square of daylight above him. The rungs felt cool and greasy in his hot wet hands. When he was not quite halfway up, the music stopped abruptly. The musical sounds were replaced by Calhoun's hysterical shrieks: "Motherfuckers . . . dirty rotten motherfuckers."

Holding tight with his left hand, Hero turned and swung out from the ladder. From that height, he had a view of it all. He couldn't help but smile watching Calhoun bounce on the bed and squeal. It gave him a feeling of satisfaction.

Bleary-eyed, the two boys sat with their hands in their laps. Calhoun jumped up from the bed only to be thrown back upon it by one of the detectives who put a cocked police special to his temple. "Fiddleman," Calhoun screamed, "you Jew prick, I'll have you for this. You got nothing on me."

Hero's ears burned. He hated Calhoun and everything he stood for. Calhoun knew his rights. He stretched and perverted them for his own advantage. Calhoun probably didn't know that he was a sick psychopath. But Hero knew for sure and couldn't think of anything that would suit the man better than a slug in the heart.

A look passed between them and Calhoun read Hero's feelings. He stared up, the whites of his eyes bulging, a pulsing reptilious sag over his shining wet jowls. Hero saw him as a fat black comedian. The guy that wears a beany with a propeller on top, on television. Hero couldn't help getting into it with him. "You're going to jail, Snuff Man. Unless you cry a little. Cry a little and show off for your tricks." Calhoun held Hero's stare.

Dwight pulled the naked boys over to the side of the bed to find out who they were, but Calhoun didn't look away or blink. When he finally grinned, Hero recognized as he always did why Calhoun made a point of not laughing.

With his mouth closed, he appeared to be a clean-cut, almost handsome black. Heavy but classic and mean-eyed . . . Mr. Slick. But when he grinned, with his unusually long eyeteeth and pink gums, he appeared a baboon. All he needed to make the picture complete was a polished red rump. "When you smile, you look like a gorilla, Calhoun. Don't smile at me."

The grin went. He said, "You fuckhead punk."

One of the detectives moved on Calhoun with his pistol held back to smack him, to demand a little respect, but Hero yelled, "No, don't do that." Then, "Which one were you going to kill, Calhoun? Whose balls were you going to rip off first—or is this just for fun? Keep the old black tubes cleaned out . . . You kids want to be in the movies?"

The blond boys looked first at each other in surprise and then up to Hero. The one closest to Dwight began to blabber. His voice was surprisingly deep, like a dead end kid. "Movies, yeah, that's what we want to know, the movies. That's what he said."

"Shut up," Calhoun screamed. He kicked the kid good on the ribs, but sat quickly back on the bed to escape a pistol-whip reprimand.

Sensing an unexpected break, Hero came back down the ladder. He walked to Calhoun. Close to the bed the air smelled of fetid sex and inelegant, sickening sweet cologne.

"Where are the movies, Calhoun? Tell me and I'll give you a break." Hero had to chuckle out loud at that one.

Calhoun lay back on the bed like a king. He put his arms behind his head and smiled his propeller beany, baboon smile. His clean-shaven armpits shone crusted white with deodorant.

Suddenly, Calhoun pulled the pink towel away and grabbed his penis. He squeezed it hard, gorging the smallish pink-and-brown-spotted head out from between his thumb and pointer finger. He sat up. "You see this, Jew boy?" Spittle flew onto Hero's bare legs. He stepped back. Calhoun's face shook with fury. He stretched his penis, pulling it at Hero. "See this,

Fiddleman? Well, stick it in your Jew asshole. You got shit on me . . . unless you want to bust me for this crap?" Using his forearm, he swept an open bottle of vodka, glasses, some white pills (probably Quaaludes), and a bag of marijuana and some rolling papers off of an end table with a crash. Pointing at the mess, he screamed like a spoiled brat, "That's what you got on me . . . some petty-assed shit nothing. You want movies? Go in the closet and look. Have a fucking ball."

He let go of his penis but strained his head toward Hero as far as his sweating neck would stretch. His eyes bulged but he spoke in a rasping whisper. "Go on, Fiddleman. Take your tennis balls and your tennis suit and go look in my closet. You'll find a couple of cans of film in there, go on. If you like Margo Lane's big pussy or John Holmes's big prick you can watch all day long, but that's all that's there, asshole. Legal stuff . . . you ain't gonna find what you're looking for here. You schmuck. You think I'm stupid, huh? You think I ain't got brains?"

Flopping back onto the bed, Calhoun reached for the purple telephone on the other end table. Hero shook his head no and Dwight put his foot on the telephone. Calhoun squealed, "I want my lawyer. I know my rights."

Standing over the huge black man, Hero pictured what a wonderful full-on drop kick to his head would do. Followed by his best mitsu karate chop over the bridge of the stunned man's nose. And then to slam the shattered bone and cartilage splinters up into his brain with the driving palm of his hand. Oh, yeah, Hero swooned to himself. To use my black-belt expertise right now. To lay all I know on him at once. The thought and the air conditioning made him shiver.

Hero turned and went back to the shining ladder. With his hand on the first cool rung, he turned and spoke to Dwight. "Look the place over, carefully. And keep a close eye on him." Two detectives were already at work in a closet.

With Calhoun's indignant voice shrieking about his rights in the background, Hero climbed the ladder.

He looked through the chromium rungs of the ladder at the wall. It was a gray wall or silver with some purple in it. The wall held his attention and Hero felt suddenly, inexplicably exhausted. He spoke quietly to himself: "I'm getting too old for this," and he rhymed, "My ego it hurty, for years over thirty."

He laughed and couldn't help looking forward to the day's end, to Kay, his poetry class this semester, to things exquisite.

Calhoun screamed, "What do I do if I have to take a piss, Hero? Am I supposed to ask permission from your boys, the gestapo? Am I supposed to say, 'Steppin' out, boss,' like a beggin' nigger, like my old man beggin' on the Georgia chain gang? Hey, Hero, I gotta piss. How about it, boss? Steppin' out, steppin' out, boss, to pee."

He was moving from the bed to the toilet. Hero shook his head no and the uniformed sergeant threw him back onto the bed.

"You can hold it, Calhoun. If you can't hold it . . . give him a glass or jar from the kitchen. While you're at it, save it. We'll run a urinalysis. I'd like to know what he's on, if he's on something."

Then he paused to throw a line back down into the room. "Incidentally, Calhoun, you're under arrest. Read him his rights, Dwight. I'm considering the charges. Book the kids too."

Calhoun screamed, "You fuck—" but settled down.

Shielding his eyes from the glare, Hero pulled himself up through the trapdoor into the blazing Venice, California, afternoon. Squinting, he saw her and she saw him at the same time. She was naked and holding herself. Hero said, "Hello," as friendly as he could and stood up onto the dirty tarred roof. He felt lethargic under the sun. She was on some sort of a slatted wooden sun deck. He watched her eyes go slowly from his shield to his gun to his face and back again.

A frantic expression overcame the girl's countenance. She clutched at herself, raking her bare shoulders with her nails. She tottered. "Back," she screamed, "back . . . stay back or I'll jump." She stumbled to the corner of the building and stood there swaying.

Picturing the net beneath her, Hero yelled, "So, go ahead and jump. If you're going to jump, jump. Let's get on with it. It's your life."

Tough love, he thought. The worst thing you can do is beg or plead or dignify the act by trying to persuade them not to do it.

Fuck it, jump, but remember you're dead a long time. I won't be an enabler, Bonnie Harper from South Dakota with the pretty white hair. Platinum, Hero thought. Jean Harlow, Kim Novak. He bet that Calhoun went nuts over it. Rubbed his blue-black meat in it.

Bonnie Harper appeared puzzled. An expression she held for some time before bending at the waist to crane her neck and look over the side of the building. Whatever she saw caused her to jump and move quickly down the edge of the roof to a place ten or so feet away from her previous position. Hero observed that her pubic hair was not blond at all but almost black, and grew unchecked out onto her legs.

She looked down into the alley again. She leaned over to yell something down that sounded like "Hello" before she waved. When she stood upright, she swayed and caught her balance by grabbing out and clutching a corner of a fire brick with her hand. She swayed and talked to herself.

Hero thought she was a pathetic-appearing little thing. Thin and bedraggled, bruised, fucked over. Her hair was not pinned back as he'd first thought but chopped short. The sun and the angle showed her hair not to be real platinum at all but more of a processed pink or orangish white. She wore one large gold hoop earring that hung lopsided in a funny way, as though half torn from her ear, and absolutely nothing else. Her bust was practically nonexistent, her nipples tiny without much pigment. Her hips were broad and bony; more hip than shoulder, pear-shaped. Even from where he stood, Hero thought he could see her dirty, half-painted toenails. Shit, he said to himself. He sighed.

Bonnie Harper's body jerked. She looked up as though she had just come to. She walked in a careful tiptoed fashion back to the corner where she had originally been seated. Hero wondered for the first time about her bare feet on the tar. Wobbling, she managed to pluck a matchbook from out of a crack in a brick and smile insipidly. She waved below and laughed. Then she began giggling and walking quickly, disjointedly back and forth from place to place, stopping at each turn to wave at the men below.

When she'd remember Hero, she'd look to him, gesture with

the flat of her hand and say, "Back . . . back, just stay back."
And Hero stayed back. Much less sure now what to do and not
telling her to go ahead and jump. He envisioned the firemen in
the alley below running back and forth from place to place,
frantically hoping to be at the right place at the right time. The
thought was humorous for a second or two but quickly began to
make him angry.

Bonnie Harper stopped pacing long enough to pick a roach
out of the matchbook, place it between her lips and light it with
several matches. Hero was sure that she scorched her lips as
well with the quick, searing flame. The aroma came to Hero
just as Dwight's voice came from behind.

"You okay, Chief?"

Hero turned to see Dwight's curly blond head up out of the
hatch. "Yeah. Stay down. She's dusted. Can you smell?"

Dwight sniffed. "Yeah. Shoot, angel dust. Okay, we're
sitting on Calhoun."

"You find anything?"

"Lots of fireworks, not much else."

"Look in the bookshelves . . . in the books. Take the joint
apart. Might as well give him something to scream about."

"You got it, Chief." Dwight disappeared from view.

Hero squatted and waited. He waited until the girl had
inhaled two good gulps of dope, until she had checked him
twice to find him sitting down and calm. Then when she turned
her attention back onto her fingertips and the roach, Hero
sprang.

He was across the roof in an instant and had hold of Bonnie's
arm before she knew what had happened. She didn't flinch.
Swaying in his grasp, she merely looked at him with a pair of
tearing eyes that swam aimlessly in her head. She strained to
focus while her body went through quick, seizurelike involuntary jerks. Her body odor was awful. She tried to get the dusted
joint to her mouth with her other hand but Hero snapped the
roach from between her fingers and let it fall to the roof.

Bonnie Harper took a long time to find her words. Her
eyelids hung and would not stop twiching. Staring blankly into

Hero's face she stammered, "I . . . I . . . I going to be in the movies . . . a . . . a . . . a movie star." Her head fell over onto her shoulder until she was able to jerk it back up.

"You mean Calhoun was going to put you in the movies?" He shook her hard. "Is that it?"

"Uuhuh . . . my friends . . ." She seemed to forget her words. Hero shook her.

"How did you get here?" he asked sternly. "Your friends? Did your friends bring you, or Calhoun? Which was it?"

He waited but Bonnie Harper from South Dakota was way too stoned to talk or do anything but hang limply in the sun.

Hero wondered about getting her downstairs. About the slippery chrome ladder and what a project it would be. He craned his head over the ledge. They were down there staring up, a bunch of firemen with the biggest ass net he'd ever seen. It made him laugh. A net as big as the alley. Huge, of round white shining nylon with a sparkling-clean-looking red dot, a red rising sun in the middle.

"Hey, you guys . . ."

Shielding their eyes, they searched the sky and found him.

"Hey, she's coming down. Stay where you are."

Hero forced the girl to the edge of the building. "What . . . what . . ." she babbled.

"We're going to do a little screen test on you, whacko, but there's no net, just concrete. And if you're not dead from falling on your face, we'll pick you up and let Calhoun put you in a movie and kill you." He shook her. "That's what's in store for you here, Bonnie. Someone was going to fuck you and kill you at the same time and make a movie of it. Maybe cut your head clean off for the audience."

Hero figured that she probably couldn't understand what he was saying, but he wanted to try and scare her. He'd been 'dusted' and knew you could hear what you wanted to. You could panic. An impression might be made. Her life might be spared, she might get hip. She was staring. Her eyes were focused. "Hang around here and die." Hero said it to her directly, sternly, and she went limp.

Hero let go of her and she looked up from the hot black roof with a hurt look over her face. "You let me fall." The way she said it, like a crybaby, made Hero think of his youngest sister. She talked baby talk too.

Using all of his strength he swaddled and grabbed her into a bundle. He stood up, close to the edge of the roof. Clutching him, Bonnie Harper began to scream. Her back was to the alley, her chin dug into his shoulder. She screamed bloody murder: "No . . . No . . . No . . . No . . . dear God, No . . . please." She pounded his back with chicken-winged fists that seemed to crumple after each blow. Hero leaned out and threw her.

He aimed her just right, not that he could have missed if he'd wanted to. The net was everywhere beneath them. But to make it perfect, he directed Bonnie Harper at the red dot when he pushed. He gave it all he had and was ready to laugh with the fire boys about his accuracy, his athletic prowess. He threw her really good and yelled, "Here comes Bonnie Harper from South Dakota."

When she parted from him, he leaned to watch. Her screams echoed off of the alley walls. Her legs flailed at the air around them and out she went like an astronaut cut loose in space. He watched all of her go out past him but a hand, a last desperate hand that clutched and held on to his strong black hair, and with a scary unexpected tug, he left his feet and went down with her.

While he was airborne, besides giving in to laughter, he threw his hand to the side of his chest to hold his revolver in place. He turned one shoulder first and was able to roll both shoulder blades horizontal for the landing. Bonnie from South Dakota screamed all the way down but they landed with a whoosh, next to each other but not entangled, safe and sound, with Bonnie like a ball, onto the red zero and Hero flat on his back.

The fire boys didn't seem to get what was so funny. Hero left Bonnie crawling nowhere on all fours against the slippery nylon, spittle hanging from her face like a rabid animal, and jumped off the net over a fireman's shoulders. He yelled, "Thank you" to them all and spoke to one of his men that was close and all ears. "Put the girl in a car, give her a blanket or two and don't scare her, she's dusted and liable to do anything. Just keep her close and call the paramedics. I'll be back shortly."

Hero ran back up to Lincoln Boulevard, to the front of Calhoun's studio, over the broken glass, into the main studio room. He sauntered back to the rear of the place where Calhoun continued to sit on his bed naked. The two boys sat huddled on the opposite side of the bed. The place was a shambles.

Chromium Levolor blinds had been drawn up tight, allowing sunlight to pour into the rear of the room. Dwight stood in front of a bright window examining thin strips of film against the light. Several dark cans of film sat next to him on the windowsill.

The detectives were sitting down looking through books, throwing them aside when they were finished. There were other police now too, in the closets, in the bathroom.

"How are we coming?" Hero asked out into the room.

"Where'd you come from?" Dwight wanted to know.

Hero told him. There were some laughs. A seething Calhoun said, "I wish you'd broken your fucking back."

Looking at him, Hero knew that he meant it. An officer got close to speak confidentially. "Nothing but a small amount of dope, Chief, and fireworks. Lots of fireworks. But the movies are just porn, straight over-the-counter junk. Nothing rough."

Dwight was there to listen when Hero asked, "How much dope?"

"A couple of grams of coke. Some of it is brown, probably smack. Some grass, not much."

"Okay. Mark it and bring it all along. Who's here? Anybody from the lab?"

"Everybody. Tom is back there too from Homicide."

"Good. Let them finish up."

Hero went back to stand in front of Calhoun. "What happened to you last year on the fireworks arrest?"

Calhoun gave him the finger. "Ask my lawyer, asshole."

"Did the judge give you probation? It seems to me I

remember him putting you on probation. All this stuff here is breaking probation."

Calhoun laughed.

It was inconsequential bullshit: the drugs, the fireworks. And God only knew what Bonnie would give them. Probably nothing but cause to bust the place and he was going to need that.

"Who's the girl on the roof?" he asked the blond boys.

They looked at each other before the homelier of the two, with moles on his cheek, questioned, "You mean Bonnie?"

Hero tried but probably didn't hide his disappointment. Shit, he said inside.

"Bonnie's a friend of ours," they said.

"There, you see, asshole," screamed Calhoun. *"They* brought the little cunt around, not me. She's a gang fuck. You know what a gang fuck is, Jewboy? Shit, you got nothin' on me . . . nothin' but lots of explaining to do to the police commissioner, the ACLU, and everybody for this. Leaning on me, always leaning on me."

Calhoun giggled and gave Hero the finger. Hero's ears burned. He felt himself lean toward the gloating black that looked like Idi Amin. He teased himself. He would drive a thumb into an eye, he would pull off an ear. But he reached quickly into Calhoun's blubbery mouth instead.

Hero drove his thumb in along Calhoun's wet molars to grab him by the left cheek.

Wide-eyed, Calhoun bayed. He hung there. The officers in the room minded their own business.

"Calhoun," Hero said, staring him forcefully in the eye. "I'm only going to tell you this once. I am all done listening to your mouth. I don't like you, Calhoun. Be very careful what you do or someone's apt to pull this thing off."

Applying pressure, Hero twisted his thumb and could have pulled the flesh off that fat black's skull. But he let go to take his hand away.

Eyes watering, slopping like a cow, Calhoun seemed to mellow. He nodded as though in agreement and swallowed hard. Still, behind his conciliatory expression, Hero thought he detected a sly smile begin to creep into the sweaty fat face.

But Calhoun said, "Don't . . . don't worry, Chief. I won't do it again. I won't say nothin' to you again . . . about nothin' . . . ever. Tee hee hee."

"Cuff him," Hero said, walking away.

Hero watched over his shoulder. The picture of Calhoun sitting there being shackled like an animal made him ask himself for the zillionth frustrating time what the fuck is going to become of the poor urban blacks, the people he seemed constantly up against. Sometimes he thought he was at war with them. He knew them.

"There ain't no jobs, man. I'll collect welfare for a while but end up in jail. There ain't no other way for me, man. That's my future. Fill up the jails."

Watching Calhoun shake in the handcuffs, Hero stood and quietly shook his head. Then he laughed sarcastically to think, anybody with the same name as Amos and Andy's lawyer is bound to be a fruitcake. Dwight got close.

"You okay?" he asked.

Hero stayed pensive. "No . . . yeah . . . sure I'm okay. I was just looking at that loser and getting pissed off."

"Oh, no. Come on, Chief, don't. . . ."

"Do you know what Kay says?"

"No," Dwight sighed. "What?"

"She says it's because they never had a proper diet when they were kids. Just sugar and junk . . . that it's inhibited their growth. Do you believe that? Is that possible?"

"Didn't seem to slow down the athletes," Dwight popped off. They both laughed at the truth in that. "Don't worry about it, Chief . . . please. I keep telling you there's nothing you can do. We're cops. We enforce the rules, not make them. So, come on, don't go off on one of your trips."

Walking for the front door, Hero told Dwight to arrest them all. The closer he'd looked at the blond boys the more he'd figured they were male whores. "Bring them in, check them out. Get them out of Venice. Push Calhoun for kidnapping. Until we know better, that's the way it looks. Call the Harpers in South Dakota. Tell them we've got Bonnie. See what they want to do. What else?"

"Push Calhoun for all the petty ante stuff too?"

"Absolutely. Everything and anything. Fireworks, dope. Do it all."

Dwight said, "You got it." He turned and walked back toward Calhoun.

Outside, the hot bright Venice afternoon was on the wane. The Pacific Ocean, a mile to the west, was already working on the air. It was perceptibly cooler. The pollution was clearing up. Picking up the tire iron, Hero thought about a run later. With the December breeze the Los Angeles air could get good quick and sometimes even stay that way.

Looking around, he couldn't deny a tinge of claustrophobia. There was an anxiety, a neurosis about Los Angeles, about Venice, that he could feel. He felt it now and surprised himself by wishing he were someplace else.

Hero chuckled and figured that he was experiencing the tail end of the Christmas holiday blues. Or a reaction to Calhoun. Or the Doc, the unfinished game of racquetball, or all of it. The changes, the trauma of the day, were twisting his head.

He thought that he might jog home. Considering it, he decided to drive up to the Santa Monica bluffs, park his car on San Vicente and run home. Kay would drive him back after dinner. They could keep the top down and take Stretch for a drive. They all loved the area at night. To make the drive from the marina up into Santa Monica and back again. Through the quaint, narrow one-way streets that ran north and south along the Venice beaches. Stretch, Hero's dachshund, stood in the jump seat behind Kay with his tongue hanging out, enjoying the roller skaters, the bar action, the Venice crazies.

Thinking about it, those wonderful quiet nighttime drives, brought to Hero a feeling of warmth for the city. I hate the fucking place but I love it—the pace, the energy. And when it's right, when it's beautiful, when the salt air is crisp and the street lights shine pure without auras in the blackness, there's no place like it, no place.

Getting into his car, he made a U-turn and headed north up Lincoln Boulevard. He slowed in front of Calhoun's studio for Dwight who was out in the street waving his arms.

"He's on his way in now, Chief, screaming. Boy, is he pissed off. I guess we've got enough different stuff to hold him for a while, enough to ruin his day." Dwight knelt down next to the car. "So, we'll see you tomorrow, right? Back to work?"

Hero said, "Yes, I'll be in early to catch up. Anything else doing until then?"

"Oh, yes . . . damn." Dwight snapped his fingers loudly. "I almost forgot. The mayor has called everybody in on it. You know who Reverend Weighgood is? The pray TV minister? Sunday morning, Channel 5?"

Hero pictured the mostly bald, black-robed television preacher. "Sure—who doesn't? What about him?"

"His daughter is missing. Disappeared from a theater in Westwood where she was interviewing for a job. A nice kid, he says. Not the type to run away or go anywhere without telling him. But who knows these days, right, Chief?"

"Yes . . . right. Can't the West L.A. guys handle it?"

"Not as well as you, everybody knows that."

Hero laughed and asked, "Did you have a good Christmas?"

"Yeah, fine. Not as much fun as last year though, with you, when you took me with you to Hefner's mansion. Gosh, all those beautiful . . ."

"Those days are gone, Dwight. For me, anyway."

"Yeah," Dwight said, standing up and kicking the street with the toe of his shoe. "Well anyway, Gates and Bradley are pushing everybody into the Weighgood thing. Because of the old man, his audience, his connections, I suppose."

"We'll get into all that in the morning. I'll see you then. Call me on the boat tonight if you need me, if it's important." Checking the rearview, Hero slapped Dwight's thigh and roared off down Lincoln Boulevard.

FIVE

Thinking about the Reverend Weighgood and his daughter made Hero want to rhyme about them, to write a poem. It seemed like the kind of "real" or "natural" situation that his poetry professor talked about. A thing with its own energy. A thing that you could "let happen," that would apply itself to the page in front of you. But he had his good new poem to finish.

Hero had been through lots of changes in the short time since he began it, but his poem was almost complete, on scraps of paper, in his daytime calendar and in his head.

Driving past the Santa Monica police station, Hero glanced at their operations to see how they were doing. To observe the coming and going of the particularly good-looking young cops that the city was hiring. Good cops, too, he thought. They smile away a lot of trouble.

Hero took Colorado west past the Holiday Inn and Santa Monica pier onto Ocean Avenue, and headed north for San Vicente. The sun was only slightly overcast now, but huge and orange, hanging out there at the horizon, causing the Pacific to reflect light blue, pink, red and apricot; a spectacular coral sea.

He figured the sun hung over Hawaii or farther, maybe out over Vietnam, that God-awful Asian sweatbox that, try as he did, he could never quite get out of his head.

There was pretty good visibility; he could see the outline of Point Dume to the north. He took a deep breath. The air was cleaning up fine. The bad taste was not there, the taste that came in mid-July and stayed through October. Winter smog could come and go in a day.

Passing the end of Santa Monica Boulevard, Hero kept an eye on the grassy knoll to his left, the place where he would run. The knoll, a part of the Santa Monica bluffs where, but for a block or so of sandy beach that lay out past the Coast Highway below, California meets the sea. The natural conclusion of the Western Hemisphere.

The grassy bluffs were clean-looking and well kept these days. All of the huge trees were trimmed regularly and the place was like any proper green park. Watching the joggers, he felt antsy, anxious to run. Some of them were women and it was comforting to know that despite the oncoming darkness they would be safe to finish their exercise in peace. It hadn't always been that way.

Not so long ago, because of inadequate lighting and ill-kept lawns and trees, the bluffs had been a haven for indigents, bums and worse. After dark the inhabitants of Santa Monica's skid row and other misfits would slink across Ocean Avenue to sleep on the park benches or under the protective boughs of the big overgrown trees. The place was constantly strewn with empty bottles and junk.

In August 1979 the city of Santa Monica had decided to take action and reclaimed the grassy knoll. They installed arc lights that made night, along the mile-and-a-half stretch, seem like day. They cut and manicured the lawns, trimmed back the boughs of the trees and began patrolling the area on horseback and with Cushmans. They made it a special, safe place to come and enjoy one of the choice ocean views on the West Coast. The bums either moved on or went to jail. And simultaneously, The Terror, the west side killer of women, stopped his attacks.

It was mostly conjecture and Hero may have been the only

one that believed his own theory, but he was convinced that The Terror had lived on the knoll. Hero had been a detective third in Homicide, Venice, at the time and all of the leads, all of the trails, went west to the bluffs. Everything he saw and didn't see, his instincts, told him so. And one witness.

Margaritte Sullivan was a sergeant in the Santa Monica Salvation Army. One sunny summer afternoon she and a group of her fellows, her soldiers, were working the bums on the knoll. They were trying to save one particular soul when they were assaulted and beaten by a bunch of the grassy-knoll gang. The police had to break it up. An associate of Margaritte's, a large woman named Lacey Stone, had been torn up pretty good and humiliated sexually by a hulking giant of a man with incredible strength in his hands. Margaritte swore she saw the same big-shouldered man behind them twice, ducking away so as not to be seen, while they walked Lacey home.

That evening Lacey Stone was found dead in her kitchen, her throat yanked out. The twentieth female victim of the west side Terror.

With a brute force that made it all the more frightful, he tore his victims' throats out clean. Autopsies revealed it was done with a minimum of groping, strangling or bruising. A powerful but neat swooping tear, and a throat would be gone. Some of the women had borne other ravages as well, before, during and after death. Acts that left traces of semen or urine or both over their bodies, in their wounds, in their vaginas and rectums.

The press said that unlike "the strangler" who closed his victims' throats or "the ripper" who disemboweled his women, this killer "tore" his victims. He was a "tear-or of women." The name caught on overnight and from that early first morning news edition, the beast that mutilated women in Los Angeles throughout the late 1970s became known as The Terror.

His last victim was the lone female proprietor of a West Los Angeles liquor store on Westwood Boulevard.

Then began a tension-filled period of wondering, a cessation of hostility by The Terror. Everyone waited. The papers and news shows counted the days. But the killing had apparently stopped.

The knoll was cleaned up, summer ended, people went back to school or work and anxiety over the killer gradually disappeared.

It took a long time for women to completely relax. But with all of the other insanity in the news, after the passage of some months, people's fear of The Terror faded.

Most everybody thought he was dead. At least that's what they hoped. As when Jack the Ripper stopped killing in London. But not Hero. Hero stayed obsessed with the homicidal maniac, the slayer of women, for a long time.

He still thought about the brute whenever one of his sisters came alone to visit or when his mother, here from New York, would go out by herself to stroll around the marina. He could worry about Kay all the time, when she ran or shopped or went on interviews. He had to make a conscious effort not to let himself think about it.

Although he didn't always understand them, Hero respected the women in his life, and held in high esteem the notion of women in general. So it was with a particular revulsion and anger that he would read, reread and memorize every detail of every available report or lead on The Terror. Even today, thoughts of the sadist were never far from his mind.

The result was that he felt he knew more than anyone about The Terror. He knew he was big and strong, that he murdered plain, ordinary-appearing women, that at one time he had lived on the knoll like a street bum and that for some reason in 1979, after twenty-two known murders, all executed in a similar larynx-wrenching fashion, he had stopped killing.

Hero closely watched the cause of death of every woman murdered in Los Angeles County, and casually kept an eye out elsewhere. He would go to examine a victim's body if it had an unusual neck wound.

Hero went to great lengths to force The Terror's hand, even chiding "the cowardly creep" in the press, but The Terror would not surface.

"The guy has got to be dead. Suicide, or in jail, or moved away. . . left the country probably," Dwight would say, hoping to stop Hero from digging.

But Hero would shake his tenacious head, "Huh, uh. I know

he's still around. I can feel it in my bones. He'll show. There's something keeping him from it. But one day he'll show and when he does, I'll nail him to a cross. Goddamn, will it be a pleasure to nail him." Hero would rub his hands together and grin like a kid.

Down-shifting, he lurched the black Porsche forward and roared east up San Vicente. The sun was going into the sea behind him. He passed a gang of kids in a Rent-a-Truck having a good time picking up Christmas trees. They would burn a huge two-story dried pile of them at the UCLA Commons later in the week, really something to see.

Turning left through the grassy island at Eleventh Street, Hero parked west back toward the ocean and the quickly dying sun. He secured the car top and windows and locked his wallet, badge, gun and holster, ignition and house key ring into the trunk of the Porsche. He sat on the curb to lace the lone trunk key into his right athletic shoe and to retighten and tie all of the laces. They were high-top shoes. Leather Nikes for indoor hard-court use. Not the best by far for running, but they would do.

There was something beginning to germinate in the back of his brain. It was the kind of inkling, like the growing recollection of an overlooked responsibility that can come over you and give you the chills. He stopped to concentrate, but the notion wouldn't come.

Standing to stretch and then tuck his shirt into his shorts, he remembered. My poem, that's it, my poem. Maybe I'll finish the son of a gun. Maybe now is the hour.

He didn't want to force it, but with the inclination, the willingness hanging around in his head, he went back through the routine of unlocking the car to retrieve a stub of a pencil and some paper from the dash. He tucked the pencil and paper into his tight breast pocket, secured the car and key and after clearing the traffic, walked to the middle of the street, to the thirty-foot-wide grass division that separates east- and west-bound San Vicente Boulevard.

He did deep knee bends and recited his shortest, sweetest poem out loud to get warmed up. Besides his lengthy poem entitled "To Feel," it was his favorite. His classmates liked it too as did Professor Talmadge, who sent it to the papers. The *L.A. Times* printed it and called him the Poet Cop. Hero was certain that the main reason it had appealed to the press was that it was so unpolicelike. But he hadn't minded the publicity this time. It brought him an undeniable feeling of self-esteem. It encouraged some latent part of him to keep at it and feel good about himself.

From kneeling to standing and back again he went, many times quickly, with his knees cracking, and he said,

"The Bureau

The governor's a whore
and much more
the mayor has no hair
and's unfair
the chief is a thief
and with clarity
gives charity
to mouths that don't even care."

Liking his poem and laughing, he ran. The day's events immediately began to surge through his mind. It was a disconcerting physiological phenomenon that happened every time he began running. It came with the initial jolts in his legs, the pounding of blood and oxygen. If he didn't resist, the anxieties of the day, like the negative thinking that came just before sleep, would go away. He let himself focus on Calhoun and all of the other crap, the sick people he had to deal with, and it was gone.

Picking up speed he meditated. He thought about the white pilot light he imagined in his soul. He concentrated on the blue-white flame and let his eyelids hang. Warming, his body felt good.

The grade down those eleven blocks to the bluffs overlooking the ocean was smooth and gradual. The kind of easy descent you're not aware of until you turn at Ocean Avenue and begin the run back. Until your legs and lungs send the message, "Hey, this thing slopes up." But Hero wasn't going back up. He would turn south across Ocean Avenue and run the grassy knoll to the Santa Monica pier and continue south into Venice, down Main Street to the marina. All of it, it seemed, a slight downgrade, a wonderful run. Kay would bring him back or if they crashed, Dwight could come by in the morning and drop him at his car. Everything was okay, good, even Kay, moving in.

Breathing deeply, he began to perspire. He stretched his legs out and concentrated on changing gears, like on a bike, putting it into third. A thought of Dwight came and his God-given talent. He heard him: "Gosh, Hero, aren't we going to run any faster? Come on, let's get a workout. I could jog at this pace all day." But Hero laughed and pushed Dwight away for the white light and the fabulous swelling sensation in his legs. Not long, graceful, natural athletic legs maybe, like some people's. But good, strong dependable legs just the same.

Feeling peaceful yet determined, Hero stretched his arms above his head and murmured, "Oh, yeah . . . Oh, yeah . . ." to describe his invigoration. It was this physical stuff, the energy that is life and the injustice, the exasperation of living that he was trying to capture in his new poem.

He knew the completed sentences of his new poem by heart. He said them to himself as he ran. He said the words slowly and listened to them rhyme. He turned it into a cadence, a rhythm, saying the phrases at the dropping of his feet. He recited his poem deliberately, not contemplating its ending but hoping when he got there he would be able, this time, to find one.

Spurred by his growing enthusiasm, he let himself go. Stretching out, pushing it, an idea came. It was full of Calhoun and slavery and the roar of corpuscles through his veins. He encouraged his imagination.

Juiced on oxygen, with no concern for the miles ahead, he began to sprint for Ocean Avenue. He hauled huge breaths of sea air into his lungs and conceptualized his poem on paper, completed. He matched the words and rhymed them. He did it again and timed his endeavor in such a way as to bring himself out and across Ocean Avenue onto the knoll under an arc light as he finished. "Goddamn . . . shit-o," he screamed, crossing Ocean Avenue in four strides.

A beige Rolls-Royce convert sat in the shadows at the curb. The top was down. A lone, shining blond-haired girl sat in the passenger seat with that door open onto the grassy knoll. The knoll's pay phone, the only outdoor telephone booth around, sat brightly lit not five feet from her. Hero knew she was waiting for her lover's call. Lots of them used that phone. Sometimes they waited in line. Sometimes they went off with each other. The cheaters' phone, Hero called it. The other good one he knew about was in Rancho Park across Pico Boulevard from Fox Studios. That was a special safe cheaters' phone too. No possibility of a bug and no private dick could get near without being observed.

Hero censored the blonde from his thoughts and ran for the railing that overlooked Pacific Coast Highway, the darkening beaches and the sea. Catching his breath, using the flat top of a square concrete post, he wrote it down, everything he knew. And then he wrote the ending. He breathed hard and perspired onto his work. He wrote fast but carefully. Not abbreviating words that he would be unable to decipher later.

Finished, he held it up and looked at it and said, "Wow, beautiful—fantastic stuff." He recited the ending again and had the title. He said, "All—right," and was tremendously proud and excited.

A sigh of relief trembled through him. Soaked with perspiration, his chest heaving, he paused to stare out over the busy Coast Highway and the brightly lit beach houses three hundred feet below. He glanced to the south and let the dazzling lighting along the Santa Monica pier and a pale slice of moon above Hermosa hold his attention.

He turned to the vastness before him and shivered. With the sun and afterglow long gone, there was no horizon, no juxtaposing heaven and earth. There was nothing but an indistinct gray boundlessness. Sensing the planet's curvature, he leaned out toward it and inhaled deeply. He was at the bow of the world.

Overwhelmed with oxygen, what he'd written and where he found himself with the creation, he said, "Thank you, Father," and looked down at his feet in humility. It was a special high, a perfect spiritual moment.

Suddenly, a chill came to him accompanied by a stomach full of paranoid anxiety. Something told him his poem was sophomoric and stupid and should never be seen. He heard Professor

Talmadge say, "Ugh and yuk . . . Yuk, yuk, yuk." He felt the fear of self-recrimination and said, "Shit."

Hero stood there huffing into the cool oncoming night, the pencil in one hand, the paper in the other. He dared himself to read it again, now. Now that you've come down, now that the running high, the oxygenation is wearing off.

With his chest out, trying to act undaunted, he marched to the closest good street light, said, "Come on, pal," took a deep breath and read aloud.

"The Heart of Integration

Hold the pressures perfect
in balance and pump
the good being done resurrection
A color so true
that nothing is new a flow
with not one imperfection
Double and bubble
with nary a trouble
happiness merchant galore
The white and the red
carry on head to head
one hopes that neither has more
Middle to bottom
to top to arms
all to go back
to the oxygen farms
Down South pray don't tattle
the same thing in cattle
Our agent is free with his charms
So tarry not long
with that menacing throng
who belch of my discontent
but value much more
the know of the score
his rights to be given not lent."

The blonde laughed uproariously in the phone booth behind him. Hero turned to see her become serious and whisper into the receiver. She caressed her flat stomach and pubic area

61

repeatedly with a thin, milk-white bejeweled hand in an inadvertent yet nervously excited gesture. Smoothing her skirt, he thought. Just smoothing out the wrinkles.

Hero turned away and didn't move again when he heard her giggle. He held still and relished what he'd written. He told himself that he knew better than to judge his work. That that wasn't his responsibility. Professor Talmadge said, "Just write it and rewrite it. Rewrite it until it is correct and then, like a child, it goes out into the world to see what it can do . . . by itself, on its own merit. So don't *you* judge it." Still, Hero said to himself with a smirk, I like it. I like it one hell of a lot. He laughed, tucked the pencil and paper away, waved to the blonde who was rubbing herself anxiously and feeling great, ran south.

Staying off the tar walking path, he ran on the firm grass beneath the trees. Perspiration quickly returned. He concentrated on landing on the outsides of his feet, on turning his toes inward the way Alberto Salazar, the marathon champ, said to do it. He wished he were wearing his Tiger running shoes.

And then suddenly, she appeared as if from behind a tree, running without making a sound. She was ahead of him and off to the right, pulling away, a long-legged brunette in a matched light-blue running outfit. For fun, Hero sped up to run over and behind her. Somebody to pass, he told himself with a cocky laugh.

When he ran, he loved to catch and pass as many runners as he could. It made him feel like a big shot, a famous runner. Besides, he couldn't help himself. His nature was to win.

Feeling good about Hero, he turned it on. He would come out of the dark behind her, pass her casually, effortlessly. Perhaps even smile on the way by and say, "Hello, don't feel bad. I'm a pro and a poet. You can't expect to—" But she saw him too.

She probably heard him breathing because she glanced over her shoulder and, after hesitating for an instant, bolted like a frightened deer. She sprinted for twenty or more yards before settling into a strong kick.

Hero said, "Shit," and chased her. He tried but the closest he got was at California Street when she slowed to make sure the traffic ramp was clear before continuing on.

With the added illumination from Ocean Avenue, he got close enough to observe her short, dark coppery hair bouncing wet against her neck. Her damp skin reflected a sensual shadowy glow under the irregular lighting. And he saw the pinholes. The small worn-out areas on the back of her tank top where racing numbers had been pinned so many times as to leave torn traces in the light-blue shiny material. A marathoner, he thought. Sure as shit I picked a heavy. He thought briefly about stopping, but wouldn't.

He hated his competitive spirit, his obsession with winning. His frustrated fear of the resentment he would hold against himself if he lost; at anything. It was the shits. His lungs were on fire. He was dying. "Let her go," he mumbled in a desperate gasp. "Let her go—slow down. There's no one around to see or care. You'll never make the marina, never. Go slow. Go home to Kay. Kay is waiting." But he kicked through the intersection as fast as he could run. He had to give it one final shot or come apart trying.

Pouring it on, like a sprinter in the hundred meters, he decided to race her to the outdoor john across from the Bellevue Restaurant or at Broadway or wherever it was. Close as it was, he knew he'd never make the pier. She wouldn't know the race would end at the toilet. But he would. He might win.

At Wilshire Boulevard he almost had her. The pain in his knees and chest was excruciating. He thought his scalp was coming off. He forced his mind to Urie, the great Czech track coach that brought Bannister and Landy through the first four-minute mile. "When you feel pain, thrust yourself against it. Pain is the great purifier." Yeah, shit, he retched to himself.

He was on her heels. Adidas competition runners without socks. But she was definitely running faster now too. Her legs. God, what legs. Brown, svelte. The brunette was svelte. She had a svelte, greased-lightning, bat-out-of-hell body.

He was going for her. He drew alongside. He couldn't look at her. Don't look at the competition. Don't try to figure their heads. It will break you. Her breathing was quiet, controlled, petite, unnerving. He heard his own gulping inhalations. He tried for the lead with everything he had but couldn't pull away. She ran faster, dirty rat. So did he. The fear, the anguish, was unbearable.

Hold on, don't shake apart, don't fall. It's the finish, the finish. Run, son of a bitch, run.

Every pore in his body felt open and stinging; desperate. His feet seemed like lead. The elastic at the top of his left sock had broken, allowing it to flop unmercifully, a bruising ton of cotton against his shin.

He held his breath to strain every muscle. Above the scream of pressure in his head there was the slap, slapping sound from his car key against his leather Nike. He wondered if she could hear it or if she was distracted by mundane shit like that. Now that he noticed, it would slap at his brain forever, until he fell on his face to puke the nauseating obsession away. Haul ass. Help me, God. If You do that sort of thing.

He passed her. His head swam. How could he express the love he had for her, the respect. She was a brunette. His mother and four sisters were brunettes. He loved them all dearly; this one now too. A hundred yards more at most.

He felt faint. Sugar, glycogen, spent. My gut, Jesus, my gut. The john was close, coming in and out of focus. Suddenly, so was she. In his periphery, next to him again. Seeing her, he had to constrain his rectum. He had the urge to defecate in his pants. He had to urinate too. Subconscious for sure. A reason to stop at the toilet. He gave it everything he had but she was unquestionably ahead when they came abreast of the public place.

Stopping, he marched briskly around in circles. He was out of control. The gristle in his knees raged. He sucked air. He held his head down, oblivious. His hands were on his thighs. His lungs were on fire. He might have been sick but she distracted him.

She was back, jogging, dancing around his inner circle. "What are you, a fucking Indian?" he gasped. But she didn't hear and asked, "Why are you stopping?" He looked up to find her bouncing lightly in place. A lovely faced, smiling brunette girl. Wet, but without the slightest trace of oxygen debt.

Hero said shit loudly to himself but bucked up. "Me? Oh, I've... I've got to go to the john. And I don't love you anymore." He managed a laugh.

She said, "Don't feel bad. Walk back and forth with your nose up in the air so you won't throw up. See you around." She ran off toward the pier.

Hero said, "Oh, okay, lady," and went into the stinky john.

He stood in front of the urinal. His body was pounding. His ears rang. He breathed the stifling urine-fumed air. He waited, shrunken penis in his trembling hand, and finally produced a silly dribble of urine. Clear too, expunged of all nutrients.

Feeling a fool, and holding his breath for clean air, Hero went back to the large, tiled open exit. A pay phone on the wall next to him caught his eye. He wanted to call Kay. To have her come and get him. Checking the coin return, finding it empty, he gave the idea up.

Outside, he breathed deeply of the good air and looked carefully in both directions. Long gone, he said to himself. The brunette was nowhere to be seen.

He ran in place to see that his legs still worked. They were tight and swollen and pained him. He wondered if the brunette was laughing. It didn't matter. He had had no choice. There was no continuing. She was better, maybe. Not that he couldn't be that good if he tried. Shit, if I worked out, ran every day like she does, I could go forever too. He did deep knee bends and touched his toes.

"Are you a movie star?" a mincy-sounding voice came from behind.

Hero knew that he looked a bit like one of those famous guys, so the question was not off the wall. He stopped what he was doing to turn and say, "No, I'm not a movie star," to a sick-eyed public-toilet queen who lurked nearby.

Hero remembered afterward the main impression he had of the man was that he appeared more frail than perhaps anyone he had ever come in contact with before. Frail with an incredibly desperate bearing. As though he would literally expire if he didn't get what he wanted. His clothing looked damp. He probably, Hero figured, wants a golden shower. He's a urine head. But that was wrong.

"Do you want a blow job, movie star?" The frail thing smiled embarrassedly but stared deep into Hero's eyes while licking his lips to demonstrate how badly he wanted it. "I need it . . . I love it when it's swollen."

"No, I don't want a blow job, and I'm not a movie star. I happen to be a cop."

The fragile man didn't blanch but spoke instead matter-of-factly. "So, what about it? I know a marine that's butcher than you, who all he likes to do is suck cock and fight. Besides, I know lots of cops who like to get sucked."

Hero said, "Yeah, okay," and turned to run off when he stopped himself. "Hey listen, have you got a dime you can let me have?"

"Will you let me blow you?"

"Well . . ." The frail one's eyes lit up. Hero laughed at himself. "No, now listen . . . aw shit, forget it." Shaking his head disgustedly, Hero took off down the knoll for the pier but the queen yelled out behind him, "Okay . . . here you are."

Hero stopped, went back for the dime, thanked the frail homosexual and called the houseboat.

He wondered how she would sound answering his phone. Their phone now. Her phone? Whether there would be a domineering hint of permanence in her voice that would put him off. That might get him wondering. Would she fuck it up? Could it be fucked up? Kay answered.

As usual she was cheerful and glad to hear from him.

"Can I sleep on your couch?" Hero asked.

She laughed adoringly and replied, "Oh, Hero, you sure can. If I can be there too. I love you so much. Where are you? I miss you."

Breathing deeply, he let the relaxed, sincere tone of her voice seduce him, dispel his anxieties. So far so good, he thought, conjuring the sweet smell of her blondness.

It had begun when he was supposed to be watching fireworks from the bluffs on the Fourth. He'd stood in the crowd in back

66

of Sue with his hands down her blouse massaging her bare breasts, when he looked to his left and saw Kay. He'd gone gaga for the first time in years and stared at those blushing, downcast Siamese cat's eyes, at the powerful genuine expression therein. And after more than six months he still hadn't been able to take his eyes away. The real fireworks that night went off in his pants and in Sue's disposition when she knew he'd followed Kay and memorized the license number on her car.

Hero felt a thrill about getting home to her. God, it must be love, boy. A home life. A good woman. The real thing. It's about time, I hope.

He told her what had happened and that he was exhausted, but as he spoke, thinking about her at the houseboat all cozy with dinner waiting, he changed his mind. He said, "I'll see you in twenty minutes."

"I could come and get you. Should I drive up for you? Meet you along the way?"

"No. I'll finish my run. It'll do me good. It'll teach me to use my head after this. I'll be right along."

"Oh, Hero, Dwight called. He left one of his crazy messages . . . said you'd understand. I wrote it down. Wait . . ." After a moment she returned to read, "Another one is missing from the Westwood theater." She waited for his reply and when it didn't come, asked, "Does that make any sense to you? Another one is missing from—"

"When did he call, Kay?"

"Fifteen minutes ago. Is it important?"

"I don't know. I miss you, I know that. I'll see you shortly."

He felt beat but he ran.

"Another one missing from the theater? I wonder what the hell that's all about. If it has anything to do with that . . . Weighgood girl?"

SIX

Thinking about Kay and smiling, Hero moved with a slow easy lope down Venice's Main Street. He jogged past the glamorous new multimillion-dollar restaurants built by the cocaine kings with their extra millions. What the hell, let's dump it into antiques, stained glass and brass. Build us a bar and restaurant; who cares? Where's the plane? When's the next run? What day is it? What planet? I'm higher than the plane on this pure stuff.

Hero laughed and guessed that the old street looked nice with the renovation, the new smells, the opulent facades. With all of the snazzy people, the movie and music stars.

Hero ran past Kay's favorite health food market where she got the delicious essence bread that she wouldn't eat but that he loved. When he arrived in front of Sewell and Webster's design center, he looked back at the brightly lit street. He ran backward for a while into the dark and, cocaine kings or no cocaine kings, he was glad things had changed. That the violence had subsided.

As the central thoroughfare through the city of Venice, Main Street had always been Hero's beat regardless of the department he was in. He knew it when it was lined with broken-down dives. When the dives were full of junkies full of mostly hard dope. The entire area had been unsafe at night. Everyone had been prey to muggers. When you walked through Venice with your girl, they'd take your money and your girl—and your life if you protested.

Hero had helped clean the city up. It made him feel good seeing it now.

Just past Donkin's Inn, Hero was able to see the lights of the houseboat at the end of the pier. It was a snug-looking colorful spot in the distance with the Christmas lighting Kay had put around the windows. He was exhausted and chilly and fighting the urge to walk, but he wouldn't let himself give up. Go slow, he told himself, but don't stop.

Reaching his dock, he vaulted the locked gate and landed to smell cooking potatoes with his next breath.

Stretch began to bark. Goddamn, he thought, tired and aggravated. I wish he'd recognize me. But it was no use.

Good old Stretch was eleven years old. Seventy-seven years as humans count them. Hero figured it was too late to teach an old dog new tricks. But the old guy was loyal as hell and a good friend. He listened to Kay, too, and liked her. Besides, he had worked for years smelling out dope and was one of the depart-ment's best dogs.

Stretch was obsessed with the smell of marijuana and would run to it every time, which had more than once been a source of embarrassment. Running aboard a friend's boat to stand in front of a locked door sniffing and howling loudly. Jumping out of the car to sniff and chew at a stranger's pant leg. Or to stand guard growling over a purse in the market or a doctor's office until Hero or Kay would make him stop.

They would scream at him and tell him he was retired, but that didn't slow the dachshund down. He had been raised on a farm that trained Shepherds for narcotics work and had, by accident, ended up at the head of the class.

Hero and Kay loved the old guy so they kidded about him. They said they could dress him up but not take him out. Stretch almost always stayed home. "To guard the fort," they told him, and he liked that. But he did too good a job.

The dock swayed under him. Water slapped. Hero jumped aboard. He heard Kay's voice from inside, "Yes, it's him, Stretch, it's him," and he heard Stretch go a little nuts, barking and chasing around. Then he was through the door that still jingled of Christmas to face them. Beautiful blond Kay with her hair up in back held by chopsticks, Hero's favorite style, and Stretch, his dachshund pal with the wagging tail. They all smiled to see each other and Hero felt warm inside.

Kay kissed him on the cheek and pulled him along through the houseboat and out the sliding glass back door to the steaming hot tub. No major changes were evident along the way. Things were neat, clean and warm-looking; orderly, like when she stayed over. She had assimilated perfectly.

"Come on." She held out her hands for his clothes which he quickly dropped to the floor or gave her. "Okay, jump in and soak. I've got a super dinner for us."

Hero groaned, "Oh, good God" when he slid into the hot bubbling water and said, "Yes, I know. I smelled the potatoes a mile away."

"Regular *and* sweet potatoes," she said in a proud way.

Moving back inside she nearly tripped over the torn hem of her green silk robe and Stretch. Kay screamed out and caught herself on the door jamb. Hero yelled, "Stretch, goddamn it," and the dog ran back for his spot next to the bed. Hero's voice echoed out over the marina and then all was quiet.

With only his head above the hot steaming water, Hero relaxed and let his eyes go with the sights. The yachts and condos, the hotel across the bay, the dark open sky and the reflections everywhere of every size boat and sparkling rippled lighting; and the cut of new moon.

Hero had purchased the houseboat from a disgruntled San Francisco architect in December 1976 for twenty thousand dollars, and had lived aboard ever since. Today it was worth a hundred or more. The architect had had the boat built in Sausalito and towed to Los Angeles, but he never could get into the southern California scene. After a year of trying, he was ready to give up and move back up north.

A week before Christmas of '76, Hero arrested three big-time dope dealers and impounded their fifty-five-footer seven slips away from the boathouse. He met the architect by chance on the night of the bust. Four days later the deal was made. Hero paid cash. The end slip's monthlies were one hundred and eighty-five dollars, plus gas, electric and telephone. Cheap, and he loved it. It served him well and the marina owners, private cops, the boat and local condominium owners, were delighted to have Hero Fiddleman from Venice Division close. They extended him every consideration.

Kay met Hero on the way to the shower. She handed him a cut-crystal glass of sherry with one hand and gave his penis a tug with the other. "This should make you feel better, big boy." She talked like Mae West. "Are you my magic man?" she asked. She stared him in the eye and blushed profusely.

Goddamn, he shuddered to himself, downing the sherry in one gulp. The sweet alcohol was into his bloodstream instantaneously. It added a hot itching sensation to his already stiffening penis. He looked down at it and back at Kay with a grin.

"Ohhh, no," she said, putting her hands up to protest and backing away. "I've got dinner, and . . . and you're soaking wet. Why don't you hop in the shower and . . ."

Hero put the glass down and grabbed her. Drawing her close, he made his lips wet with sherried saliva and kissed her. Gently at first, licking her lips, and then ravenously. With her arms straight down between them, she fondled his penis. She squeezed it as hard as she could. She rolled it between both of her flat palms and broke the kiss to whisper, "Rolling pin . . . I'm your rolling-pin girl. I make you good dinners. The oven is on, but right now . . . *my* oven is . . ."

"Is hot?" he inquired anxiously.

"Yes," she confessed, looking away shyly.

With her head against his shoulder, she brought his hand, which seemed to him a muscled hulk amid her soft touch, and placed it over her smooth-skinned belly. Gently, she encouraged his fingers down to feel the luster of her vigorous pubic hair and to touch under, between her legs.

"See?" she whispered.

Hero's sphincter slammed shut. His penis throbbed and he had to catch his breath when he touched the syrupy slickness over her inner thighs. Kay tensed and held her breath while he traced the wetness up to find her pouting vaginal lips. Tickling, touching ever so softly, he ran his fingertips back and forth along the thick juicy protrusions until he pushed aside her upper labia to graze her clitoris with a knuckle. Kay swooned and fell into his arms.

Losing her robe along the way, Hero carried her to the king-size bed, but as he laid her down, she broke away to run into the kitchen to "fix things so they won't burn." Hero took the opportunity to put Stretch out in back by the hot tub and close the sliding glass door. Lying back onto the bed he rested his jaw in his palm and watched her move around the kitchen naked.

He observed her long smooth legs and "high cunt," as he called it. He pictured what he thought to be Kay's unusually high, pronounced clitoris, and dreamed how easy it was to contact with his tongue or coarse pubic patch. How it would stand up hard and purplish pink. He stroked his thick erection and used his other hand to toy with the wetness over the head of his penis.

As she bent over the oven, her bust hung. Not huge but meaty and nice with incredibly sensitive nipples that they fought over squeezing and pinching when they made love. She glanced to see him watching and smiled to ask, "Do you like having me here, to come home to? Are you comfortable?"

Hero replied, "Yes, yes I do. Very much. You're so beautiful."

"Is that all?"

"No . . . no, but you do make my eyes feel good." He laughed.

She smiled and said, "I love you."

And Hero said, "I love you, too."

He stopped playing with himself to watch her closely. It never ceased to amaze him. She had everything, and yet she was definitely cockeyed. "Slightly crossed," were the words she preferred. But no matter, her eyes had wandered and focused funny from birth. Surgery would help, perhaps even correct the defect, but Kay was afraid of being cut. She disliked herself in glasses and never wore any of the ten or so pairs that lay around except to drive. Besides, the ailment worked well for her.

Her eyes appeared perfectly normal on camera but unusually sexy, alluring. Two limpid blue pools with the most intense pupils that could charm the coldest heart or sell the stupidest product. Kay's eyes held a compelling expression that advertisers went crazy over.

It didn't bother him in the least, but Hero knew she dreaded having her eyes wander when he could notice. She concentrated and held them perfect, which she was capable of doing most of the time, unless she was exhausted or forgot to keep up the effort.

It was this constant straightening, disentangling exertion that came from her pupils like a hot black ray that helped make Kay a modeling star. She could turn it on too, turn up the heat the way she was doing now, as she came to stand in front of him.

She removed the chopsticks from the back of her hair and shook her head to allow her blondness to fall heavy and luxurious down over her shoulders. She stood on her heels, with her legs apart like a gun slinger. She burned him with her eyes and after a moment rubbed her belly in a circular motion. Blushing but speaking directly, she asked, "Have you got something for me, Magic Man?" She dropped to her knees next to the bed. "Let me see the magic wand."

Hero lay back to produce his perfectly erect glistening penis.

Using her face, tongue and lips only, Kay maneuvered her mouth up and over the distended purple head of his penis. Her mouth was hot, her tongue rough in a sandpapery, yet sloppy way. She used her tongue to perform some magic of her own under the head of his penis, along the sensitive zone. She used her fingers to manipulate then squeeze his testicles in a slightly painful fashion that he loved. It made his head pound. He cried out but she squeezed a little harder and he groaned with pleasure.

Hero touched her shoulder, then held her there with both

hands to force her onto him, to move her faster. Her skin was wet. She smelled fabulously, of sex and LEDE perfume, his favorite.

He leaned up onto his elbows to watch saliva spill out of her mouth down and around his pulsing, blood-vesseled penis. It was sexy to watch the terrible stiff thing slide in and out of her lovely face. It made him writhe on his buttocks. Holding her silken blondness out of the way to watch, he fucked her pretty mouth hard. Kay didn't wince but took it all. Finally, he let go of her and fell back.

After a good amount of time, Kay lifted her mouth away with a slurp. His penis fell to his belly with a wet slap. "Are you the Magic Man?" she asked softly. Hero sat up to see her beautiful red-cheeked face covered with wetness, her eyes crossed.

Smiling and feeling full of passion, Hero brought her up next to him. She concentrated her eyes straight. They stared deeply into each other until Hero wasn't sure he had anything left, no secrets. It was a strange new sensation that brought with it an inkling of giddy self-consciousness, but he went for it.

"I love you," he said.

And she smiled endearingly to say, "Oh, Hero, I love you too. . . good God." She squeezed him tightly to take his breath away, and broke away to scold, "Well, how about a trick, Mister Magician . . . and how about later? I had a whole ritual planned, black nightie and all. I'd planned to make good love later on, after. . ."

"We'll take care of that too." He smiled mischievously. He put his tongue in and out of her ear and asked, "How about some magic, want to see some magic?" He flexed his stiff penis against her thigh.

Wriggling in anticipation, she whispered, "God, yes . . . yes."

Moving on top of her, he concentrated on throwing his internal control switch. She comes first, before I get mine.

He was into her easily, wet and deep. He held his pubic mass firmly against her high clitoris, until Kay shuddered. Clinging, they stared into each other's eyes and he ground on her. Kay blushed but kept her eyes open wide. Her jaw hung. Hero twisted onto her, around and around, back and forth, keeping contact.

Kay's eyes did nutty things. They rolled up into her head and then became two swirling blue whirlpools with her pupils gone out of control. She closed her eyes and began breathing heavily. Hero concentrated. He wanted to give his woman a good time, to welcome her.

He counted ten slow, but firmly put, strokes and pulled out to go onto his knees in front of her. Her vagina was sloppy, succulent flesh over his face; her taste a lush feminine sweetness. He teased her clitoris ever so gently around and around with his tongue, but was careful not to push. Thrashing, she pulled at his wet hair, but couldn't get a grip.

He took his time. She made him the most excited he could ever remember being, but he kept his cool. Whenever he could sense her beginning to build in a serious way, he'd take his mouth away and move up to stroke her ten good ones again with his penis that now stood perpetually fixed, a straining, drooling dead giveaway. A testament to unanimity: the little head and the big one in the same place, finally, hopefully, in love.

He went back to his knees and ate furiously between her legs in a selfish, all-devouring, cannibalizing way before he settled into teasing her clitoris again.

"Hero, honey... come up—finish me with your cock-... please," she begged.

But Hero licked the top of her crack easily and carefully until she moaned and raked his back with her nails. Then up again he went to drive her ten, fifteen good ones before going back to his knees.

Kay began pleading, "Please... pleeeeze," but Hero said, "No," scoldingly, and repeated the procedure again and again until she appeared prostrate and faint. Past exasperation, her mind seemed gone. Her body lay melting before him.

He said, "Okay, blond beauty, your dark animal man is going to hold the cheeks of your ass and fuck you hard until you squirt the best one ever. You will come for me, won't you? Make my prick real juicy?"

"Uh huh," she moaned.

He slid his penis into her and let it soak. Reaching under, he grabbed one soft buttock in each hand and squeezed them alternately, firmly, to get her attention, to hurt her just right.

"Well?" he questioned.

"Oh, God, honey, no more teasing. Do me . . . do me up right, my baby. Fuck me until . . ."

"All right." Hero cut her off and began to work.

He was the writer. Sometimes when she was describing how she liked it, it went against what he knew to be good poetic composition and made him laugh. "Oh, Hero, use your long well-tuned staff of life in my dark cavern . . . make the stars explode in my . . ."

"All right, all right—I love you."

"Oh, I love you too. Don't stop what you're doing."

He didn't have to hit her many times before she caught her breath and tensed. Using shorter, firmer strokes, he held contact. He put his tongue deep into her throat, squeezed her bottom black and blue and she went. She clutched and twisted and the syrup in her vagina surged to thick rich cream.

He stayed with her all the way, through the decline, milking her until she slowed to crack a blissful smile. She sighed long and hard, said, "Wow," and giggled with her eyes struggling to uncross from her nose.

Leaning back away from her but staying inside, Hero stroked her burning hole and watched the action. He loved to watch his glistening darkness against her pink and blond vagina. The room smelled of their wetness. He arched his back and swooned. Perspiration flew over Kay.

His penis was so perfectly stiff as to come all the way out of her and find the way back in easily without a searching probe or aiming. The head of his penis was swollen blue, the size of a fist. The night, the ocean, the room, began to ring in his ears and cloud his vision. His testicles were up tight against his groin and paining him. He kept on, all the way in, all the way out.

Straight-eyed, Kay remarked in awe, "God darn, honey, go for it. You're so sleek and magnificent with . . ."

"All right, all right, once more, just one more stroke . . .

once . . . once . . . once more . . . one . . . "

Carefully, with near surgical precision, he eased in the final time and let go.

Semiconscious, he babbled nonsense while he concentrated on the dark overwhelming sensation. The slamming synapses in his brain that sent impulse after surging impulse from his testes to the tips of his extremities. He tried to make it last, to hang onto every tingling ripple of muscle until it began to subside and then spent itself completely.

He hung over her panting. Spittle fell from his open mouth onto her breasts. After a shudder that went everywhere in him, that left him in perfect oblivion, he fell onto her, soaked and exhausted. Say it, say it, now that the heat is down. Say it, you chickenshit, say it. "I . . . love you."

"Yes, Hero, honey, my man. I love you, too. Gosh," Kay yawned. "I feel wonderful. Like the cares and woes of the world have been lifted from my shoulders. And we've got a great dinner and Governor Brown is on Buckley's show at seven-thirty. And, who knows, I might put on my new black nightie for you. If you want."

She kissed him gently on the mouth. His penis began to unfold, but she jumped up to go into the bathroom.

Feeling great, Hero yelled, "I wonder if Brown will have his beard with him?"

"Who? His what?" she yelled back over a flushing toilet.

"Governor Brown . . . his beard . . . Linda Ron . . . Oh, never mind." He laughed and lay on his face.

He laughed a good one, over something Dwight had done a month or so before. Funny it should come to me again now. Maybe it wasn't even that funny, but he thought it through again and it made him chuckle.

Dwight had called him at home one Sunday to ask the number of a prostitute. Dwight was in Hero's office at the precinct and wasn't sure where to look. It was for a lonely buddy of his down at Central Division, newly divorced.

Hero had said, "Get my book out and look under H."

Dwight asked, "H? Does that stand for herpes?" And Hero said, "No, asshole, it stands for hooker."

"What's so funny?" Kay wanted to know.

78

"Oh, nothing...just thinking about Dwight. He can be a card. Let's pass on Buckley and watch the 'McNeil-Lehrer Report' on Public Broadcast."

"Oh, that's a good idea."

She was in her new black outfit. A sleeveless silk top and bikini panties. She wore black, furry go-ahead slippers. Her hair was held in a ponytail with a black ribbon.

"Goddamn, Kay, you look pretty. Good enough to..."

"Even for a shiksa...isn't that what your father calls me?"

Embarrassed, Hero laughed and said, "Ah, yeah, even for a shiksa. Come here, blondie."

"Now, now." She wagged her finger on the way to the kitchen and said, "Dinner in five minutes, if you want to shower."

Hero bounced up, turned on the television and headed for the bathroom.

"You know what, honey?" she called.

"No, what?"

"I miss New York."

Hero thought that that was understandable, shrugged, answered, "Yeah," and hit the shower.

They had had a ball in New York. Staying at the Plaza. With coffee, strawberries and violins every evening at the Palm Court.

Rena, Hero's youngest sister, an actress/model, had thrown a blast for them in SoHo to end all blasts. Kay was known there as a model. Hero saw that that made her feel good.

Hero had bought Kay a pair of round emerald earrings at Carimati's and they'd walked up north along the east side of Madison with their noses in the crisp clean air.

They'd laughed and hugged and shielded their eyes from the wonderful December sun that burned so intensely as to turn the entire sky gold and the sidewalks white and light up the city for as far north as you could see.

Hero's mother had been great, his father a pain, but in all, they had loved it.

Toweling off, Hero let Stretch in and yelled to Kay, "Love is in the air, speaking of New York...remember?"

Kay answered, "Oh, gosh, do I. What a good time. When can we go back?"

"Soon. This summer, April . . . whenever it's convenient."

He turned the television up and paused to watch Robert McNeil interview a congressman about the SALT treaty and the current delivery systems for nuclear devices.

"I finished my poem. It's called 'The Heart of Integration.'"

Kay responded enthusiastically as usual and asked to hear it. After retrieving the wet notepaper from his shirt pocket, Hero recited his poem to her while she put a tablecloth over their big bed. She adjusted the television's volume so she could hear him better. When he was finished, she stood perfectly still except to nod her head up and down in serious thought. Then she smiled and said she was genuinely impressed.

"God, it's a fabulous poem, honey. You're so talented. I love it. They'll love it at your school, just love it."

Hero sat under Kay's professional hair dryer while Kay put the food trays onto the bed, their favorite spot to eat.

"Fabulous," was the word Hero used to describe the dinner of fresh salmon, baked potatoes and salad. They drank Cold Spring water. Less sodium than Perrier. A find from Minnesota.

While eating, they watched and listened to McNeil and Lehrer interview the congressman, a general, a nuclear physicist and a Soviet expert from Yale.

"I did a crazy thing at the market today," Kay reported.

"What?" Hero asked.

"Well, I was standing in line with a few last-minute things for dinner, and a big fat man—big and smelly—came barging into line in front of me with two six packs of beer and a bag of potato chips. He just pushed his way right in front of me and said, 'Oh, you don't mind, do you, dear?' Then he turned away, taking for granted that I wouldn't care. He just turned his back on me.

"He smelled terrible, just terrible, the kind of terrible odor that burns your nostrils. And I could see the broken blood vessels all over his neck and back above his filthy tank top. I stood there blushing and sort of . . . flipped out. I started to scream, 'Yes I mind, yes I mind. Get into line in back of me.

Who do you think you are, anyway? Yes, I mind. I mind.' Jeez, honey, it was just awful."

"So?"

"So he went back in line and I paid and went out to the car. I sat and turned on the air conditioning to cool myself off and I realized something. You know what I realized?"

"No, what?"

"I realized that I wasn't mad at the fat man."

"No?"

"Nope, it was me. I was mad at Kay for being such a coward, such a chickenshit all my life. You know? I didn't tell you this, that a low rider in a pickup truck pulled up next to me at a stoplight in Westwood last week and spit all over the windshield of my car."

"Was it an accident? Maybe he—"

"Oh, no, no accident. He looked right at me and gobbed all over my windshield and said, 'Rich bitch . . . I hate fucking BMW's.' But forget him. It's me. I just sat there mortified instead of . . . of . . . doing something."

"What did you finally do?" Hero asked angrily, wishing he had been in his car behind Kay.

"I just sat there like a lump until he went away. I turned on the windshield wipers and it all washed off. But instead of just sitting there like a coward, I wish I'd been able to tell him off, you know, call him an asshole or tell him he was a pig . . . or something. I don't know."

Hero patted her knee and understood her frustration. "There are a lot of assholes out there, Kay, what can I tell you? But you did the right thing. He may have been looking for an excuse to jump out and smack you . . . or worse. Just be cool and keep on going when that happens."

He smiled and finished the salmon, but that wasn't where his head was. He was thinking of arming Kay. Of installing a small .25-caliber automatic under her dash. He envisioned the asshole spitter jumping out of his truck to face a woman's small pistol. It made him smile.

Having grown up with women, knowing them, respecting

them the way he did, he could get himself sick thinking about the animals that preyed on them. The low-down cowardly men who get high, who get their nuts off pushing it on a defenseless female. It's like a guy that's cruel to animals. Goddamn, he told himself. I hate those sick motherfuckers.

"It's a good thing that you unloaded at the market. How do you feel about it?"

"Pretty good. I feel like I accomplished something today, for myself . . . like I grew up a little. How's dinner?"

"Fantastic."

"What do you think about the interview?" She nodded toward the television.

"It's a good show but the subject is all bullshit. It's all bullshit. Money, politics, that's all. How's your weight?"

Kay blanched. She began cleaning the dishes. Hero helped her.

"I mean, you look super to me. I mean, I love you whatever, but don't you have any interest in going back to work? I'm not trying to push . . . just be supportive. You always say you're so happy when you're modeling. Don't you feel . . . ?"

"No . . . my weight isn't right."

"Well, I don't mean to pry, but why? How wrong is it?"

"Wrong enough. It shows in my face. I weigh one-twenty-two. I should weigh one-thirteen or fourteen."

"Well, you've never said anything about a weight problem. Why can't you . . . ?"

Slamming a stack of plates down, she turned on him. "Why can't I lose eight or nine stupid pounds? The truth? Well . . ." Tears welled up in her eyes. "Well, and I'm not trying to put anything on you, but the truth is, I worry about you, out there with the crazies. All the responsibility that you take on yourself, protecting your men, always out in front. I feel hollow when I know you're out there, and I eat. It's as simple as that. Food fills the void."

Hero was shocked. He held her. He brought her back to bed, turned off the television and lay down with her to hold her.

"I never knew that . . . that you worried."

"I know, it's gotten worse. Anticipating moving in here, and now being here. I care so much. I get . . . scared." She began to cry on his shoulder.

"Shit, honey, that's terrible. I don't know what to say."

"It's my problem, Hero, and I'll deal with it. I knew you were a cop coming in. I knew your job, but it gets to me sometimes. But it's my problem."

"Well, then, why—?"

"Because I want you to know the truth, and I need your support, and . . . and I want you to be extra careful . . . of yourself. You're my man, you know. I'd die if—"

"Don't worry, honey. Christ, I know what I'm doing if anybody does in this job. I'm good at what I do. I'm not even in Homicide anymore. I don't—"

"Bullshit, that's just bullshit. You run it all. You're the chief of detectives. You work where you want to work. And you're always in the middle anyway, regardless. You might just as well still be in every department. You left a little bit of yourself everywhere anyway. They all come to you, depend on you. Well, the hell with them, Hero. They're all big tough guys. They can look out for themselves. I mean, what would happen if . . . I got . . . pregnant?"

"And we wanted it to stick?"

"Yes."

Hero jumped up. "Are you?"

"No." She dried her eyes and laughed. "No, but it's something to think about. Policemen get killed all the time. Especially these days."

Hero held her close, rubbing her neck and shoulders until he knew she was asleep. Petting her hair, he began to float himself until the telephone jangled them both awake. "Goddamn," he said, getting out from under her.

Kay said, "Sorry, I thought that I'd unplugged it. I haven't even washed my face." The phone rang again.

"Go back to sleep. Your face will wait until tomorrow."

"No it won't."

She got up and staggered into the bathroom. Hero answered the phone before it could ring again. It was Dwight, sounding excited.

83

"Sorry if I woke you, Chief. It's early, you know, but you sound asleep. Did I wake you?"

"Oh, ah, no, Dwight, we were just sitting here staring at each other waiting for your call. Yeah, we were asleep, but it's okay. I've got to walk the dog. What's up?"

"Well, I wouldn't have called but I thought you'd like to know. It'll blow you away."

"I'm listening."

"Well, Calhoun was out in a couple of hours just like you figured."

"Oh, swell, Dwight. That's just what I wanted to—"

"No, wait, wait a minute. There was a shooting in a warehouse downtown on San Pedro Street, just a few blocks from Central Jail. And guess, just guess what they found?"

Hero didn't answer.

"Well, they found a studio, a movie studio with lots of porno stuff. And a torture chamber. Lots of straight porn films. And two snuff films being processed and printed for distribution. And guess who pays the rent? And guess who brought two drunk marines there tonight to try and tie up and suck off, so they say. And guess who the drunken marines blew to pieces . . . shot his head damn near clean off?"

"No, you're putting me on."

"No, I'm not putting you on. Calhoun is dead as a doornail. Shot to pieces by a couple of tough guys from Pendleton. What do you think about that, Chief? I guess it was bound to happen."

Hero said "Yes" quietly and, of all things, a poem about Calhoun the goon began to wind its way into his mind, but he dismissed the thought to ask, "Are you positive?"

"Sure as shooting. Rollins called me from downtown. Wasn't sure about bothering you. Asked me what I thought. It is absolutely Calhoun, no question."

"Thanks for calling, Dwight. I'll see you . . . Oh, Dwight, pick me up in the morning. My car is in Santa Monica. I ran home this evening. We'll have some coffee on the way in and talk."

"Great . . . Oh, did you get my other message, about the theater in Westwood?"

"Yeah, what's that all about?"

"Don't know . . . weird. Another woman lost from the theater . . . like she was swallowed up. Happened last night. We just got it this afternoon."

"So, have the Westwood guys been through the place?"

"Sure—nothing. It must be somebody hanging around the neighborhood or forcing them out the exit. Who knows? They're just gone, that's all anybody knows, disappeared without a trace. I guess the Reverend Weighgood is putting the pressure on good too."

"I suppose. See you in the morning." Hero hung up.

His memory of Calhoun faded fast but the women disappearing from the theater stayed with him.

"What is it, darling?" from Kay, who came in to crawl under the covers and swoon.

"Nothing, only Dwight."

"Anything important?"

"Not really. A new weird one, that's all. A clinker. The kind of disappearance case that almost always has an obvious clue dangling somewhere that everybody has overlooked. The kind I like." He laughed, kissed her on the temple and headed for the door with Stretch. "I'll be right back. Keep things warm."

Kay moved to his side of the bed and swam around under the covers. "I'll be waiting. And Hero?" She was up on one elbow, without makeup, her eyes straight, smiling in her usual self-assured way.

"Yes?"

"I love you. And I'm not afraid. I'm proud of what you do. And honey . . ."

"Yes?"

"You'll find the clue to this new case, and solve it, or I don't know my man."

Hero stepped outside with Stretch, but replied, "You can bet on it," before he shut the boathouse door and breathed deeply of the cool night air.

SEVEN

Jean and Joan Pilgrim were born on November 15, 1949. The identical girl twins were delivered by Caesarean section fifty seconds apart at Good Samaritan Hospital in Des Moines, Iowa. Dark complected, organically healthy and quick of reflex, they progressed normally their first few weeks, side by side, in a crib built for two.

During their eleventh week, while nursing one morning, Jean suddenly became stubbornly territorial. Following suit almost immediately, Joan would eat only from her mother's left breast while Jean possessed the right. They would starve rather than switch and with an uncanny instinct for which nipple was which, they could not be coerced or fooled into changing breasts. Their father, who was inclined to accept the guidance of astrology, laughed and said it was surely because the twins were Scorpios.

As time passed, Jean and Joan began to pinch and gouge at each other. Considering it a stage, Mrs. Pilgrim fastened mittens bearing appropriately crocheted initials over their tiny hands. But Jean was able to free her right hand and with an incredible display of strength, deafened Joan's right ear.

From that point on, everyone could tell that there was something very wrong between the Pilgrim twins. It showed in their eyes. When placed close to each other, they would abruptly stop whatever they were doing and stare at each other with a dark-eyed hatred that gave observers the willies. Yet when they were separated for long periods, the girls would· scream as though in the most awful pain until they were back together again. Their grandfather said that the Devil was at play between them. They were watched constantly.

Even though Joan was never told the truth about her loss of hearing, there was a sense about her, a lingering begrudgedness, that made it plain she knew just exactly what had happened.

On a clear January day in 1960, while the eleven-year-old twins played in the snow, Joan somehow got the tip of her ski pole into Jean's right eye. Joan didn't run for help, but stood smirking in cold steamy huffs behind her mitten while the thick yellow composition of Jean's right eyeball ran down her cheek, off her chin and into the snow.

Using the ski pole accident, Jean's convalescence and glass-eye fitting as almost welcomed excuses, the exhausted Pilgrim parents sent Joan away to an expensive boarding school in Madison, Wisconsin. But the respite was brief.

The twins became ill. Four hundred miles apart and their symptoms were identical. Their skin turned gray. They would not eat. They became emaciated and wept constantly. They tossed and turned and cried out for each other at night. Professionals at both locations were bewildered and waited to see what would happen.

Ten days later the girls were unable to feed themselves or walk and were reunited in their parents' Des Moines home.

When they first saw each other again Jean said, "I hope you know how much I hate you."

To which Joan replied with a happy smile, "Of course, but it's nothing compared to the way I feel about you. I hate you so much, much more."

In three days they were completely recuperated and the

88

decision was made to leave them alone with each other; to stop interceding and allow them to live as they would or, to kill each other if that was the way it was to be.

The physical altercations stopped. The attacks on each other became verbal, mental abuses that, sad as it was, the twins appeared to thrive on. Their lives together seemed an incessant bickering, a never-ending quarrel.

After high school, the not unattractive, full-figured brunettes tried to do for themselves what people had been trying to do for years. They made an attempt to get away from each other. Simultaneously, they chose marriage as a means of escape.

Neither marriage worked and there were no children, but making use of their husbands and other men, of universities and in the end their own recalcitrant natures, they were able to stay apart for nine years. During that time both of their parents died, leaving them each with a small income.

Finally, at the end of nearly ten years of separation, at age twenty-seven, the girls made a plan. In a demented telephone conversation filled with reassurances of hatred and misgiving, Jean and Joan agreed to meet in California and to live there together, under one roof, in an apartment in West Los Angeles.

People did not go to visit them. The insanity that pervaded their tiny apartment, the sense of unhappiness, made you want to run from the place the minute you entered. Jean and Joan had no friends. They went through each day the same, side by side, scowling and complaining about being depressed, lonely and unfulfilled and blaming each other for their predicament.

They didn't drink or smoke or carouse. They wore their dark hair chopped off below the ear, shiny and clean but with no curl. They wore no makeup and dressed plainly in light sweaters, pleated skirts and brown loafers, interchangeable attire that commingled, hanging in one closet. Their television set was rarely off. They went out to the movies four times a week. They had their favorite TV and motion-picture stars who were all men.

With no interest in reproduction, their sexual existence was limited to fantasy and masturbation. They slept together in the same king-size bed but were not homosexual. They owned one vibrator for masturbation and constantly fought over its use.

When one of the girls masturbated, the other frequently hovered nearby, chiding, berating, accusing her sister of sexual obscenities with one or another of their favorite screen stars. "Go on, rub at that ugly thing. Robert Redford would take one look and puke. Yuk . . . yuk . . . what a big ugly pussy. . . Oh, dear, look how hard you work at it. Aren't you embarrassed?"

On this night, to avoid the crowd, Jean and Joan decided to go to the late show at the Westwood Crown movie theater in Westwood Village. They took seats, as they always tried to, on the far right-hand side of the house away from people. The holiday crowd was unusually light.

After a while, Jean spoke impatiently. "Let me out, I have to use the toilet."

Joan paused to make her wait before replying, "You old hag, why don't you sit on the outside? You always have to go. You drink too many liquids. And besides, what a time to disturb me, the best part of the—"

"You bitch, you. You just said that the movie stinks. You're such an unkind witch. You know with my eye I can't see well when I sit on the outside."

"What do I care what you can see? I have to strain to hear wherever I sit. And my good ear still has an aggravating constant ringing all the time. Go out the other way." Joan folded her arms and sat tight.

Jean said, "You mean person. There are other people down the row there to crawl over."

"Well, that's just too bad, because I'm not moving one inch. You can hold it and pee in your pants for all I care."

"I hate your guts, do you know that? I want you to know that before anything else, how much I utterly detest you, you mean horrible girl. Now move before I—"

"Before you what? You homely unloved thing."

When Jean moved forward in a threatening posture, Joan stared at her and began to laugh. "You've got a moustache, do you know that? I can see it with the light from the screen. You look like Clark Gable." Joan laughed at that while Jean pushed by her to stand in the aisle.

Before stomping away, Jean put her hands on her hips and said, "I hate your slimy guts, do you know that? Disgusting person."

"Don't let it drip in your pants, Clark." Joan laughed.

Upstairs, the luxurious pink hallway made Jean feel better. She pushed hard on her right temple until her ocular muscles relaxed and her glass eye rested more comfortably. She sighed a breath of relief. God, she thought, I hate her. I hate her. I hate her, I hate her. God, I'd like to move. But she knew that that was something to talk about and not do. She had tried it so many times and been miserable.

Alone in the ladies' room, Jean took her time to urinate. She relaxed and let it happen, glad to be by herself. It's fun to be in the theater when it's nearly empty, she thought. Fun to roam around without your horrible sister. She figured she'd wander around before she went back. Walk around and drag her feet over the thick pink carpeting.

Jean finished, straightened her clothing, flushed the toilet and stepped back out into the pink washroom. She was aware that someone had recently cleaned the place and used Pine Sol disinfectant. It left a good sanitary smell. Without her purse, she touched her shortish hair into place and used her thumbs to smooth her eyebrows. Stepping back to observe her reflected angles, she guessed that she was plain but that her eyebrows looked fine, well shaped and natural.

Staring at her face, self-centered, Jean was startled when the bathroom door opened into the room. When she saw it was a man, she blushed profusely and put her hand to her mouth. She stared. She thought that they smiled at each other and she waited for him to go. When he closed the door behind him she saw how big his shoulders were and she couldn't help but notice his large peculiar hands, how they hung almost comically from his sleeves. She thought to move but hesitated to watch him merely to see what he was about because he wasn't leaving. He did something with his right hand and her vision went down there to the front of his pants.

The man's erect penis was in his hand. He rubbed at it and stretched the skin up over the end in an abusive, tugging way.

He made a nasal moan. She caught her breath and tried to see his eyes but looked at his penis again instead. It was by far the biggest one she had ever seen. She couldn't help wonder if Joan would like it. She wondered if she would be jealous. She fought it in the useless way one fights a sneeze, but staring at the penis, her juices began to flow.

I'm going to be raped . . . he's going to rape me, she shuddered. Perspiration ran down the insides of her arms and down the small of her back into her buttocks. She opened her mouth but stuttered. Her mind seemed suddenly enfeebled. Her temple ached.

Jean had her most private fantasies and was hard put to reject the fact that this was one of them. A strange man, a strange place, a huge veiny penis, but used carefully, coarsely but lovingly. No one to know, a modern rape, a sophisticated intrusion; not too rough, not too . . .

He was closer now and had let go of the muscular thing to let it stand by itself, wagging like the stiffest Iowa pig's tail and drooling its stickum.

She could smell him. The Pine Sol was gone and it was only him. She allowed the scent in past her brain and diagnosed it. The sensation panicked her. She stiffened and put out her palms and said, "No . . . No . . . please."

She smelled him again and knew what it was that horses smell when they don't like someone and shy away. She was shying now too, backing away. It was her instinct. The room held in it the animal's distinction, an aura of imbalance, of danger, of insanity.

Jean threw her mouth open to scream but a gigantic hand was there to stop her. The brute shook her with a snap. Consciousness went and came and went again to return with an overwhelming rush of terror. She squawked. Her glass eye fell out. It bounced once and broke onto the tiled floor. The pain in her throat abated. She saw him looking down.

And now, she hoped, she begged, mercy at last. A feeling of pity for the poor one-eyed woman. But no, he laughed the delirious laugh of a madman. A full double-lunged laugh before he overpowered her, wrenching her to the floor in front of him.

She tried frantically to resist but should have known she couldn't. Then he said something that wouldn't register. Oooooh, no—no way to get to that kind of thing. Horror of horrors, no. But he laughed and growled, "Take a good look at this," before committing the unthinkable.

Jean knew it would end like this. There was no question. She pleaded, "Please, no . . . please . . . pleeease." But her strength was suddenly gone as was her tongue and there was nothing but a thrashing, and her whisper from oblivion, "I want . . . I want . . . my sister."

EIGHT

Simon Moon packed his women in around him. Onto their backs, he wedged them into the insulation between the rafters next to him so that he could reach and touch them as he pleased. He loved the feel of the ruffled pink blouse and the big soft breasts underneath. He messed with the ruffles, stood them up and petted them back into place.

He reached into the blouse and had a cheap feel. She didn't say one word, not a peep. Into her bra, he twisted the flaccid nipple and pinched it hard but there was nothing, no lip. He laughed at his mastery over it all and clapped his hands with feelings of glee.

Andy came to Simon's mind. Smart Jewish Andy, the best divorce attorney in Los Angeles. *The* expert in family relations. Simon laughed sarcastically.

"Go to my house, to my mother, Andy. She can use an expert in family relations, a slick L.A. attorney, a specialist to cut my old man a new asshole." My blind mother—fuck, he said to himself angrily.

It made his ears burn and his hands ache when he gave her any thought; the woman who had stood nonchalantly by while he was brutalized. The dirty bitch who he always pictured with her back to him, who had 100 percent of herself reserved to kiss the old man's ass; to support the pig by her sins of omission.

Simon fiddled with the pink blouse and rummaged around in his memory for a feeling of compassion for his mother who this very minute was in Los Angeles, probably at *his* house, visiting with Carol.

Perspiring, he searched for a time when he cared. He wanted to care, Christ Almighty, but she'd never ever cared for him.

He'd become numb and it had taken a while to see her for what she really was. But then he'd stopped beating his meat, thinking about her big loose tits, and began to wear out his knees praying to see her dead.

And Andy was right, of course. His no-bullshit approach. He tells the truth. Simon pictured Andy with a toothpick in his hand, digging at his teeth after lunch and lecturing.

"Hey man, they're all whores, all of them. They whore for security. They suck your cock and fuck you and tell you that you're the best and only you can make them come, and that they love you. And they say it with a straight face . . . a straight face, mind you, that's what kills me."

Andy would laugh at the joke and slap his knee. "I mean, how are they going to survive? I ask you, how? If they don't whore, they sell it. They sell out, is what they do. That's what's too bad. That's what shits in this man's world. They have to sell out.

"You want to see a miserable sick cooze? Look at one that marries a guy that's got dough. She smiles so warm and nice and says she loves him and makes him feel real good in bed . . . or terrorizes him if that's what it takes to get his dick hard. But she plays her game . . . And then he loses his money." Andy would laugh and throw the toothpick away to draw attention to his point like the good trial lawyer he was. "He loses the dough and what has he got? A supportive, loving female? Oh, no, he's got a miserable, mean nasty cunt that's a lousy lay who turns away and starts looking again.

"But they can't help it. They're trained that way. They sell out for security, all of them, one way or another. Besides, we don't know what they're thinking. We're not supposed to know. But I know, and I'm here to tell you that they're thinking security, security, security. The shame of it, the dirty damn shame is that they've got other names for it . . . like love."

Simon broke from his frozen attentive posture to scream out, "You're right, you're right, Andy, you're right." Simon slapped the women's faces and kicked the one-eyed girl in the ribs until they cracked. Then he sat and said quietly, "You're right."

He wondered about his wife, Carol. He wondered as he always wondered whether she really loved him. Whether she really really really loved him or if she was just a bullshit, placating specialist like all the rest.

Simon smiled and felt himself blush thinking about Carol, how she would pay him compliments and then look sexy and then look secretive and away. It made Simon crazy over her, silly with desire. Carol would build him up, tell him how smart, how competent he was, even handsome in her eyes, and then she would force a blush and turn her back on him. It made him wild when she turned her back on him as though she was too shy to continue.

In bed, she would roll away and put her hand under her nightie to do something with that hand between her muscular, but lean runner's thighs and then rest her hand back over her shoulder in front of Simon's nose.

Carol would put her hand on her shoulder and wiggle the two wet middle fingers and Simon would sniff at them, lick and suck them. Then Simon would hold his own with the clock and prolong things by kissing her entire back under her straps, the tightly squeezed cracks of her armpits, but nothing more, no hands. Finally, Carol would take her nightie off and turn around toward him.

"When she turns around, look out." Simon laughed ghoulishly out into the black attic. He rubbed his stiffening penis and then stopped cold with a miserable thought.

He saw it clearly before him; he saw Charlotte, their little girl, hanging onto the bars of her playpen watching her mother suck off the Culligan man or the plumber or some coarse, brutish workman type. Then it came to him and he was so positive that his hair stood on end at the thought. Simon touched his tingling scalp and envisioned their mailman.

"It's the mailman for sure . . . for absolute positive," he said, shivering convulsively.

The mailman was a black man. He wore gray uniform walking shorts on his rounds every day regardless of the weather or time of year. Simon had seen the way that that black looked at Carol. He'd peeked through the drapes and watched outside at the mailbox while Carol brought a package to him. He'd seen that black devil rub his bare thigh and laugh. He remembered how the fucker looked at Carol's tight runner's rear end, her jutt butt, when she turned around and walked back to the house.

Simon recalled watching that black freak lick over his glistening white teeth while he watched after Carol, and it came to him right then and there. He hadn't thought of it until he thought of it, but Simon had seen Carol look back too.

She said something back to him, over her shoulder, and the spook adjusted his walking shorts. He lifted them up at the belt line and turned them from side to side to ease himself. To relieve the constriction, the pressure of the gray mailman uniform cloth over his thick, black, positively uncircumcised licorice stick.

That's it, Simon thought, as sure as shit. She compliments him and then turns her back. She wears her red shortie nightgown. That's what she'd wear for that naked slithering beast who rubs his thigh and wags his black piston. She touches her wet pussy and wiggles her fingers to let him smell and then turns her back on him.

"Ohhh," Simon moaned, "I'll bet she gets a wet cunt for that black rod."

His ears rang. He felt nauseous. He rubbed his aching hands and saw her turn back around to begin the easy licking of that scabby slave stalk.

Trembling and sweating, Simon thought about the black mailman debasing his sweet, shy Carol.

He imagined her kneeling, eyes closed, a pleasurable smile over her face, and he saw the naked mailman behind her, his muscular black rod slathered with Carol's frothed saliva.

Simon saw the naked black mailman as a sleek black Labrador hound hunched up behind Carol, his claws raking her back, his red tongue panting out of the side of his mouth.

"Fuck me, Isaac, be my pimp. I'm dirty white meat. Fuck me good and turn me out to fuck and suck for you . . . to buy rhinestone mud flaps for your long, thick black car."

Simon laughed a bit in his insanity but blabbered into the darkness, "Fuck me, and go to sleep. I'll deliver your mail. It's all for you. I'm nothing . . . nothing but bad white security meat. Kill my ass dead."

Simon loved his hard penis that pushed and pained against his trousers but he felt suddenly flooded with guilt. He cursed his erection and didn't understand why it should be so hard, but he went past the reasons and the guilt and promised never ever to think those thoughts again. Or to remember what he did with those images on this particular attic occasion. Thinking about Carol with the black mailman, Simon masturbated and climaxed quickly in abrupt merciful seizures.

Afterward he was depressed. He worried about things until his mind raced. Crawling, he found a flat plywood spot down the attic a ways and did pushups. Lots and lots of pushups to tire himself, to exhaust his body and mind; to stop his imagination. When his trembling muscles were totally expired, he squeezed out five more, said "Jesus," and let himself down cheek first onto the dusty plywood flooring. He fell into a broken sleep.

He thought he came awake one or more times from dreams that left him boggled with their sense of authenticity. He could smell his women, their dusty perfumed fragrance and the putrified, sweet, candied-apple smell of cyanide. But times were different.

The Westwood Crown theater was constructed during 1978 and '79. The place should have been completed in eight months but a major labor dispute closed the site down leaving the half-roofed skeletonlike barn of a structure to provide a break in the weather, a home for some weirdos and Simon.

It had been a particularly deranged time for Simon, before Carol, when he had chucked his legal profession and run headlong with his obsession. He lived in flops and on the Santa Monica grassy knoll until the cops got rough out there and then in the unfinished theater.

He did it to a bunch of women during that time. In his dream they chased him. Their pathetic sad eyes were everywhere; in every bus and car, around every corner, in every window. The crowds were made up of them and they came from alleyways wearing Santa Claus beards and red miniskirts.

They were afraid to say what they really thought but pounded behind him down a nauseatingly steep flight of concrete stairs. He fell. Down and down he flew into a stale blackness until he splashed into a puddle at the foot of the stairs.

The women seemed to arrive all at once and fly onto the puddle to jump up and down into the crimson slop. He felt himself splash onto the cold black walls and ran quickly into the cracks to hide. It didn't hurt but it frightened him so much when he tried to scream and couldn't that he began to pee in his pants.

Controlling his bladder, Simon crawled then walked along the attic rafters until he reached the entrance to the metal ventilating shaft. He had to urinate badly but caught himself and understood the danger that the people presented who walked in the hallway below.

Sitting on his haunches, he stared out through the grill and into the bright fluorescent pink hallway. The people appeared to move beneath halos. They walked in an aura of reflecting pinkness, expressing no personality, no enthusiasm or individuality.

He went back into the attic and urinated in a corner. Then he came and waited just inside the grillwork entrance of the ventilating shaft for the movie sounds to stop and the people to go. Then he waited some more.

Downstairs, he proceeded carefully until he was positive the theater was empty.

He stuffed himself with buttered popcorn and, remembering

about salt, that Carol always said it lay in your veins and was bad for you, he did without for the first box. Then, associating a mild feeling of depression with the bland popcorn and Carol's will, Simon salted the next boxes he ate and used too much butter. "Sickening," he said, as she'd say it.

"Sickeningly good . . . and delicious." He gave her the finger.

Simon watched his reflection in the chromium-and-glass popcorn machine. He looked in at the waves of yellow popcorn and brought his focus up to see himself smiling. "This is my place, Carol, and there's salt at my place."

He drank three large Cokes and ate two boxes of chocolate bonbons. A pencil sat nearby which he picked up and pretended to smoke. He watched himself pantomime smoking and danced around in circles like a burlesque comic, flicking imaginary ashes.

Stopping and getting close, he waved his hand before his face and removed a piece of popcorn from his teeth. He said, "You must be nuts," and answered, "Maybe . . . but I'm not going home."

Bringing a dime from the cash drawer that sat partially open, Simon pranced to the telephone. He laughed and danced around having a good time. Carol answered on the first ring.

Simon said, "I need an answer." Carol didn't speak. He could feel her coldness at the other end but it didn't matter. "Please, sweetheart," Simon said. "Don't get me wrong but I've really got to know. You're all whores, aren't you? Please, tell me the truth now, come on . . . gutchy, gutchy, goo. Please tell me the truth . . . It's important as the dickens to me."

Carol asked, "Where are you?" in one scolding breath.

"Tell me," Simon demanded. "Whores for security, that's it, isn't it? Whores for steady dependability. That's what the secret is, isn't it? That's a woman's secret?"

Simon thought that she laughed though she might have sighed, but it seemed she laughed too with her face away from the phone. Amidst all the anxiety he was supposedly causing her, Carol chuckled and Simon knew with a cold certainty that he would never get the answer. Not from Carol. She was one of them. My own wife, he thought. Well, fuck her, the cunt. She's sure as shit one of them. Goddamn, I'm super stupid to have tried.

"It's Christmas, Simon. Your parents are on their way back here from the motel. Have you forgotten? About my feelings, and Charlotte's? Come home, Simon. Have you forgotten? They will be here in . . ."

Simon put the phone into its cradle and vomited onto the pink theater carpet. He did it again and again until he was exhausted. He slumped to the carpet and said, "Forgotten . . . how could I ever forget?"

Simon was born on the fifteenth of July 1939. An only child, he grew up on a four-hundred-acre barley farm outside Kansas City, Kansas.

Simon's father, Alvin Moon, and his two big uncles, Ben and Jack, were famous bootleggers. Alvin supplied the barley from his farm and a modern two-hundred-gallon still housed in a shed out behind the farm's second barn where the machinery was kept.

Jack and Ben each owned a tanker truck disguised as liquid-fertilizer carriers. They stayed in touch by C.B. radios. Alvin had a receiver at the farm. Ben and Jack did all the hauling and distribution of the illegal rye whiskey.

The three big-shouldered men, the Moon brothers, were not hot-air blusterers either. They meant business and would kick ass together or one on one; showing off in front of the whole town. Jack and Ben Moon were notoriously rough. But Alvin Moon, Simon's dad, was the coldest, the baddest of them all.

During dinner one night, when Simon was a kid, Alvin seemed uncomfortable and fidgety as though his bottom hurt him. Suddenly he slammed his fists onto the table top and said, "Fuck this shit. I'm gonna do something about this thing." Jumping up from the table he stormed up the stairs into the upstairs bathroom and slammed the door.

Simon's mother, Florence, with one hand to her bosom, the other outstretched as though to cling, which was her usual posture around her husband, chased up the stairs after him. When she eased the bathroom door open for a peek, she screamed out in the most blood-curdling way ever, and Simon ran to see.

Alvin was nude from the waist down, squatting over a mirror that was covered, as was much of the bathroom floor, with bright red blood. In one hand Alvin held a pair of everyday but farm-sharpened scissors. In the other, he held what looked to be the fresh red innards of a chicken, the gizzard or the liver. The bleeding meaty stuff was Alvin's hemorrhoids. Alvin had suffered from a bad case of piles long enough and wasn't finished cutting yet.

"Out," he screamed, the veins pounding in his neck. "Out of here."

Simon's mom fainted into his arms and how he relished the opportunity to gently touch her, to carry her out of there into her bed. He sat next to her and petted her face and mostly held his breath the entire time. He did the same whenever she fainted, which was often. She would lie still and sometimes even smile while he held her hand and petted it. Simon could love his mother when she was in a faint. He could adore her even though it was a one-way street. She lay so quietly, except for the rise and fall of her heavy breasts, as though she were dead. Simon loved it.

Alvin had finished up on himself, to afterward sit in the tub with the water running until it ran clear around him. He drank half a bottle of rye whiskey to get going every morning for a couple weeks after that and took a long tub at night. But he worked hard every day and never squawked about the pain.

Living with a chronic gut-wrenching contempt for Alvin, Simon had mixed emotions about the hemorrhoidectomy. He had to admit that in the way that had to do with masculinity, an impression had been made. But it scared him, the insanity of the thing, and he'd had bad dreams about all of the blood.

Simon walked the long pink theater hallway and slapped the wall with the flat of his hand along the way. "No, Carol, I haven't forgotten. That part of my brain burns with perfect clarity."

Simon flashed on the man, his father, who had had the nerve to cut out his own sick asshole, and anxiously remembered the beatings he had suffered for no good reason past simple mean temper and alcoholic rage.

Alvin would lock him in the attic every Sunday afternoon. In the freezing or broiling black attic, stifling whatever the time of year. Then Alvin would fuck Florence until the house shook and she screamed to high heaven. Simon was lucky if his mom ever spoke to him but she'd scream like a wildcat for Alvin.

He could have killed them both and never stopped dreaming of the ways, but whenever he got close to doing it, he froze.

Now, back in the attic, back in his spot, Simon held hands with the one-eyed girl and brooded.

All he could ever remember his mother saying to him, ever, her favorite line, was that he must be eating something wrong at school or somewhere because his skin was bad; something made the boils come to his neck. She'd say "Yuk" and turn away.

When Simon hounded Florence for attention, she would finally say, "Get away—I never wanted you." But at least she looked at him when she said it. So he'd push her some more until she'd say it again. When Alvin was away on a whiskey run, which was most often, Simon would sneak to sit near her when she slept. To get close and smell her breath and pretend.

Florence never wanted a child. It was Alvin. He wanted an offspring. Not for loving and sharing or growing together either. And not for his pride and joy or to leave a likeness behind, or for a pal to go places with, but for ego. It had been a drunken joke, a bet. "Oh, yeah, well, put your fuckin' money where your mouth is."

Alvin went home and told Florence to perform; to pop him out a kid. She obeyed in her cowering way, as she did all things for her husband, the provider of every last thing in her life including her validation as a woman, her self-esteem. Simon was the brunt of the scheme and now knew it. He was the trump. Simon was Alvin's proof to his thug brothers and all the other Kansas toughs and the world, that his cock and balls worked.

Florence didn't like it when Simon was left home alone with her, so when the men went on a run they took Simon as far as town and left him at Coco's. Coco got most of her booze from the Moon brothers and accepted Simon without a fuss. Simon stayed at Coco's weeks on end, even months, as he got older, especially during the summer.

Coco lived in a huge, three-story Victorian mansion, painted bright yellow with white trim and surrounded by a picket fence. It sat on a nice, evenly mowed grassy lot, one of the last homes on West State Avenue, a mile and a half from the stockyards. On a hot summer evening when the breeze was just right, it seemed the Kansas City kill plant was next door.

Simon slept alone on the unfinished fourth floor, "at the peak," as Coco called it. "All right, Simon, that's enough. It's late. Get up to the peak." It was Coco's classy way of avoiding the word *attic*. Coco did most things with class.

Coco was a large-boned young woman with a rounded figure. Her hair was waved and chopped short almost like a man's, but with bleached-blond streaks running through its brownness. Coco's eyes were blue and expressive and she wore lots of black mascara, like an actress, to emphasize their soft color.

She wore beautifully colored, loose-fitting garments, often silk, and boas around her pale-skinned neck. There were nearly always large, sparkling gemlike earrings hanging from her pierced earlobes and she wore spiked lounging heels covered with black angora.

Addicted to morphine rectal suppositories, Coco enjoyed lying back, lounging around her big house, seeing to it everything was handled right; "professionally," as she liked to put it.

But the anesthetized look in her eye could deceive you. Screw with her and you'd disappear, so the story went. Coco had a photographic memory and kept all of her business in her head. She'd read *everything* and could recite most of it line and verse. She taught Simon how to read, really read, and to comprehend.

Simon learned many things from Coco and her girls. He even fell in love.

Her name was Lisa and she was fifteen. Young as she was and Lolita-ish when put together, she was not very popular with the men. Lisa exuded a perpetual long-faced sadness that could put a damper on any party.

It was this unhappiness that drew Simon to her, and the way she always smelled of Doublemint. Lisa had Doublemint gum in her mouth at all times: when she slept and even when she gave head, which aggravated the customers to no end. Coco scolded her but she wouldn't change. Simon liked the clean minty smell.

Lisa was the first girl to ever be kind to Simon. She seemed to understand him. She didn't talk about it but demonstrated that she cared. She lanced the boils on his neck, squeezed out the pus and used a hot towel to clean him up. She told him what kind of clothes looked best on him and how to get his hair cut. She would play croquet with him out on the back lawn for anyone to see and Simon was grateful.

Simon wanted to marry Lisa. He was sure he could make her smile even though she never smiled, even when he rubbed her shoulders, her long beautiful neck and calves early in the morning when she finished working.

They didn't make love but sometimes lay together for long periods in total silence; hugging, sending and receiving vibrations that seemed to make them both feel better. Simon would dry-fuck her leg a little and come quietly in his pants. He came so easily. He hung around her like a big protective dog.

One day the tension appeared to vanish from Lisa's face and soon thereafter she smiled. She began to take to Simon's unconditional kindness and change before everyone's eyes. It was a neat thing to observe, color coming into the young girl's cheeks, and early one evening before going downstairs to work, she came up through the attic hatch to him and stood up to throw her gown aside.

"Do me, Simon. Come and do me . . . please."

Simon stared and gulped and did her.

Lisa took out her gum and stuck it to a rafter and giggled in a newfound way. She cried in long hungry sobs and held onto his big bare shoulders for dear life. He crushed himself against her frailty and she burst into laughter. Lisa told Simon that he had the biggest prick she'd ever felt. She said it softly and gently, with a naughty, new sweet-faced grin that made Simon head-over-heels goony for her.

They made love all night and rather than be angry, Coco let it go and never told Alvin. Simon stared into Lisa and asked her with a serious desperation to run away with him, to marry him. He said that they were both misfits, but that love could keep them strong and that he would work hard at anything and everything to provide for her.

After listening to him sell and plead for a long while, in a way most unlike her, Lisa suddenly sat up to shout, "Okay, I'll do it." They laughed and hugged and snuck some champagne.

Afterward, Coco told Simon that Lisa had said, "Maybe I'm the most foolish girl that ever lived, Coco, but I love Simon like I never thought was possible. You know, he never judged me once or told me to quit working. He gives me a feeling of self-respect and pride. I feel the pride. And that's what counts in the long run—me. It's what Simon says."

Lisa told Coco with an unabashed, new headstrong giggle that she positively knew if Simon fucked her long and hard enough in his sincere desperate way that she would come. She said it had to do with trusting another human being, that she could feel something changing deep in her gut. Coco said she got a real glint in her eye when she said that someday soon she was going to be able to achieve an orgasm.

Simon understood that hookers didn't come, that they couldn't. He heard Uncle Jack say it to Ben and Alvin one day when they were all standing on the boards out in front of Coco's, kicking the mud off their boots. The men had been talking about Coco's girls, which one was the best faker, and Jack said, "There ain't no such thing as a hooker that can come. Never has been, never will be. Some man has fucked 'em over too good . . . usually their own Pa too . . . usually fucked 'em himself when they was still babies . . . or they didn't have no Pa at all and heard about men from some bitter cunt, or some pissed-off old maid."

They all laughed and agreed. "Don't matter, the reasons. Hookers can't shoot, and that's a fact. They got empty guns." The men laughed but Simon took it all in and believed what Jack said.

Lisa became obsessed with her thoughts of normalcy and wouldn't turn another trick whatever the price. She became perky and developed a happy, sparkling personality. Simon walked with her around town or to a show and he could feel how incredibly proud she was. It made him feel like a giant of a man, a king.

"I can trust this thing of ours, can't I, Simon. You won't let me down . . . ? I can trust you?" Lisa wasn't a nag but Simon was overwhelmed by the desperation in her eyes. He could feel her fears and insecurity as if they were his own and constantly reassured her of his devotion.

"I'll never let you down, Lisa, never."

The other women in the house warned her to watch out. Not to count her chickens before they hatched, not to set herself up for a big letdown. They had all been proposed to at one time or another by lonesome, well-intentioned men, and they were still there, right where they had been before; night after night, selling sex at Coco's.

But Lisa knew Simon, the look in his eye, and she believed it with all of her newly discovered heart.

The wedding date was set and Coco threw a small house party. It was a joyous occasion. The champagne flowed. The girls danced with each other and terrorized Simon by chasing him around, pouring champagne over his head and threatening to pull down his pants. Simon was deliriously happy.

Later, Simon and Lisa snuck upstairs to make love one last illicit time. They laughed and loved out loud with the door open for everyone to hear, and Lisa almost came. Their impropriety wasn't the wine talking or perverted sex; it was braggadocio; they were mighty proud.

A local magistrate, a friend of Coco's, was to marry them the next day at noon so they could be on the last train, the 3 P.M. train out of Kansas City for the Northwest. Simon and Lisa would begin anew in San Francisco. They had their tickets and three hundred and seventy-one dollars cash between them.

After the party and the lovemaking, Simon left Lisa downstairs with her happy girl friends to depart home for the farm one last time. Lisa held the train tickets over her heart and said, "Until tomorrow, Simon." She blew him a kiss as he drove away and everyone applauded.

Simon returned to the farm and had just finished sneaking a peanut butter sandwich when in the kitchen door strode Alvin.

Simon felt lucky that his suitcase was up under his bed.

"Whatcha up to, boy?" Alvin wanted to know.

"Nothing. Hungry, that's all."

"Well then . . . when's the big day?"

Simon gagged on the sandwich and nearly let the glass of milk slide from his hand. He stared at the floor. Alvin got close. Simon could smell the reeking of booze. Alvin grabbed him by the hair.

"Well, when's the date? When do you buy the whore out?" Slamming Simon up against the counter, he demanded, "Why can't you rent the cunt like everybody else? I've fucked her myself, you know. Fucked her in the asshole. She loves it in the ass. How about you? You ever get her there? She loves it from behind."

Alvin laughed curtly and grabbed Simon by the ear to nearly tear it off. Holding him that way, he shook him hard and said, "You ain't going nowhere, dummy, especially to marry some whore. Ain't you got no sense at all? I knew you was dumb, but to marry a slut . . . What'n hell do ya guess people would say about *me*? My dumb-assed kid running off with a whore . . . Shit, boy, you gotta be dreamin'. Now go and build me a big fire in the front room. I want to talk to you."

Simon was sick inside. He wanted to scream and cry, to beg. He wanted to talk sensibly, to explain things. He wanted to kill his father, he wanted to run, but he hung his head impotently and farted. Alvin cuffed him to send him reeling backward out the door. "I don't want no guff, sonny boy, get that fire a goin'."

Numb, Simon carried the kindling and some heavy logs and made a fire in the living-room fireplace. Alvin stoked it and made it a blaze. Then Alvin left and came back into the room with a coil of heavy rope. Simon understood immediately. A powerful chill ran through him and his eyes darted to the door but the big man noosed him twice around the neck and shoulders and held him frozen.

"You're not going nowhere, dummy. You think I don't hear about what's doin' in town? You think I'm stupid? Well, people know me and respect me and tell me things and I ain't lettin' you make no fool outta me, no way. Now as long as you ain't able to think for yourself, I'm gonna do your thinkin' for you. Marry a whore, are you nuts? Come heyar."

Alvin made a double noose around Simon's neck, pulled it up tight, put it around his hands and made him sit on the floor in front of his big chair. "Lay down, boy," and Simon did. Alvin wrapped the rope around his waist until there was no slack, and that's the way they slept.

Simon tried to move but when he did, Alvin felt the tug and would stir. Once he actually was nearly free but the big man responded to the gentle working of the rope to sit up and bark, "Cut it out, will ya." He made the rope tighter than before.

Eventually, Simon dozed and awoke with the light of dawn to the smell of bourbon and strong coffee. Alvin sat in front of him drinking from a mug. "Come on," Alvin said, dragging Simon downstairs to the basement.

Alvin made him stand next to the pile of secondhand clothing that Simon knew so well; discards from Alvin and his brothers that had clothed Simon for as long as he could remember. Always damp smelly things that hung on him, making him appear more gawky than he really was. Until Lisa had taken a hand and helped him dress properly in plaid shirts and khakis. Until Lisa, Simon thought. God in heaven, help me.

Alvin threw the rope over a beam in the ceiling and tied Simon impossibly tight, standing, with his toes barely touching the concrete. Alvin tied him the way he'd tie a steer for branding as he mumbled something about having better things to do all day. Simon watched the professional knots go into the rope that bound him, that he understood only too well, hanging as he was, he would never be able to undo.

Alvin turned before he walked up the stairs and scolded, "You ain't marrying no whore . . . no dumb son of mine. I've got a certain reputation to uphold in this community."

He went upstairs, slammed the door and locked it. The ropes cut into Simon as he hung and spun when he tried to move. He wept and wanted to die.

After a while, Alvin's pickup truck started and left the farm. Simon began to chew. It was a nearly impossible chore that he'd never seen an animal able to do, but Simon hung and spun and chewed voraciously on the rope that held him to the ceiling.

It started to come, too, that thick awful piece of hemp, but his teeth began to break or just come loose and fall out down his chest onto the basement floor. His chin and chest were soaked with blood. His jaw was on fire but he kept on until he heard it, and stopped to listen.

A creak in the floor above him. He strained to hear it again. There was no doubting, his mother was home and in the very room above his head.

"Please, Mother," he wailed. "Please, please, please...I love her. She needs me. I need her. She's depending on me. Please, if you've never done anything for me my whole life, do this one good thing. Cut me down. Mother... HELP ME..."

He screamed and begged until his throat went hoarse, raw and closed. Hoping, he held his breath and listened but there was nothing.

What he wished upon his mother was so extremely vicious, his hatred for her so intense, that he might have passed out and when he resumed chewing, something had happened in his mind. It was a snap that altered his thinking, that brought him into a new plane. It was like growing up in one pop or experiencing a cerebral hemorrhage, if one can be conscious of such a thing, but the occurrence wasn't growing up or an explosion of a blood vessel in his brain. It was a slamming open of the door to perversive criminal behavior, to sadism, to the wicked room in his mind. The insanity from which Simon Moon would never recover.

The day dragged by like some horrible ancient form of mental and physical torture. It was dark when the rope finally gave way. Simon rinsed his broken, torn mouth in the basement sink and swallowed several cauterizing mouth-washing glugs of his father's rye whiskey.

He ran through the locked upstairs door with a powerful shoulder-wrenching slam and probably would have killed anyone who stood in his way. He was crazed with questions about Lisa, how she would take his no-show.

The hood of Simon's clunker '39 Ford stood open, the distributor cap gone from the engine. Simon took the tractor. He drove it like a speed demon, in fourth gear, as fast as it would go, without lights, with both hands tightly squeezing the wheel.

He knew something was seriously wrong as he hit the outskirts of town and headed down State Avenue for Coco's. He could feel it in the Kansas City night air that blew against his face and made his eyes tear.

Simon screamed through his nose to chase the image of Lisa's face from his mind and stopped the machine in the alley behind the house. He turned an ankle jumping from the tractor in the dark but he ran anyway up the back stairs through the kitchen into the house.

In the living room he was confronted by a group of women who looked away or down when they saw him. He wanted to scream his innocence. Don't look at me like that, don't, don't, don't. It wasn't me, please. This before any concern for Lisa.

The women looked solemnly up the long staircase and that's where he ran, up the two flights of stairs into Lisa's front-room apartment. Coco was alone in the room. She sat on the windowsill in front of the open window looking out.

Simon stopped and screamed, "Coco!"

He must have been delirious because when Coco turned back toward him, it seemed she took forever to come around. Coco made her lumbersome, agonizingly slow hallucinogenic turn and Simon saw her eyes, heavy-lidded, awash in red, stuporous. Gone on morphine rectal suppositories.

Fixed in his tracks, Simon screamed at her again. Coco moved her eyes to the other side of the room, to Lisa's vanity table. Something was scrawled over the large mirror in thick red lipstick. Simon stepped aside to read what it said out loud.

"Find me, feel me, fuck me, and forget me."

Simon felt an arctic wind blow through his gut. "But . . . I'm here, Coco . . . I couldn't help it . . . Where is she?"

Coco turned to let her gaze go back out the window into the night. Simon ran to her side and leaned past her to look out. The scene was bathed in an eerie yellow glow from the mosquito light outside Coco's front porch. A group of dark indistinguishable bystanders hung together in the shadows out by the fence. Lisa was directly below.

With her wedding dress she appeared a gathering of yellow carnations dashed against the cement pathway. If there was blood, Simon couldn't see it. There was just Lisa's twisted body with the yellow dress up around her pretty neck, long and pretty and broken with her lopsided head full of curls shining yellow in the dreadful glow from the mosquito light.

NINE

Simon lost his mind and dove for the open window. Coco moved to block the way. When he hesitated, Coco pushed him back hard, a good one with both hands against his chest. Simon stumbled backward and tripped to fall onto his behind in the middle of the room.

"Don't do it, Simon . . . get it out of your head. That's what suicide is all about. It's supposed to kill two. Don't let it kill you too." She touched his hair when she floated to the door and spoke over her shoulder before disappearing into the hallway. "Let it go, Simon. Lisa was sweet but there'll be others. You're alive. Life goes on . . . You've got things to do."

After Lisa's death, Simon stayed in her room for two days without eating a bite until Alvin came and got him. On the way home Alvin said, "There now, isn't that better? You've got your whole goddamned life in front of you. You don't need some sick, dependent broad hanging onto you."

Simon could have killed him. At that moment driving in the pickup, it came to him that he positively had the strength. The screwdriver from the dash into his temple. The only thing that stopped him was after running what Alvin said through his numbing psychosis, he figured his father was probably right. Yeah, fuck that dependent shit. Who needs it? But Simon would often cry in the dark over Lisa and dream revenge.

Simon wore a sad look after Lisa, a dour countenance that worked so well he kept it on continuously. People felt sorry for him, gave him what he wanted and left him alone. He could come and go as he pleased both at home and at Coco's where he became the official paid masseur. He brooded, hung his head and walked stoop-shouldered, spying from the corners of his eyes at what was going on. No one knew what he was thinking and sometimes he even scared himself.

Simon *loved* to be at Coco's on Sunday afternoons and Thursday evenings. That was when big-busted, Italian Madelaine turned her main trick, her *numero uno* dollar John. His name was Thomas Roman III.

Looking at him, the neat way that he dressed, always in a gray business suit, starched white shirt and silk tie, gave people the impression that the man was the most elite of conservative businessmen.

The Roman Imperial, his large, modern Kansas City movie theater, was one of a chain of theaters owned by the Roman family, headquartered in San Francisco. Simon assumed that Thomas Roman III's family knew about him and had banished him to Kansas.

Thomas Roman was most fastidious. He kept an impeccably clean theater and that was the way his entire life appeared; to his fellows in the church choir, to his many friends and prominent associates in the city and state organizations to which he and his wife belonged. But Thomas Roman III was a different sort of man every Thursday evening and Sunday afternoon at Coco's.

Always the consummate gentleman, Thomas Roman would sit in Coco's drawing room, his knees drawn up side by side, his shined black shoes placed evenly and neatly together beneath him. He sat in a formal, almost stiff-backed way and drank one good Scotch cocktail.

Then Madelaine would arrive, dressed in things black and tight. When he saw her, the whites of his eyes would go red and he would blush profusely. If he was speaking he would stammer. Madelaine would get close and always position herself to stand above him. Thomas Roman would look the other way and pretend to be oblivious.

Then she would let the red leather dog's collar and leash come out from behind her back and dangle it in front of him or lay it over his shoulder or around his neck. Thomas Roman would panic. When he tried to speak, he couldn't. He would loosen his tie and undo the top button of his starched white shirt. With his eyes flashing, perspiration beginning to show, he'd ask, "What . . . what do you want?"

Madelaine was stern. She'd point at the floor near her feet and say, "Come here, Rug Man, get down here where you belong. Get down low where you belong so people can walk on you."

Thomas Roman would sit frozen in place, a high-pitched "Geeee" sound coming from between his clenched teeth until Madelaine yelled, "Don't you hear me, Rug Man? Down for your master."

Thomas Roman would beg, "No . . . No . . . No . . . Don't take me, please. I'm having the best time right here, the nicest civilized conversation . . . Please don't . . ." And implore whichever of the girls happened to be there in the sitting room with him at the time, "Please no, don't let her take me. Don't let her take me up there into that cold upstairs kitchen. Please, not up there—I can't take it. I'm serious—I can't stand it. Please, no . . . She's so cruel . . . Help me, please."

But the other women would shrug their shoulders and exit or move to the hallway or the next room to peek at Madelaine doing her stuff. Sometimes they'd sit on the stairs as she dragged him up past them by his leash and collar. Despite his protestation, you could see by the way Thomas Roman's eyes darted around that he enjoyed the female audience, as did Madelaine.

"Stop your whimpering, Rug, you no good piece of shit, and quit walking on your hands and knees. Crawl—get down on that yellow belly and crawl up the stairs. I've got your baby-blue girdle ready for you and you'd better be able to get it on by the ten count or you know what happens. Move, you lowlife, sick man. I wish Mrs. Roman was here to see you now...or your kids. God, you're pathetic. Now get along—crawl."

Thomas Roman would crawl up the stairs one by one, next to Madelaine's boots.

"Today, oh, today, lowlife, you're going to get it...or rather, you're not going to get it. You get no pussy, Carpet Face. Not that you'd know what to do with it if you had it. No cock, no-cock man, tiny-cock-and-balls man, cock-like-a-girl man—"

She'd step onto his fingers and make them crack. Thomas Roman could scream if he wanted to. It was his time. He paid for that Thursday and Sunday time, three hundred dollars per experience, six hundred dollars per week. But most often he'd become indignant and yell, "Jesus Christ, Madelaine, you've broken my hand. Take it easy, will you? This is only playing around, you know, just fun and games."

This would infuriate Madelaine and on the second and last occasion that Simon was able to sneak a peek at the Thomas Roman affair, Madelaine screamed, "Over—over onto your back and I'll show you fun and games."

She jerked the leash and collar so hard it looked as if Thomas Roman saw stars, and he quickly rolled over onto his back near the head of the stairs.

Thomas Roman begged, "Easy...easy," and Simon could forever clearly recall Madelaine, such an overwhelming impression the thing made upon him, drawing back her boot and kicking Thomas Roman as hard as she could in the testicles.

Thomas Roman let out a horrible, agonizing scream and Simon felt nauseous watching the man's body retch as he half crawled and was dragged by the neck the rest of the way to the upstairs kitchen.

After the door was slammed shut and bolted, you could hear the most awful pleading and terrible screams you've ever heard. "Don't. Don't. Be careful, don't bruise me. No, no-...careful, my wife...Oh, no, not that—not that. Oh, no . . . noooo." Then the screaming would stop for an uneasy silence before it would begin again.

Simon guessed that Madelaine twisted parts of him or did things in hidden areas, inside his mouth or rectum or behind his scrotum, because Thomas Roman never appeared injured after they were finished.

On the days in between Thomas Roman's visits, Simon listened intently for stories but never could find out what went on behind that heavy enameled upstairs kitchen door. Simon really wanted to know, too, in the worst way, precisely what Madelaine did to Thomas Roman III to make him scream and moan with such anguished delight.

Simon found himself with an inordinate curiosity in Thomas Roman III. Drawn to the Imperial theater for no apparent reason, Simon hung around the place, saw all the movies and paced the theater lobby.

One evening while loitering near the drinking fountain, Simon spotted Thomas Roman in an argument with a young couple. When he got close to them his heart pounded as though to rupture his chest. Unable to control the urge, Simon blurted that the young couple was right and knocked Thomas Roman to the floor. A delirious swell of excitement rushed through him but when he drew back his foot to kick the prostrate man in the testicles, Thomas Roman stared up into his eyes and said, "For shame . . . vicious person," and Simon ran away feeling nauseous.

There was no denying the change that began to come over Simon. Coco described it as "getting worse." He began to dread being around people. He was convinced they talked about him when they were in groups; that they snickered and pointed at him when he wasn't looking. He couldn't really blame them either. He knew he was different. He thought it was unfair, however, that women couldn't stand to get near him; that they despised him before even getting to know him.

He began to never ever speak unless spoken to and developed a morbid curiosity with death, as though it would bring some sort of relief, and it wasn't long before he started to display an irrational, suspicious temperament toward the women at Coco's, many of whom had been his friends. He knew they wanted him off the premises. He would hide from them in the attic where he felt the most secure.

Finally, the girls at the house really did begin to shun him and stopped letting him massage or touch them at all. If it weren't for Coco, he would have been turned out, but she warned him. She told him his brooding, antisocial behavior frightened people, and to change the way he thought.

Simon didn't understand what there was in his thinking to change. At times it was difficult to make any distinctions at all and he could feel paralyzed. It scared him too. He could cry or giggle uncontrollably without the slightest provocation and began to develop a genuine pleasure in being cruel.

He always thought he liked the neighborhood dogs. He liked them better than he did their owners and unlike their owners, knew all of their names. They were his pals. Yet one day with no clear reason, but constraining a giggle the entire time, he smashed up a Coke bottle, mixed it into hamburger and fed it to as many of the local animals as he could find. That night he hid in the attic and listened to them howl. There was no denying that the howling made him feel light-headed and sexy.

A whore named Marie worked long and hard to sew a beautiful white-laced dress. One night, while it hung on its form, Simon snuck down to cover it with bright red paint. Afterward, he knew that they all knew. They stared and suspected him and probably pointed at him behind his back. The guilty feeling made the hair on the nape of his neck tingle and his gonads ache. When Felix, Marie's jealous lover, got the blame, Simon was sick with depression.

Insanely, when they had suspected him the most, when he felt the most paranoid pressure from a group of women that a human male might endure, when it was time to be cool, he snuck into the pantry and urinated in the open jars of canning cherries before the cook got the wax and covers on.

Lying in the dark waiting for them to come up and get him was pure heaven. Just as it was heaven sneaking across the river bridge into Missouri. Just following them home in the dark, to stand outside and imagine doing it to them, made his head swim.

But Simon had sex. He had sheep that he fucked out on the western plain. But they started to run away when they saw him coming too. So he vandalized most of the females in the herd by pouring gasoline over them and lighting them on fire. He sat nearby watching and loved hearing them scream.

Coco called Simon in one night and explained without malice that she had had enough. That he was to get out and stay away, not to come back to her house for any reason. She said there was something wrong with him, that he had a sad, unkind, perhaps even dangerous nature. But she asked Simon to listen closely, that she was going to do him one last favor.

"Listen and take my advice, Simon. Whatever it is you're feeling, whatever that crazy mind of yours is up to, do yourself a gigantic favor and learn to *act as if* . . . as if you are all right. Pretend you are okay and maybe it will go away. . . maybe you'll grow out of it. Don't let on what you're thinking. Pretend . . . pretend you're . . . normal. Otherwise, you may have to go to a . . . place . . . a school or institution or something." She chuckled a bit to take the onus off what she'd said.

Simon loved being bawled out by her. He sat on the floor and hung his head while she spoke. He hung his head because he was so sad and to hide his smirk. But he heard her too and was locking her advice away into an important region of his brain, in around self-preservation, when the doors came down.

Coco offered the demon a disguise and he grabbed it. Then the Kansas City police were suddenly everywhere, busting the place, gathering people, pushing Coco.

"And who are you, fella?" they wanted to know. "Some trick or john?" They laughed coarsely.

Simon smiled in a pleasant way and it was remarkably easy. He rubbed his aching hands together and calmly said, "Who, me? Oh, no, just a normal guy, hanging around."

"Well, you're coming with us. You're all coming with us."

"Sure, whatever you say. I have nothing to hide."

Some important politician or police official had been offended for one reason or another and despite the usual payoffs which were intact, wanted to teach Coco a lesson. They were all pushed into two paddy wagons and taken to jail.

Coco laughed at the hypocrisy of the thing, saying every last one of the arresting officers were customers. Even the big red-faced sergeant who looked the other way when he sternly said, "The law is the law."

They were all free before dawn the next day anyway and it was then that Simon made a decision that would affect the rest of his life.

They all stood in a group in the street outside the jail laughing and talking while Coco counted heads.

A sleek-looking man Simon didn't recognize stood away from the group at the mouth of the alley. Smoking a cheroot, he leaned with one foot up on the sidewalk that ran in front of the jail. Simon had to squint because of the morning light coming up behind the man. He was impeccably dressed in a black homburg, a dark custom-made suit and white boutonniere, at that time of the morning yet. Simon looked from the ragtag bunch he was with, disheveled from the night in jail, and back to the handsome stranger.

"Who is that?" Simon asked Coco.

"Oh, that's Nathan, my lawyer." She stared for a time and after seeing Simon's reaction, laughed and said, "He is beautiful, isn't he? Look at him standing there. He's got a license to steal. A license to take your money, as much as he wants, with his silk gloves and a smile. What a way to make a buck."

Simon would always remember the impression Nathan made on him that morning; the feeling of admiration that he felt for the man.

"How does he do it . . . be a lawyer?"

Coco picked up on Simon's fascination right away, and after a moment's deep thought, snapped her fingers to say, "That would be a good place for you, Simon, a great place to . . . hide . . . in a law book. That would take all of your concentration."

Rubbing her cheek and thinking, she said, "I'm only going to say this once, Simon, but if you want what he's got, you can have it. You might be . . . a little . . . off." She laughed.

"You may be a little whacko, but stupid you're not. You're a darn good reader, an excellent reader, and reading comprehension is the name of the game in his line. Come on, let's go talk to him and ask him. . . ."

"No, no." Simon pulled back and wouldn't go.

"All right, suit yourself, but I'm not going to be seeing you anymore to remind you. You know I meant business back at the house?"

Simon nodded sullenly.

"Then listen. You *can* be a lawyer if you want to badly enough. Just go to school. Start wherever you have to and work your tail off. And don't forget . . . "

"Act normal?" he interjected.

Laughing, Coco said, "You've got it."

Simon saw it all clearly; the handsome, well-respected, rational man of the law, bathed in a halo of morning sunlight. It was an almost theatrical event, a golden illusion, one that Simon would recall a thousand times.

Coco said, "Come on, let's walk for home. It'll do us all some good."

Simon got close and asked, "Does Nathan ever come to the house?"

Coco was in a schizophrenic mood and already beginning to give Simon the cold shoulder. She answered his question but wouldn't look at him. She made it obvious she was as good as finished with Simon.

Somehow she'd gotten one of her suppositories into her, and stoned out of her head, she lectured and entertained the group all the way home.

"Does he . . . does he ever see the girls?" Simon demanded.

"Nathan, no, he's a strange loner of a man. His wife died of some awful disease and he raises his kids alone. He works hard . . . really hard. I've asked him to come over, to have his pick anytime, for free, but he always has the same answer. He always smiles and says it's just his work for him these days. I tell him, 'Nathan, all work and no play,' and all that stuff, and he gives me his learned smile and says, 'Well, Coco, you know what Sigmund Freud said.' And I say, 'Yes, yes, yes,' hoping to shut him up, but he goes on and tells me anyway, 'All a man really has is his work.'

"And then I tell him that Freud was a cokehead and probably gave that quote when he believed his work was testing cocaine for the world.

"Can you guys see the old goat? Old Ziggy, snorting away gigantic lines of cocaine and saying, 'Oh dear, yezziree, dis iz quvite an interesting profezzion here, dis testing of da new chemicals dat getz me very happy. Oh vell, zo much for zee vucking zsychy. Put your noze in dat pile of zsnow over der, and gootbye mit da schitzo, hello mit da halleluya time . . . and de helium ride . . . up, up and avay. Oh vell, vat a poor overworked vellow I am . . . but, I zuffer trough. I guess all dat dis poor doctor haz, iz hiz vork . . . All dat a man really haz iz hiz vork.

"'You got that, Hector? Hello. Put zat big mountain of zsnow over der on dat big mirror. Oh, datz nize. Zo now I gotz to go climbing dat big bad old Mount Kilimanjaro. Oh, golly, zee work dat I go trough. I tink dat I'll write a book today. Shit, der hello, I tink I'll write me a volume of books today. Nope, I tink I'll put ze pen in mine noze too. No, no, I vill put ze pen in mine azz and let mine words blow out of mine azzhole like zey usually do. Oh, fuck ze writing. Ve all gotz heads like apes anyhow—just give me a funnel and a shovel vile I make a big blizzard in mine noze. Hi ho, hi ho, itz off to vork I go . . . and all I gotz iz mine vork.' "

The gang of them cracked up with laughter and good times, but not Simon, who wandered away picturing himself handsome and well respected, a lawyer in a halo of bright orange light; acting normal.

Simon spent a long time licking the plump girl where it would do the most good. Though his concentration was indistinct and he understood it might well have been his fault, it angered him nonetheless that she wouldn't come. He slammed her good and told her she was fat. "Get your shit together, fatso . . . you're not trying. I know the fat girl's game. Hookers can't come and fat girls won't." Simon flashed on sharp Jewish Andy.

Andy knew the score. He had a fat girl friend and bitched plenty about her being fat and where her head was, but he was hip.

"Crazy, isn't it, Simon? For a woman to stay fat for insulation from men, for insulation from love. To stay fat so's not to have to face the look of love from a man? It scares the shit out of them. What a drag."

Under cross-examination, Simon's wife Carol admitted that some women, she wouldn't say how many, used symptoms like overweight or dressing dowdy or dressing in unattractive patterns or wearing broken-down shoes; that certain women who knew better did it for protection.

Simon let himself down into the shadowy pink theater hallway and headed downstairs for the pay phone. Thinking about calling Carol made his temples pound. He was slick with perspiration.

When there was no answer, he threw the telephone against the wall and screamed, "Shit," hysterically. His mind raced. He tried to glimpse and relish as many of Carol's sexual indiscretions as he could while the images flew past into a frustrating psychic jamb.

Frantic, he called again, again and again, until his mind went blank and he found himself slumped down onto his cramping haunches, his back to the hard pink wall.

Holding himself, he rocked. The telephone receiver hung nearby. Its persistent throbbing tone made him think of a distant warning signal of some kind. Like in a war movie, a submarine under attack. "Dive . . . dive," he shrieked and laughed, but slammed the back of his skull against the wall over and over until his head swam in a sparkling pink cosmos.

He didn't move for a long time. He stretched out where he was, onto the carpet. Lying on his right side with his arm stretched out, he let his head slump over onto his shoulder. Drumming his fingers against the carpet, he stared at the durable shocks of wooly pink yarn as they parted from the weight of his fingertips.

Something made him realize that his outstretched arm was asleep and that he was mesmerized. He looked up to find himself staring into the eyes of a woman who stood at the foot of the theater stairs.

She was a redhead, physically large, wearing too much makeup. Her right hand twitched nervously near her side until she put both hands onto her hips in tight fists to demand, "Who . . . what are you doing here?"

Simon smiled but she looked back in disgust. He felt himself flush.

"What are you doing? Who are you?" she demanded. "Get out of here, right this minute."

Simon thought she was probably five foot ten and saw that she had a cloth banking bag, a bag for receipts, under her arm. She stood aside to indicate with a stern pointer finger what she expected him to do, where she wanted him to pass.

"I'm not fooling. Now get out of here, now, before I call the police. Come on." She gestured past herself with her finger.

"This is my place," Simon said.

The big redhead became indignant. "You? Why, you're crazy, out of your mind. My husband and his partners own this theater—and he's getting the car right now to come and pick . . ."

The redheaded woman stopped her sentence midstream, caught up by something in Simon's eyes. She stammered, "I . . . he . . . is . . ."

Simon could see what she was.

"My husband will deal with this. I strongly suggest that you . . ."

Simon got to his feet. She turned and bolted for the stairs. He chased her. The exercise felt good.

She headed across the lobby for the theater's front plate-glass doors. It was black outside. Night or early morning, and raining.

She reached the doors and threw them open, but Simon was there too. He caught her and pulled her back around to face him. She smelled of Spray Net or Lauren, probably both, odors he detested. She tried to pull away and Simon smiled at a thick black false eyelash that had fallen down into the middle of one eye.

"Leave me alone, let go of me, you . . . you animal."

Simon seized her by the neck. He dug his powerful fingers in through the flesh and cartilage of her throat, grabbed her windpipe, and yanked.

Her eyes nearly popped as her throat came out in his hand. But she managed to do something instinctive, defensive. She broke a high heel in her effort, but was able to trip him a bit so that he lost his balance.

Leaving the cloth receipt bag at his feet, uttering a gulping sound, she broke out of the place. With her hands clutching her throat she ran north up Westwood Boulevard into the soft downpour.

Standing in the open doorway watching her crazy lopsided, broken-shoed run, he was made to think of a Thanksgiving turkey back on the farm. The cocky red-topped fowl that ruled the roost all year, beheaded and thrown into the yard to bleed out. Flopping around all over the place, directionless, pissed-off with no head. He could hear her gobble.

He breathed deeply of the cool, clean, damp air and felt invigorated.

The big redheaded woman made it to the corner and out into the middle of Wilshire Boulevard, which was completely devoid of traffic, before she went down into a heap. She raised herself up onto one stiff elbow. She reached out pathetically with the other hand toward the north before collapsing again onto the glistening wet black. Simon picked up the cloth bag, closed the theater doors and locked them tight.

With his forehead pressed against the cold glass, he surveyed the concrete in front of the theater. It was wet and clean. He strained to see the sidewalk up the street in the direction she had run. There was nothing. No telltale trail. No red. There was only the slick wet surface of the gray cement sidewalk and the darkness.

Back inside the attic, Simon lit his candle for the first time and discovered an adding-machine tape and twenty-six hundred dollars in the cloth bag.

He liked the candle. It made things cozy and secure, especially with the rain. He looked through his old magazines and paperback novels. He read the first thirty-one pages of *War of the Worlds,* and slept, holding hands with the one-eyed girl.

BOOK TWO

The holidays had been slow for police business. Hero stood next to his desk quickly perusing the reports and various handwritten messages that his men had left for him while he was on vacation. Nothing important, he said to himself. They didn't need me for a damned thing. Just like last year, slow. A good time to take off. Yawning, he didn't want to get started.

He had a sip of Good Earth tea and opened his mail. Reading, he went to the other side of the room and pulled the blinds. Bright warming sunlight flooded the room. He opened the window. Squinting, he scrutinized the morning. He looked out across the damp parking lot and thought that rain does great things for L.A. Gets rid of the fucking smog for fifteen minutes.

Nothing in the mail either, he thought. He threw the junk letters into the trash. Two pieces missed the wastebasket to slip under his desk. As he bent to retrieve them, a sharp pain shot through his lower spine causing him to cry out and stand up straight. "Jeeesus." He rubbed his back. "That fucking Dwight."

The ambidextrous devil had beaten him two games straight in handball the evening before—21-13 and 21-9. You tried too hard, old boy, he told himself. You can't play handball with him. Stick to racquetball. Or go and kneel in the left corner of the court and practice. Hit balls with your left hand till it falls off. Do it all day, every day for a year or two. Then maybe— "Aw, shit," he said laughing. He slid carefully into his chair which creaked loudly.

Checking his watch, he buzzed the desk sergeant to see if Dwight was in. "Is he ever," the sergeant said. "He's in the middle of a screaming match with a man and woman in reception." Hero let go of the intercom switch and in strode Dwight. He looked fatigued.

"Goddamn, Dwight, you looked hassled. Did you work too hard last night at winning? You jack-off, my back is killing me." He laughed and so did Dwight, but Dwight was into business.

"Odius is here, and Placenta, and they're screaming their hinies off out there. Listen, do you hear that? All the way up the hall?"

Hero tried but couldn't hear anything.

"I told you about these crazies, didn't I? About Odius and Placenta? Did you read my report?" Dwight began to shuffle through the papers on Hero's desk.

Hero stopped him. "What is it, Dwight? What do they want? Why are you so uptight?"

Dwight stopped to think. "Yeah, I am, aren't I? It's because I missed breakfast. I'm carbed out. Come on." He opened Hero's office door to the hall. "Come on, walk with me to the candy machine while I get some cashews. I need some energy."

Leaving his office door open, Hero walked with him. "Did you read my report on them?" Dwight asked. "Don't kid me."

"No, I haven't had a chance. Is it a big deal?"

"Well, judge for yourself. Placenta is Dr. Emily Schoen- baum, the gynecologist that runs Western States Adoption

Center and Sperm Bank over on Ocean Park. A real crazy old dame, eccentric. Ever hear of her?"

"Maybe. Is she hot? She's a real doctor, isn't she?"

"Yes, she's a real doctor all right. A good one, supposedly. Delivered a thousand babies during her career, but . . ."

"But what?"

"But her lover is this guy, Odius. A real creepy-looking Valentino type. Dresses in black. Apparently they've been lovers for years."

"So?"

"So, it turns out that Dr. Schoenbaum—she calls herself Placenta—has been using *his,* Odius's sperm to artificially inseminate . . . to impregnate everybody. Every woman that she has impregnated artificially has gotten a child from Odius. Can you believe it?"

"That sounds like a lot of bullshit." When Hero laughed in disbelief his back pained him. Standing perfectly still, he rubbed his spine.

Dwight worked the machine until it produced three bags of nuts. Now Hero could hear them screaming at each other, up at the end of the hall off in Reception. He watched the desk sergeant move briskly across the hall to bark something that echoed throughout the polished concrete building. The bickering stopped.

"See what I mean, Chief?"

"Yeah. Dwight, when I lean against the wall, rub my lower back with the heel of your palm, will you? I must have strained it."

"Sure, Chief."

Hero leaned against the wall with the flats of his hands while Dwight rubbed the small of his back.

"It's not true of course, is it? I mean, is it supposed to be the truth? It sounds ludicrous."

"Ludicrous, hell, I think it sounds downright cruel. But yes, it's my opinion that it's the truth. I believe them. There, is that better?"

Hero stretched and bent over from the waist several times. "Yes, I think so."

"I really had to go some to beat you last night, Chief. I—"

"Knock off the bullshit, Dwight. Just tell me what the doctor wants with me, before you call the D.A. and tell them this crazy-assed story. Let them figure it out. I don't believe it."

"It's not her, it's him, Odius. He wants you. He's heard about you, and he wants you to get his kids back, to find his missing kids, the whole bunch. Placenta says there's a couple hundred of them."

Hero stopped. "You are shitting?"

"No, I'm not. That's why I wanted to talk to you before they got to you. To decide what to do. It's crazy, if it's the truth— potentially big and messy."

Dwight opened and meticulously poured all three bags of cashews into his right hand and began to eat them one at a time with his left. He offered one to Hero, who refused.

"Goddamn, what a story, what a fucking story," Hero said, stopping to watch Dwight.

"Are you left-handed, Dwight? I see you eating with your left. Are you a lefty? Once and for all, don't shit me."

Dwight laughed. "No, Chief, no, honest. I don't think so. I'm not sure. It doesn't make any difference which hand I—"

"Yeah, yeah . . . okay."

Schmuck, Hero said to himself, then, "Well I suppose I'd better see them. Does this guy, Odius, know who the kids are, or where they are?"

"Not yet, but he's all over the doctor to tell him and she looks to be weakening. She has all of the records locked away but she sure as shootin' could tell him if she wanted to. Every last name and address . . ."

"And Odius expects us to cut the files loose and get him the kids, is that it?"

"Yeah, Chief. His kids. He says they're his. That they're missing persons."

Laughing, Hero said, "What total bullshit. Who the hell does he think he is?"

They walked back into Hero's office. Hero sat on the edge of his desk to finish his tea. Dwight sank into the davenport. He kicked off his loafers and put his feet, covered with clean wool socks, into the stream of sunlight. Eating cashews he said, "You know, the sick part is that some judge might do it, that's what I think. Odius seems real determined, says he's getting old and wants his kids around him. I guess it would take a pretty big house."

They laughed but Hero stopped to say, "I'm sure you're right about some judge making it possible. Brandon would do it for him, wouldn't she?"

Dwight nodded in agreement.

"So would Judge Christianson downtown. And how about that little self-righteous Oriental chick over in the D.A.'s office, Shirley something. She'd get Odius his kids."

"Sure thing. And the press . . . think about them for a minute."

"Yeah, shit, the press. They'd have a field day, ruin a couple hundred—my ass, how about the parents and families—ruin a thousand people's lives. But what a story for those sharks. They wouldn't give a damn. What a mess."

Hero lowered himself into his creaky chair to think.

"Yeah," Dwight said, "and complicated. Your back okay now?"

"I think so, thanks."

"Good, well, that's why I wanted to brief you. I came in early and they were already here champing at the bit. They knew you'd be back this morning. I called the boat but missed you. You're lucky you came in through the garage. "Oh"— Dwight sat forward on the sofa—"there's something else too. Ready?"

"Dwight, don't always ask me if I'm ready. You always say that before you serve the ball too. Yes, I'm ready. I'm always ready, now serve, I mean talk. What else?"

Dwight removed a neatly folded sheet of teletype from inside his sport coat and held it out to Hero.

"Read it, Dwight. You know what's in it. Is it in my stack?" Hero reached for the pile of papers on his desk.

"No, Chief. It just came in this morning. I got it because I was here early. It just happened this . . ."

"What, Dwight? What happened, Jesus, come on. I want to get to that goofy gynecologist."

"A woman was killed this morning, murdered. She was the

wife of one of the guys that owns the Westwood Crown movie theater."

Hero perked up. "The theater?"

"Yep. She was found half a block away. Somebody or something tore her throat clean out. The same exact M.O. as you know who, from three years ago. Throat completely gone."

Hero stared blankly. He chewed at the inside of his lip. "The . . . The Terror?"

Dwight nodded his head up and down smugly and ate cashews.

Hero felt a chill come slowly over him. "When? Where?" He sat on the edge of his chair.

"Sometime around three A.M. I called the desk over in West L.A. for what they've got. Thought you'd want to know."

"Go on."

"Her husband left her in the theater with the day's receipts—about three in the morning—and went to get the car. It was drizzling. When he came back to get her, he stopped in front of the theater and honked. His headlights just happened to point right out into the middle of Wilshire Boulevard. You know the place, facing north? Can you picture it? There's a slope down there to Wilshire.

"Anyway, it made it just right for his headlights to shine onto a dark clump out in the middle of Wilshire Boulevard. He sat there until it came home to him, until he realized what he was looking at. He jumped out and ran to her."

"Was she dead?"

"Probably, but he didn't think so . . . wasn't sure . . . so he rushed her over to UCLA Emergency and of course she was dead on arrival. Throat pulled right out of her. Clean as a—"

Hero's telephone rang. It was Darryl Gates's office. The Los Angeles chief of police. Hero shushed Dwight and wrote "Gates" on a piece of paper that he showed him. Dwight raised his eyebrows, finished the cashews, brushed the salt off his hands, put his shoes back on, crossed his legs and sat back attentively. Gates came on. He spoke fast in a hushed but urgent tone. He asked if Hero had heard.

"Yes sir, we were just talking about it."

"Take a look will you, Hero? Sneak over and let me know what you think."

"How close a look?"

"Well, don't let any of your urgent business slide, and try not to alienate the West Side guys, but have a look, okay? Although nobody should give you any heat over there. They'll probably be glad to see you. I'm bringing the whole city in on it. I just left Bradley. This reverend fella and his connections are leaning on the mayor real hard. I haven't answered their calls. And the press, shit, the fucking broads will panic if they think . . . Anyway, have a look, as a favor to me?"

"No problem. I was going to go over anyway. I just came in from vacation today. Anything more on the disappearances I should know?"

"I wish there was, but nothing, zilch. They're just gone from the theater, two females. That's all we've got. And now this fucking thing."

"I'll take a look at the body, too. I'll know right away if. . ."

"Yeah, we're lucky the body is at UCLA. But if it's him again, Christ Almighty, don't let on. Don't tell anybody but me. In fact, keep all this to yourself."

"There's one man I trust, my partner."

"Dwight?" Gates asked.

Surprised, Hero said, "Yes."

"A good man. All right, let me know, call me." He hung up.

"How do you know Gates?" Hero asked.

"Tennis, remember? He's an 'A' player. I met him in the police intramurals, the quarter finals three or four years ago, before he was chief. He's a good player."

Hero said, "Oh, yeah, I forgot," and they both laughed, remembering Dwight had beaten him easily in straight sets.

"He likes you."

"Me? Gee, that's nice."

"Yeah. In the meantime, he's shitting a brick over this theater thing. Looks to him like it might be The Terror too. Wants us to keep it quiet."

"What's he want you to do?"

"He wants me to nose around and give him an opinion."

137

"And?"

"And nail the son of a bitch if I can, I suppose."

"Wow, here we go again."

"Yeah, and you know, Dwight, I hate to say it but I hope that it's him. I hope he's surfaced again."

Hero was onto his feet, pacing and stretching from the waist.

"Yeah?"

"Yeah, that would be just fine with me. And you know?"

"What?"

"All of a sudden my back feels brand new."

ELEVEN

Hero walked fast and businesslike with his chest out when he went into Reception, but Odius was waiting with his energy up.

"Fiddleman?" Odius demanded.

Hero nodded. Odius threw his red-lined black cape over his shoulder and glided over to him. Jesus, Hero thought, a dancer. A real cha-cha-cha.

"You've got to help me, Inspector Fiddleman. Help me to get my children. I'm fifty years old and . . ."

"Wait, no, don't listen to him," from the doctor who came running now too, her hands outstretched to grab Hero.

Hero put his hands up to stop them. "Hold it, both of you."

"But, but—" from a pleading Odius who smelled of garlic.

"I said hold it. Now stand still and don't talk, either of you. Dwight."

Dwight came in behind him.

"Dwight, take this gentleman down the hall and get his side

of the story. You won't need Sondra." Sondra was the Venice police stenographer.

Dwight looked in Hero's eyes and seemed to understand.

"Get him a cup of coffee and keep him with you. Listen to the whole thing. Got it?"

"But . . . but, Inspector, I've already told him all about—"

"Don't breathe on me, mister. Stand back. Dwight will take notes this time. I'm sure there are aspects of your story he's missed. Get the whole story, Dwight."

Dwight nodded and ushered Odius out and down the hall to an interrogation room. Odius was saying, "I don't see why. . ." but Dwight took charge.

Hero brought Dr. Schoenbaum down to his office. "Placenta," she said. "Please call me Placenta."

She was sixtyish and from her expression, definitely off the beam. Never fixing on anything for long, her eyes wandered over him and around his office. He didn't speak but sat on the corner of his desk observing her, which seemed to make her anxious. That's okay, he thought. I'm anxious too. Anxious to get over and see that body. Anxious to finish this thing up.

Finally she looked at his chest and said, "I don't know what I'm doing here. I want to go."

"Sit down, Placenta, over there. You're here to find out what's going to happen to you for abusing your responsibility, for breaking the law."

"No, no, that's not why, that's not right. Odius is the one. He's trying to—"

"Forget about Odius. You're the one going to jail." He sat down at his desk and folded his hands.

Placenta worked her mouth as though to firm her chops. Her color paled. "J-jail?"

"Sit down."

She sat on the edge of the davenport. Hero picked up his telephone, punched a blank line, waited drumming his fingers and said, "Hello? Whose office is this? I want Rudy Garcia in the district attorney's office. No, I don't mind."

Placenta was getting up, but Hero directed her to sit back down and not speak.

"Hello, Rudy, Chief Fiddleman. Yeah, sure. Same to you. Listen, if you've got a minute I want to relate a story to you. I want to know the culpability...how much prison time is involved."

Placenta adjusted the shawl over her shoulders and nervously picked at imaginary lint.

Laughing and making small talk along the way, Hero repeated the story that Dwight had told him about Placenta and Odius into the dead phone line. He changed the names. Placenta did not protest but merely hung her head, indicating that he had the story very close to right. When he had finished Hero said, "Well, Rudy, what do you think?"

Placenta looked up and began furiously chewing a hangnail while Hero pretended to listen.

Finally, Hero said, "That bad, huh? Really...Sure, I agree. It's a dirty damn deal. Ruin a lot of people's lives. No, I'll call you back with the details. Thanks, Rudy." He hung up and stared at her as hard as he could, trying to make her feel guilty.

"Ten years, Placenta, if you're lucky. Your clinic is finished, of course. We'll board it up. Your reputation, goodbye to that."

She hung her head and said, "I didn't know. And Odius?"

"We'll find something to hang on him, but he hasn't done much that's against the law. You're the one. He'll go free. *You* are going to jail. You're the one that's washed up, not him. He'll be sitting at home with all of his kids. Why haven't you told him who they are?"

"Something...has kept me from it."

"Do you know who the families are?"

"Yes, oh, yes, I keep impeccable records. You see, Odius was such a perfect specimen...a perfect donor...such an intelligent, perfectly limber..."

"Was he a good lover?"

Placenta answered, "Yes, oh, dear yes," with the silliest grin before she froze, grasped her shawl as though to warm herself and stared out the window.

"So, where are the records?"

"At the clinic," she said soberly. She drew a string up from around her neck that held a lone key.

"To my files . . . there's only one."

"Are there copies of your records?"

"No, just originals, but they're safe and sound." She dangled the key.

"How about downtown, City Hall, how about their records?"

"There are none. I have them all, I told you."

"No, Xeroxes anywhere—*anywhere?*"

"No, no, I told you." She dropped the key back into her bosom. "What are you getting at?"

"A bonfire."

Dr. Emily Schoenbaum clutched her key through her thick satin blouse. "Oh, no . . . never . . . dear me . . . those records are my life's work. Oh, dear, I would never so much as . . ."

"Burn 'em or go to jail, lady. It's as simple as that." He picked up his phone. "Well, ?" he asked. "I've got things to do. Decide."

"Odius—he would die."

"So will you, in prison. Are you still fertile?"

"Me? Hardly."

"Well, then, adopt one. Find a baby that looks like him—a good dancer—and tell him it's his."

She looked at him for the first time. "I've never thought of that. But only *one*. He'd—"

"Find a bunch of them if you want. Loose children up for adoption. But *not* someone else's. Come on."

He escorted her to the reception area. "You drive—do you drive?"

"Odius has the keys."

"Ben," Hero yelled to the desk sergeant. "Go get her car keys from her boyfriend. He's down with Dwight. Tell them to sit tight. We'll be right back."

"What are we going to do?"

"Keep you out of jail."

"But Odius is going to just die. You've never seen him when he cries. It's so sad. He's such a sensitive man. Not like most men."

Hero looked at her and said, "Yeah, sure."

Ben returned to toss Hero the keys. Hero motioned Ben to come close.

"Ben, find out that guy's real name, Odius who, or whatever. Run him. Find out all you can. I'll call you shortly."

Driving over, Hero said, "I want you to know I appreciate your invitation. I've always wanted to see your clinic. It was nice of you to come and get me."

She looked at him strangely and wrinkled her brow questioningly.

He said, "This is all your idea, Doctor. All of it. I'm just along for the ride—you got it?"

She nodded and neither of them spoke again until they were in front of the clinic.

Hero knew the facade well. He'd been by it innumerable times. He had always regarded the clean white-tiled building as respectable looking. A crew of painters were working on the place next door. Their paint truck sat blocking her driveway. She said it made her mad but let it go and parked down the street a few doors.

Walking up Washington, Hero was surprised to find the Atlas Pawnshop two stores down from the clinic. Atlas was the name of the pawnshop famous for illegal buying and selling of guns and hot goods. They had been tossed several times but managed to stay in business. Pawnshop permits were a piece of cake in the city.

It really wasn't his department but he couldn't help glancing in the dark place anyway as they walked by. There was nothing to see inside but blackness.

They passed the painters' truck before entering the clinic's side door and Hero lifted a small unopened can of turpentine from the truck's rear bumper and brought it along. They acknowledged her employees but Hero urged her ahead to her private office which was on the other side of the building. The sterile white room was in perfect order and faced out into a parking lot through sliding glass doors. A large white metal filing cabinet sat in the corner of the room. Hero sneaked the turpentine onto her desk. When she turned she noticed it immediately.

"What's that I wonder?" she asked.

"Turpentine . . . highly flammable. One of the painters must have left it."

"Painters?" she questioned.

"Why not show me the files I've heard so much about?"

The doctor stared out into the parking lot next door and didn't move. He knew what she was thinking, that she didn't want to, or couldn't do it.

"If it makes you feel any better, I can tell you that I don't see another way. I mean, what the hell is going to happen if you unlock those files, to anybody? I'm disappointed in you. You're supposed to be a smart woman. You can begin again."

"But Odius."

"Hey lady, fuck Odius." He went with his temper. "Put your hands behind you. Anyone who can put . . . Odius . . . before all of these families—I said put your hands behind you." He handcuffed her lightly. "—deserves to spend the rest of her life in the can. I've had it with you." He turned her brusquely for the door.

"Where should I do it?" she asked.

"Do what?" he asked, forcing her to do the thinking.

"Burn the files. There they are, that entire top section." She nodded back to the white cabinet.

"I don't know, it's up to you. It's your property."

"Would you take these off, please?"

Hero removed the handcuffs. The doctor went to her office door, opened it and yelled, "Melinda."

"What are you doing?" Hero asked.

"There's a metal garbage can outside." She gestured to the vacant lot to the north. "Out at the rear of the lot, but I don't think I can—"

"Yes, you can. You don't want anyone else involved."

Melinda was there, an attractive black girl. "Yes, ma'am?"

Hero shook his head. "Never mind, Melinda."

Melinda went away, closing the door to the hall behind her.

Dr. Schoenbaum pulled the drapes the rest of the way open, opened the sliding glass door and went outside in search of the can herself. Soon she returned, dragging a galvanized metal garbage can. She dragged it up and over, into her office.

"Will you help me?" she asked, out of breath.

"Nope."

She pulled the can, which already had a small amount of garbage in it, over to the white file. She used the key from around her neck to open the cabinet. The heavy top section rolled open automatically and there they were, neatly filed for anyone to see. Scores of manila folders with names and addresses on the tags. In the wrong hands, Hero said to himself, a catastrophe.

Soberly, she did it. Her arms and shoulders moved back and forth in a mechanical way, over and over, each move the same. Clutch a batch of folders, lift over and drop. Lift over and drop until the big drawer of the filing cabinet was empty.

The can nearly tipped over as she pulled it past the sliding glass door's track, but she managed finally to get the can out into the lot.

"Further," Hero yelled.

She dragged it another ten yards.

Returning for the turpentine and matches from her desk drawer, she smelled strongly of perspiration. The can of turpentine shook in her hands as she emptied it onto the folders that choked the garbage can. She lit the entire book of matches and threw it in. The can roared into flames.

With her shoulders in a hunch, she dragged herself back inside to fall into her desk chair.

"Is there any other way of tracing those children, Doctor? Think."

She shook her head slowly and said, "No. It's all there. I know what you wanted. It's done, believe me."

"Do you remember any of their names?"

"No. Well, maybe one or two. I wasn't interested in names. Don't worry, it's all done. Fire and ash."

"Then let it end here, Doctor, all of it. Your memory as well. Is that understood? I don't want to ever hear your name again, connected with anything illegal or even improper, or I'll be down on you like a ton of bricks."

She looked up.

"I'm not shitting, Placenta. Keep your nose in the right direction."

She shook her head up and down.

"If you're worried about Odius, don't be. Let me deal with him. I'll talk to him. He won't give you any trouble. If he does, you call me, understand?"

She nodded and stared at her hands.

"Don't act so unhappy. You just did something very good, for everybody concerned."

He walked out to the fire and kicked the can. He kicked it again and again until he was sure there was nothing inside but burning black ash.

Before walking back up to the street through the lot, Hero paused to stick his head back into the doctor's office.

"You don't happen to have any of his sperm left around do you? You wouldn't—"

"No, I don't, and no I wouldn't." She began to sob and Hero left her.

Hero walked back past the Atlas Pawnshop to the pay phone on the corner. When he got Ben at headquarters he asked him to get Dwight on the phone too and make it a three-way call.

Dwight spoke as soon as he got on, saying that Odius wanted either to be released or to call his lawyer.

"What do you want to do, Chief?"

"What did you find, Ben?" Hero asked.

"Odius is his alias. Real name is William Townright. Born New York City, 1924. The guy's got a long record of misdemeanor and petty larceny arrests. Nothing pending, no wants."

"All right, Dwight, I'm going to ask you to put him on the phone with me. Thanks, Ben."

Ben hung up.

"Put him on the phone, and then drop him someplace quick on the way down here. I want you to come and get me. I'll be at the phone booth next to Schoenbaum's clinic. It's close, down on Washington. Got it?"

"Yeah, sure thing, but what's up?"

"There are no more records on the families or the babies. They're burned up. I may be asking for it, but fuck it, it's simpler this way, equitable. It's not totally foolproof but they'd have to go through a ton of bullshit to find them. And we'll be watching. Okay?"

Dwight said, "Ah, so. Sounds smart. Real smart move, Chief. Let me go get him."

Waiting for Odius, Hero turned around to see two Mexicans entering the Atlas Pawnshop with three television sets piled on top of each other on a rolling rig. He said, "Sheeit," laughed and shook his head in disbelief. "Broad daylight, too much."

Odius answered.

"William Townright, is that you?"

Odius answered tentatively, "Yes, it's me. How did you—"

"Listen, William Townright, and listen good. This is Chief Fiddleman. I'm down at Doctor Schoenbaum's clinic and there are no records of what you're talking about. So quit hassling her about it."

"But—but—"

"It seems she's in love with you. That's why she told you that story."

"But, why that's—"

"Now listen. I know all about you, about New York and how you've led your life, and I want you to get this right. Are you listening good?"

"Yes," in a monotone.

"All right, I'm telling you to forget this obsession of yours. What you had in mind, if it had been true, was a chickenshit idea. You'd have ruined a lot of people's lives."

"But—"

"Wait a minute, Townright. Don't but me. It all speaks of your character, what a shitheel you are."

"Now just a minute, I don't have to listen—"

"You don't *have* to do anything. But on the other hand, you'd better goddamned well do something. You'd better put on your cape and go out into the community and fly right. I don't want to hear a fucking word from you, or about you ever again. If I do, I swear to you—are you listening?"

"Yeah."

"I swear to you I'll bust your balls. Have you got that? Go

out and lead your life like a gentleman, with some integrity, and I'll leave you alone. But if you push this thing, I'll have your ass. One way or another I'll have your ass, and Townright?"

"Yes."

"I've got many resources—you understand?"

There was a pause then. "But my children, my little ones."

"Knock that shit off, Townright. It was a fairy tale. Now straighten up and promise me that you're going to be a good citizen, that I don't have to send *somebody* out to find you some night."

That did it. Hero could feel the fight drain out of him.

"I don't think you want me as an enemy, do you, William Townright?"

There was a sigh, then, "Okay. . . okay."

The phone shuffled back to Dwight.

When Dwight came on, Hero said, "Tell him I'm pissed, and that I mean what I say. See you at the phone booth and step on it. I've got something on my mind, a quick stop or two I want to make."

"Yeah, something on your mind. The Terror, right?"

"Give me back to Ben, Dwight, and get rolling. Come on, I'm waiting."

Hero told Ben to send a couple of men down to the Atlas Pawnshop and dump the place one more time.

"Tell them to make sure the store's got receipts for everything. Check everything in the place against the hot sheet."

Hero was tempted to take the place himself but he knew it could get involved and didn't want that. His head was filled with what he might find at the UCLA Medical Center, in the morgue.

Stepping out into the day, Hero walked anxiously around the booth twice before stepping back inside to call the houseboat.

Hearing Kay's voice made him feel warm. When she spoke, it was as though she knew he had things on his mind, business problems, and didn't need any more unanswered questions in his head. Her sober good cheer brought him a feeling of security; her beneficence, a feeling of calm. Gone were the days when he would tolerate an erratic female in his home. Home is where you go for peace. Thinking about your home should make you feel safe. The tone of Kay's voice told him she was there, responsible, making a quiet place to lay his head. Old-fashioned maybe, but nice.

"I'm on my way down to Young & Rubicam to do a tape for them. They've been driving my agent crazy."

"Fantastic, Kay. Back to work?"

"Well, it's for Clairol. They just want my hair. I just toss my hair around and they shoot it in slow motion. Just the back of my head."

They laughed.

"Shit, what a perfectionist dope. You know you're the most beautiful girl in this town."

"Well, I'm a hundred nineteen on your scale, so I'm getting there, and I must say I'm all fixed up and look pretty good."

"There, see?"

"We'll see."

"How's Stretch?"

"Fine. He sat right next to me on the floor while I put on my makeup, or draped over my foot. He's a good old hound."

"Yeah, he's a dachshound. And there's a foxhound and a bloodhound and then there's me. Do you know what kind of hound I am?"

"No."

"A cunt hound. I like to stick my nose in your big high crack and lick the goods." Sensing her blush, he tingled.

"Hero," she sighed. "Now... now you've made me—"

"...Wet? Well, that's understandable because..." Imitating B. B. King, he sang the blues. "Because I'm a cunt hound, baby, just a sniffen over you, yeah. Well, I'm a cunt hound, baby, and I don't aim to sniff your shoe."

"Hero, you fucker, cut it out. My makeup is starting to melt." They laughed.

"Okay," he said. "So have a good day. Oh and Kay, plan on going with me to a late movie tonight."

"Oh, Hero, great. Which one?"

"I don't know. Check it for yourself. The late show at the Westwood Crown movie theater, in Westwood. Deal?"

"Deal. But I'll talk to you before then. I love you."

"Me too."

After he hung up he thought for a moment with his hand on the phone and said, "What a neat girl."

Then Dwight screeched to a stop outside, and Hero slammed from the booth to join him.

TWELVE

Well," Dwight said, driving up Washington, "Odius, A.K.A. William Townright, is disposed of. That's done. I dropped him at Chez Jay's. He said he needed a drink. You really handled that smart, Chief. Ballsy. A little bit off color, maybe." He laughed. "But smart. Stopped it cold."

"I hope so."

"I'm sure of it. Odius was of a different mind when I left him. Do you want to eat? It's eleven-thirty."

"No. Let's go over and look at the body. I want to see that woman's throat, *real* anxious to see it. Can you wait to eat? Wait and I'll buy you lunch at the sidewalk cafe. Deal?"

"You're damn tootin', Chief. It's a deal."

Dwight took Twentieth Street across town to San Vicente and San Vicente to Wilshire and to Westwood. The sun was under a cloud and the pollution was trying to come back, but there was enough of a breeze that women held their skirts and hats running across intersections. That was always a good sign.

An ocean breeze to help blow the shit away. Send it down to Palm Springs where the Chamber of Commerce calls it desert haze.

"Smog? Don't be silly. Never in Palm Springs."

Dwight talked about the old days, when he first came on the force, as he liked to do when he was alone with Hero.

Hero's head was someplace else when Dwight asked if he was boring him. But Hero smiled and said, "No, continue. Talk about whatever you like. Listening to you is relaxing. It helps me think. Turn here, Dwight, and go up Federal. We'll go in from the side. I'll show you where I park when I go to my poetry class. It's close to the hospital."

"Is the morgue in the main UCLA hospital?"

"Yes, in the basement. Want to hear my new poem?"

"Yeah, for sure."

"It's called 'The Heart of Integration.'"

"Yeah, go ahead."

Hero recited his newest poem to Dwight as they drove onto the UCLA campus, over the clean, winding black-topped streets, past the green lawns and ruddy firebrick buildings that brought to Hero the feeling of ageless substantiality every time he was there.

When he finished his poem, Dwight said he was genuinely impressed with Hero's knack with words. It pleased Hero more than he let on.

They parked and walked across campus to the UCLA hospital, where they took the escalator down to the morgue.

The basement was at least fifteen degrees cooler than the rest of the building. Stepping off the escalator, Hero shivered out loud. Dwight reacted sympathetically with a similar shudder. The corridor was brightly lit with artificial light. A dissimulated reflection came off of the greenish walls, coloring everything in varying shades of heliotrope.

After the young, long-haired Chinese intern had seen their shields and IDs, he took them back to the slabs, as he called them. The intern had a smart-alecky, know-it-all smile frozen over his face that appeared moist, damson wax under the light.

The room of drawers, the slabs, was long and silent as a

tomb. "Eerie place," Dwight said as they walked.

Hero cleared his ears and said, "Yeah."

"Ripped her real good," the purplish-black-haired Chinese said before he checked the number on the drawer with a sheet he held in his hand.

"Have the guys from downtown been here?" Hero asked.

"No, they're not coming. A few came last night, but the body is going downtown later."

As many times as Hero had been to the morgue, it never ceased to make him cringe when they pulled out the drawer. Hero suspected that Dwight wasn't bothered at all any more, if he ever was. They never spoke about it. Judging from his anxious posture, leaning closely now over the young Oriental's shoulder, he had no apprehension. He was eager, keenly interested, nothing else.

The drawer slid open. The Plexiglas bag was unzipped and Hero thought about Kay. How she had stopped using plastic in the kitchen. She cited some new study that said storing foods in plastic could be harmful to your health, perhaps even carcinogenic.

I don't guess you will mind much though, will you? He directed his thought to the corpse before him.

When the plastic wrap came back, Hero felt his heart stop. He stood there agape, unblinking. Dwight spoke first, "Goll-ly, Chief. What do you think?"

It was The Terror's work. There was no question about it. He saw that at first glance, but her face . . . the panic, the horror in her eyes. . . .

"Jesus," Hero said with a crack in his voice. "Don't you guys close the eyes?"

"Depends. Not this time. Orders are not to touch it. It goes downtown. Looks like something scared the hell out of her, huh?" He laughed.

"You can say that again," Hero said solemnly.

Dwight said, "One fell swoop. What power. . . unbelievable."

Hero nodded in agreement. But, goddamn, he thought, the eyes, I wonder what she saw? I wonder how it happened?

153

"Heavy, huh?" from the intern.

Hero didn't respond, and walked away motioning Dwight to follow. At the end of the room, Hero stopped and put his hand on Dwight's shoulder. He stared down at the highly polished black tile floor. The intern came by to ask if they needed anything more. Hero shook his head without looking up.

Dwight said, "No, and thank you," before giving Hero his undivided attention.

"Well?" Dwight asked finally.

"The fucker is back, Dwight, just the same as before. It's him, but—"

"Yeah?"

"But I've never seen their eyes before, have you?"

"No. I was thinking the same thing."

"Jesus Christ, man, what's it mean?"

"It means he's a . . . terrifying son of a bitch."

"Yeah, terrifying. Murdering fucking animal. We've got to get him, Dwight, before—"

"Yeah," Dwight interrupted. "Yeah, I know."

On the way out, the chief of UCLA's Pathology Department, Dr. Bernard McClendon, stopped them. Introducing himself, he asked, "Are you Fiddleman?"

Hero nodded and the doctor asked, "What do you think?"

"It's not what I think, it's what I know, and you?"

"No question about it. I've been here seventeen years. It's the same thing all over again. I autopsied two just like her, two, three years ago. Gates asked that I give you my opinion. I hope you guys can catch him this time."

Hero said, "Yes," and got on the escalator with Dwight.

"Keep it to yourself, Doctor," Hero said, moving up and away. "And tell your staff the same thing. We don't want to start a panic."

The doctor said, "Certainly, I understand," and disappeared down the hall.

As they reached the main hospital corridor, Dwight said, "Frustrating as the dickens. I'm not even sure what to look for. I can't even conjure up an image of the guy, The Terror. I mean, who or what do you suppose it is?"

Stopping, Hero paused to think. Finally he said, "Dwight, you've given me an idea. Since we're here, come on." He urged him back down the large tiled hallway to the nurses' station.

Showing them his badge, he used their telephone. Waiting for the hospital operator to answer, Hero handed another phone to Dwight and asked him to call their Venice office and check in.

Connected to the office of Dr. Roland Choates, UCLA's chief of psychiatry, Hero waited for his friend to come on the line. Choates was an intuitively brilliant old character whom Hero had consulted on special cases in the past. He was a man who enjoyed life, drank too much brandy, was an habitual pipe smoker and an incurable womanizer.

Choates called Hero "the poet cop." But he had said "Forget about poetry. It's time to write a book, a novel. Remember what Hemingway said, 'Go out and live—experience it all until you're thirty-five, and then write about it.' You've seen plenty. Get to it." Choates told Hero he had what it took to write novels.

"Well, Hero, as I live and breathe, come on up." Then he whispered, "I've got a new secretary that you'll like. But hurry up, I've got a class."

As they took the elevator to the seventh floor, Dwight brought Hero up to date on a few things at the office and explained that everything was under control; no emergencies.

Referring to the men at the precinct, Hero asked Dwight if he kicked ass for him while he was on vacation.

To which Dwight replied, "Yes, Chief, I always do. I stay right on top of them."

Dr. Choates's secretary, Georgia, was a small girl, probably a student, about five foot or five foot one, who couldn't have weighed more than ninety pounds. She wore a white, stiffly starched uniform and cream-colored horn-rimmed glasses that showed two puddles of blue behind powerfully refracted lenses. Although her hair was cut short like a boy's and she needed to wax her upper lip instead of bleach the hair there as she had been doing, Hero and Dwight smiled and agreed with their eyes that she was a sexy little thing. Almost like a perfectly formed little midget, a little doll, Hero thought. Delicate, frail, the bones in her forearms no thicker than a stiff you-know-what.

When she held open the door to the doctor's office, Hero stared at her proportions and couldn't help wondering what she was like in bed, so tiny and all. Then he thought about Kay and felt guilty.

Doctor Choates waved them in and mouthed a hello as he wound up a telephone conversation. They walked to the window of his office and looked out. The good air was holding its own. They could see the ocean.

"Dwight, why don't you take a shot at her. She's real cute, liable to be wild in bed. Why not get her number? I saw her staring at you."

Dwight shrugged his shoulders and said something about the day.

"Jesus Christ, Dwight. You've got a libido like a snail."

He shrugged again and said, "Yeah, but it's my libido."

It was true, too. Dwight rarely dated and didn't have a single girl friend that Hero knew about. There was nothing funny about the guy that way, just that he was always content merely to hang out, to be a third wheel.

"How about you, why don't you take a shot at her?" Dwight wanted to know.

"Because I've got a girl."

"That never stopped you before."

"Yeah, well this one's different."

"What is it with her? Why is Kay so special? What is it you see in her, Chief? Not that I don't—"

"I know, I know. It fits, Dwight. What more can I say? All of it, everything, fits."

The doctor got off the phone with a slam. They turned to find him producing a bottle of brandy and three glasses. They exchanged greetings all around and Doctor Choates poured them straight brandy.

"Dwight thinks that Georgia is hot stuff." Hero smiled and Dwight protested embarrassedly.

"Oh, goddamn, I know what you mean." He went quickly to his closed door and listened. Back at his desk he spoke softly but enthusiastically. "You wouldn't believe it . . . fucks like a mink . . . bleaches the hair on her pussy. Oh, God, Hero, you wouldn't believe it."

"How old are you?" Hero asked.

"Sixty-seven."

Laughing, Hero and Dwight exchanged glances. "You old cocker, you."

They sipped the brandy. Doctor Choates lit his pipe, checked his watch, sat back and said, "I've only got a few minutes, old pal. What'll it be?"

"Doctor," Hero began, pacing back and forth in front of the desk, "I need to ask you something, about the motivation of a—"

"Alienation of affection," said the doctor bluntly.

Hero stopped pacing. "What do you mean?"

"The Terror. That's what you're here about, isn't it? It's got to be a man whose mother or some woman, probably the one that raised him, deprived him of love. It's called sensory deprivation. Lack of love, touching, rocking when we are young, can cause brain damage. The damage warps the man's moral judgment, his sense of right and wrong, and, most important, produces a repressed rage that leads to extremely violent behavior."

Dwight said, "You're kidding," from across the room and asked, "You mean literally damaged, or. . ."

"I mean literally, physiologically damaged. Yes, small scars, like from a burn, on the cortex of the brain."

"Good God, but how in the hell did you know?"

"Oh, come on, Hero, I know everything that goes on around here. I know what kind of shape that body's in downstairs. Fact is, it's my right to know. I'm on the staff. So, what do you think of that?"

Excited, Hero said, "So, we're looking for a guy that was sort of—"

"Shit on," the doctor said, "or totally neglected, ignored. If you ignore a baby gorilla, don't touch him or hug him, if you

157

take his mother away as soon as he's born, and grow him up that way, shit, he'll tear your head off. Mean, uncontrollable, brain damaged. But really crazy around females. Instinctive, still angry at their mothers."

Impressed, Hero said, "Is that all theory, or fact?"

"Fact. Retestable. Did the studies at Johns Hopkins and Kentucky. Everybody agrees now. Sensory deprivation, lack of love toward an infant, can cause brain damage. And here's a real goody for you."

"Go on."

"They feel happy for a while when they get even—fulfilled, tremendously relieved. That's why he keeps on doing it. It feels good. He probably knows it's wrong but it gets him off. It frees him for a period of time, a sort of sweet revenge."

"But why would it have stopped, and started again?"

"Well, I'm not so sure about that."

"What do you mean?"

"I'm not as convinced as you, apparently, that it's the same killer. Mind you, I haven't seen the body, but . . ."

"Let me guarantee you, Doc, it's the same guy. I am absolutely convinced. How about it, Dwight?"

"Oh, no question. From what I can see, exactly the same. Throat torn clean out. No bruises, just an empty neck cavity with the pipes hanging. But you sound like you've got something else on your mind, Doc."

"Aha, Dwight, perceptive lad. There is no semen or urine in these wounds, Chief Fiddleman. Remember the others?"

"Now, how in the fuck do you know that? I don't even know that."

"But nevertheless, it's the truth. Now, do you still think it's The Terror?"

"Positively. No question about it. They didn't all have semen and urine over them."

"Oh?"

"No, hell, no. Maybe the couple that came through here did, but they all didn't. That wasn't a commonality, like the throat thing Dwight mentioned. And your chief of path agrees. I'm telling you it's the same guy, Doc. Believe me, I can smell it.

And assuming that I'm right, just assuming, what happened to him? Why did he drop out of sight for almost four years?"

Doctor Choates laughed and finished his drink. "He's been on holiday. How do I know?"

"Come on, come on, you've got something in that head of yours."

"Well, use your noggin. Think about it." He paused to knock the ashes from his pipe into the metal wastebasket. He checked his watch. "I've got a class."

Hero stood waiting, his hands on his hips.

"He got involved." The doctor shrugged. "Something took his mind off his obsession, if it's the same person."

"It is, I'm telling you. What would it be? What kind of diversion?"

"Hospitalization, drugs, some medication that worked, a job, a combination of the above, or. . ."

"Yes?"

"Hell, I don't know. Maybe he fell in love and got married. That would keep him busy for a while. Check all of the newly divorced men in L.A. You might not find The Terror but you'll sure as hell find any number of guys capable of murder." He laughed. "I've got to go, but seriously. . ." He put his hand on Hero's arm. "Seriously, Hero, that's probably what you're after. I don't know if it helps, but it's not very hard to figure. It's classic. The guy that tears out women's throats is pissed off at his mother."

"Real pissed off," said Dwight.

"Well," the doctor said at his office door, "real pissed off is right. They can make you or break you, our mothers. Sorry, I've got to run."

"Wait, we're coming too. Come on, Dwight."

Dwight and Hero bade the doctor and Georgia goodbye and hit out down the seventh-floor hall for Venice and some lunch.

Hero drove on the way back and they were both lost in thought until Dwight said, "Boy, if ever there was a guy who seemed to have all the answers, it's that Doctor Choates. Don't you think so? He even looks like he knows it all."

"Yes, he knows a lot of stuff."

"What kind of person is his wife?"

"He's not married."

"No? Well, why the wedding ring?"

"In memory of June."

"June?"

"Yeah, his wife, June. She hung herself seven or eight years ago."

"You're kidding. Shoot, you never know."

"He's got lots of answers, Dwight—for other people."

They parked in a no-park next to the St. Charles Hotel and walked the few yards west to the boardwalk, the wide concrete recreational pathway that runs north and south along the Pacific Ocean from Santa Monica to the marina.

The area had a weekday feel about it. The Christmas holiday was keeping people away, and the intermittent sunshine. The weekend, Hero expected, would be a mess. Particularly if the weather stayed decent.

They walked north toward the restaurant. The open-air merchandise stalls were vacant but for here and there: a display of dresses, Indian jewelry, a roller-skate rental truck with its tailgate down holding a longhair, stretched out flat on his back, getting high.

Hero was glad Stretch wasn't along. He'd be underneath the truck in a flash, barking his ass off. Marijuana, handcuffs, come on. Let's get this guy.

Passing the next corner, they stopped to observe a bunch of wrestlers or body builders grouped together just up Market Street to the right. Migrants from Muscle Beach two blocks south, they were clad in tight, colorful posing briefs. They stood shoulder to shoulder, barefoot, their muscles abulge, greased and glistening under the sun .

Hero stepped aside to watch the hulking bruisers encircle a young man and a girl. The shortest but bulkiest muscleman, a dark type covered with black body hair, was arguing with the girl. In the middle of the girl's explanation of something, he stepped into the center of the circle with them. He appeared to befriend the slight young man who wore a puff sleeved white shirt like Romeo.

160

The muscleman spoke confidentially to the taller thin young man. When the young man bent down to listen, in a quick move that told Hero he was a professional the wrestler drove the top of his head up under the young man's chin with a jaw-wrenching slam. The concussion echoed all the way down the block. The young man left his feet and dropped to the street, unconscious.

The wrestler kicked his victim, laughed and beat his huge hairy chest. The girl screamed hysterically and flailed out at him, blows he easily deflected. Then he stopped laughing and punched her, knocking her down onto her knees beside her fallen friend. Laughing, using their bare feet, the big men began to roll the unconscious boy back and forth between them. They flopped him over from front to back. His arms and legs flew along disjointed, lifeless. The girl screamed and pleaded.

Figuring the young man's brains had to be taking an awful beating, Hero ran to the big slippery wall of flesh and pushed through, yelling, "That's enough, enough. You're going to kill him."

Surrounded by the smell of strained, sweating tissue, Hero stooped to have a look at the injured man. A close examination showed him to be a teen-aged boy barely capable of his soft scrawny beard. He bled freely from his nose, eyes, ears and mouth.

"They've really hurt him, I know they have," the girl screamed.

Hero didn't think so but before he had a chance to do anything else, someone greased and powerful, who knew what he was doing, stepped in behind him and forced him into a hammerlock.

Hero said, "Aw shit," and his brain went cold.

He despised being grabbed from behind. It made him think of Nam, the constant fear, especially if you had any kind of authority, any responsibility for your fellows. It hung over you, a never-ending pall, the nervous, jumpy, irritable, unanswerable screaming question, "What's behind you?"

It didn't matter whether you were out on patrol or not, or if it was day or night. Daytime in the cities could be the worst. Grabbed, snared from behind and garrotted with a piece of nearly invisible wire that would slice easily through to your spine. Left dead but gasping, for your money and credentials.

"Let it all hang out," Dwight yelled, his voice high with excitement.

Hero didn't waste time testing the strength in the arms that held him. Check it out, see what you're up against. Feel for a weakness. Fuck that shit, we're going to lunch.

"I hope you know what you've grabbed, pal, you rotten, smelly, dirty-dealing motherfucker, 'cause you're goin' down."

Going past the wrenching pain in his shoulder and arm and the loss of breath from the forearm across his neck, Hero showed off. He gave him the full treatment.

He slammed the heel of his shoe into the wrestler's bare toes; not once but three times fast, as hard as he could. The wrestler screamed, "Yow . . . ow . . . ow . . ." and the powerful hairy arms relaxed. Hero threw a mitsu karate driving elbow, horizontally, straight back into the man's heart. The splat sound from the blow was in the air and a loud gushing moan that came, "Yuuuk" and a fart, but Hero was hunched quickly over as though to touch his toes. Reaching between his legs, he grabbed the wrestler by his scrotum. Hero went hard. Palming the wrestler's testicles, he squeezed them with most of his might. He squeezed them as he would a handball, walking to the court, aggressively, with determination. Hard enough to bust the ball if that was possible; you never know if you don't try. Hard enough to show the ball who was boss. Hard enough to win.

Hero knew a rupture when he felt one. It was the natural conclusion of the move. Before he let go, he felt the wrestler's testicles surge into a swollen state thrice their size. Hero spun around to see the short, stocky wrestler who had done the punching, clutch his belly and fall away to begin vomiting convulsively into the street.

The rest of the distended gang stood unmoving, staring silently in disbelief.

"Who's got ID?" Hero yelled at the bunch of them. He saw Dwight sitting on the fender of a parked car watching, smiling.

The hysterical girl had calmed to attend her boyfriend who was conscious now and up on one stiff elbow.

"I asked for ID. I want some ID, now."

The wrestlers stood as though mute. Their friend continued to vomit into the gutter. The acrid smell hung in the air.

"In their trunks," the girl said. "They keep ID in their trunks."

Hero brought out his badge and watched their faces fall. With the truth out, they all produced a folding of bills and driver's licenses from their briefs.

"Give my partner your driver's licenses."

When Dwight had collected their IDs, Hero said, "All right, pick up your friend, *and* the kid, and take them over to Venice Receiving. Make sure that everybody is okay. We're hanging onto your ID until you get back. We'll be having lunch at the sidewalk cafe, or come by the Venice Precinct. What's your name?" he asked the girl.

"Marie. Gino, he's my brother, the pig." She gestured with a fist at the end of a stiff arm for him to go fuck himself. "He got what he had coming, the bully. He can't control my life."

"Yeah, well, you go along and keep an eye on things. I want you to come back too. Give me your ID."

"Mine? No, I didn't—"

"Give it to me, or I'll take you in."

"What for?"

Hero moved toward her angrily and she quickly handed him the driver's license from her purse.

"You go with them and get everybody patched up and come back too, got it?"

She nodded and helped her boyfriend.

"All you guys, got it?"

Acting downtrodden, the bunch carried the boy, helped Gino to his feet and began to move slowly up Market Street in the direction of Venice Receiving, an easy ten-minute walk.

Watching them, Hero laughed. He laughed because it had been what he considered a lightweight encounter. No real malice. Almost fun, a quick workout. And because of the appearance of the group as they walked away.

"Nowhere in the world," he told Dwight. "Nowhere in the

world but Venice could you see such a sight. Have you ever seen so much muscle with its tail between its legs?" Dwight's laugh was reserved.

"Some of those guys are good athletes, Chief. Some of them are good guys too. Pumping iron takes a special kind of—"

"I know that, Dwight. Hell, I like to lift myself. It's just funny to see, that's all, the big lunks." He laughed again and his eye was drawn across the street into a shadowed alleyway.

Brushing himself off, straightening his clothing, he continued to stare at a clump of a thing that seemed to be moving in the shade close to the ground. A derelict, he told himself. A bum waiting for the late-afternoon wagon to come and take him home to the drunk tank for the night. The area was full of them. Panhandling was good along the ocean walk, the restaurant garbage cans a dream.

They were walking away when Hero had to go with his inclination. There had been something about the moving clump that demanded a closer look. Sort of an aura of desperation. Hero crossed the street to the mouth of the alley. One quick glimpse to see that it was a bum, a drunk, and nothing else. He walked into the alleyway.

The clump was the back of a man sitting on his haunches. The disheveled person was weeping and wiping at his face with a coarse brown paper bag. Closer, the man's hand came away from his face with the bag covered in fresh red blood.

Stopping just behind him, Hero spoke to his back and soaking wet hair. "How badly are you hurt?"

Sobbing, the man spoke as though through blubber, or phlegm. "You . . . you don't want to know. Are you a cop?" He sounded acutely sober.

Hero answered, "Yes, let me see." Bending, he gripped the man's shoulder and turned him around.

Hero was unable to moderate his gasp, the loud involuntary utterance of revulsion that resounded in the alleyway.

He snatched back his hand exclaiming, "Holy shit!"

The man had no face. His eyes, pitch black and rheumy, made Hero want to scream, to bolt and run. Two deep-black pissholes in the snow. A snow of sloppy red.

Dwight said, "Jeeez, what happened? His face is ...God..." from behind.

There was nothing. No features, no nose, no cheeks, no lips or eyebrows or skin. Just the bony white front of a skull and some ravaged hanging red meat and the eyes.

Trying for calm, Hero choked his words out over his shoulder. "Dwight...Dwight, go and whistle..." He thought about putting his own fingers into his mouth to whistle and cringed. "Dwight, go and whistle for the wrestlers. Get a couple of them back here."

"Are you a cop?" from a grating sick, probably malignant voice box.

He dabbed at the bloody front of his head and Hero shivered to say, "Jesus, don't...not with that rough bag...Christ Almighty."

"Are you a cop?" from the rattling dark toothless pit.

"Yeah, yeah, I'm a cop. Good God, mister, what happened?"

"You don't want to know. Kill me. Please. Take out your gun and shoot me. Help me, please."

They stared at each other. Dwight was whistling and yelling out in the street behind him and Hero let his eyes lock with the most horrific stare he'd ever seen. It was hotter even than a kid after he'd stepped on a Claymore. After the smoke cleared and he sat up to see his legs gone below the knees. He'd stare up at you and it was this same terrified, impotent look. But then the kid would faint or die. This guy held the look. It went on and on. The power, the insanity, the pain, shit.

"Loan me your gun. I'll do it myself. Pleeeease."

Mesmerized, Hero reached and touched the butt of his .38, but stopped. "Goddamn," he said, throwing his hands down at his side. He said, "Goddamn...Goddamn." He was relieved to hear Dwight coming with the wrestlers.

"Give me that." Hero snatched the brown bag away and opened it up. It was a grocery bag, "better shopping for all," and large. Hero batted it out from the inside to get it back into shape and put it over the man's head. "Leave it that way, try and hold it on, you hear?"

The man raised one hand from the wrist and let it fall again in a futile gesture of compliance. The other hand came up to hold the edge of the bag. Then Dwight was there with three out-of-breath wrestlers.

"Take this guy, too. Keep the bag over his head. He's had a bad fall. He's a bloody mess. I wouldn't want you girls to be scared."

They looked at each other and laughed with heaving pectorals. Dwight laughed too, and shook his head in the blushed way he did when he admired Hero's nerve, his resourcefulness.

With one fell swoop, saying, "Hold on," the biggest wrestler took the bagged man way up onto his shoulders to sit. "Hold on," said the wrestler, "I've got your legs."

The wrestler took off jogging and the pathetic man rode away, holding the bag over his head, bouncing atop the wrestler's huge shoulders.

Laughing, Hero gave Dwight the high sign and they jogged too, for the corner.

"What's so funny?" Dwight asked.

"Thinking about Receiving, those nice nurses. Can you imagine? 'Oh, hello there, what's under the bag? Don't be afraid, let's just have a nice look now . . . YEEEOW . . . What the fuck?'"

Dwight laughed too and asked why they were running.

"I've got to wash my hands."

Dwight shook his head and said, "Oh," matter-of-factly, and they were there.

"Dwight, go and call Receiving and warn them about the characters headed their way. Tell them about the man with no face, that we have absolutely no idea how it happened. Most surely it was *not* from a fall. I'll wash my hands and get a table."

Dwight ran through the bar area headed for the phone booth. Hero waved hello to the manager and ran into the kitchen. Careful not to touch a thing but a bar of soap, he turned on the hot water with his elbow and scrubbed up. The water was scalding but he washed and scrubbed until he thought his skin might come off. Then he dried off and did it again.

They sat next to the railing near the sidewalk in the sun. They ate cold poached salmon, drank a beer, and talked about Westwood Village, the scene of The Terror's last killing, and the Westwood Crown movie theater. Hero would take Kay there tonight for the late show, to have a look around.

Then a thought came.

"Dwight, put a man in the theater."

"A man?"

"Yeah, one of our guys. Don't tell anyone, even the owner. Tell him to show his badge if he gets pushed, but to try and stay there for a while."

"Even after they lock up?"

"Sure, why not. Maybe a couple days. Just to see what he can see. Have him hide in the can or backstage somewhere. Tell him to watch the show a bunch of times and to just hang around. Tell him to dress like a repairman, in coveralls, like a workingman killing some time, taking some time for himself. If the management busts him, show his badge, otherwise don't." He thought for a minute and said, "Yeah, that's a good idea. Let's do that."

Shrugging, Dwight said, "All right, but you've got to know that the West Side guys have been all through that theater. I mean, good grief, what more do you expect to find?"

"Who knows, but I've got to start somewhere. You've got to admit that it's awfully coincidental. Two disappearances and a killing, right there. I don't know, maybe I'm nuts, but I want a close look for myself. And put one of our guys, one of our top guys, in there and let's see what happens. Okay?"

Dwight was somewhere else but snapped back. "Yeah, oh yeah, Chief, got it. Consider it done. You know, I can't stop thinking about that guy with the bag over his head. What an ungodly mess."

Hero shook his head and finished his beer. "Yeah, I know what you mean. The implications: bizarre, crazy time, a man without a face. Jesus."

THIRTEEN

Simon was lying in the hay-
loft devouring *Male* magazine when he saw the postman come.
He saw something manila-colored go into the box and knew it
was what he'd been waiting for. The powerful numbing fear of
rejection cramped and slowed him as he ran up to the main
road. A moment later it was in his aching hands.

From The Educational Testing Service in Princeton, New
Jersey. For Mr. Simon Moon, 913 Talamon Road, Star Route
3, Kansas City, Kansas. And in the bottom left-hand corner of
the envelope, the black-as-black momentous words, "Test
Results." His heart leapt out of control against his breastbone.

He tore the well-glued thing open and let the envelope fly off
down the road. One stiff orange card displaying a graph. One
hundred possible percentage points. The ninety-seventh per-
centile was boldly circled in black.

That was a day he'd never forget. Back in his room, he
followed his plan. He packed his bag, brought what money he

had saved and, taking no chances, went out his bedroom window over the roof to jump onto the oak tree and down to the ground less than twenty yards from his old car.

It started on the first try and Simon kicked up a ton of dust getting out of there. Tearing up the rise on the country road, he slowed to look back over his shoulder at the place with the swirling dirt cloud now beginning to settle. Exhilarated beyond control, he screamed, "Stick it in your ass, you motherfuckers . . . stick it in your fucking assholes." Flooring it, he cried out in shrill delirious laughter and went a hundred nonstop all the way to Wichita.

At Wichita State University, Simon concentrated on political science and acting normal. He worked nights as a bartender and bouncer at The Corkscrew. He had learned to put what he considered a sociable smile over his face and wore it constantly. Nonetheless, most people stayed clear of him, until he met Libby.

Libby Peuter had money, property and prestige. A six-foot, gawking coed who walked with a lumbersome, arm-swinging drag, she wore her hair long, straight and blond, down to her waist. Big-boned, she was large all over except for her breasts which were small and unattractively proportioned. Although she couldn't enter a room without clumsily banging into something, the girl was the brain of the university. That's how she met Simon. She sought out the person named Moon who was almost always one rung below her when the quarterly grade point averages were posted outside Bishop Hall.

Libby hung around The Corkscrew and when things were slow, loved to stand next to Simon. She'd ask him to hang his long arm over her shoulder and they'd stand there sipping beer, listening to the jukebox, not saying a word.

Near the end of their sophomore year, she proposed to him. She proposed that they "blow this hamburg of a town" and that he hang his long arm over her in Chicago where they could marry and live on her money, in her very own apartment across from the lake, and attend Northwestern University. After obtaining their bachelor's degrees, they could go right on to law school where her father's name and reputation, his donation of the Northwestern Law Library, would precede them. And that's how it happened, approximately.

Simon graduated third in his law school class behind Libby and some freak named Lloyd, who barely uttered a single syllable the entire time.

After graduation, Libby had a baby and Simon went directly into the Chicago District Attorney's office as an assistant D.A. That's when it began to hit him. He had become a lawyer but didn't know what else to do; how to act, where to go from there. The wind still blew through the hole in his gut and he most certainly wasn't happy except in his dreams, fantasizing his women. His dream girls, as he laughingly thought of them. He slew them almost every night, over and over, but he knew it was make believe. Besides, he acted normal.

His sex life with Libby was perfunctory and mechanical. But in so being, a turn-on.

Libby either had a particularly tiny vagina or couldn't get loose; he never knew. She was never naturally lubricated and put Vaseline on him each time. But she performed often and dutifully.

"Do you want to fuck?" she'd ask, reaching for the Vaseline, and Simon would hover over her thinking of his dreams while she greased him up. Libby grimaced through it all as though in the most awful pain and said from the first stroke, "Are you ready? Are you coming? I think you'd better come now, please."

Sometimes, when he didn't care about her, when he forgot about her money and that she looked out for him; after he got it in, he would pound her and she'd cry out, "Ouch, ouch, ouch," with each stroke, and always scream, "Good God, you're killing me."

One night after sex, Libby lay smoking a long Vaseline-tainted cigarette. "Simon, I want to ask you something. Yes or no, I'll understand, okay?"

Simon said, "Sure, go ahead."

"Well, how would you feel about my bringing another woman into our relationship?"

Laughing, Simon answered fast and glibly in his prosecutorial district attorney fashion, "A blonde, redhead or brunette?"

To which Libby replied in a serious, preoccupied tone, "A blonde, Simon, a beautiful, dainty little blonde, . . . very young. An absolute beauty."

He'd never looked Libby in the eye until that moment; at least not that he remembered. But he did it then and saw her for what she was. Nothing in recent years had ever hit him in quite the way that lesbian thing did. Thinking about it later, the feeling that came to mind was when he'd been thrown from Lightning, an erratic plow horse back on the farm. He saw stars and forgot for an overwhelmingly nauseous moment in the blackness who he was, what he was about.

"I would like it a lot. It would please me very much," Libby said further.

Stunned, Simon sat there smiling innocuously, the feeling gone from his face. He said, "I—I—" but was unable to speak.

When Libby saw the expression on Simon's face, when she realized what she had done, she tried to recover the moment by saying it had all been a joke. She laughed with her head thrown back, her mouth open wide, and slapped her big bare thigh.

Then she begged him to forgive her. But Simon had changed and didn't want to be with her anymore.

The last time Simon saw Libby was in the corridor outside the Chicago courtroom where the final decree of their divorce was granted.

They were no longer married and as Simon walked away, feeling hollow inside, Libby called to him and came running to say, "Do you know what you should have, Simon? A three-cornered hat, buckle shoes and a big white bow for around your neck. You should be a Quaker, Simon . . . you fucking Puritan."

Then with tears literally squirting from her eyes, she stepped back to scream, "You fucking square Puritan asshole." Her voice echoed off of the marbled walls. People paused to stare, and Simon broke Libby's jaw.

They both saw it at once. She lay on the floor in the stone corridor with her jaw dislodged from her skull, staring. In his delirium, Simon followed Libby's eyes down to see his suit pants standing out and wet, the pleats gone from the power behind his perfectly erect penis.

■   ■   ■

Simon had made the wrong acquaintances in Chicago and taken substantial bribes to reduce sentences. After Libby, he wasn't sure of anything he was doing, even in business, so he ran. Feeling as though he were in jeopardy, knowing the law well enough to see that, he left everything but his money and flew to Los Angeles. He had read and heard about the Western city and liked thinking about it. "The land of dreams and impossible schemes." What does it mean? Simon wondered. What goes on out there?

Simon stayed at the Beverly Wilshire Hotel and wore his best smile. Keenly aware of the importance of externals, he bought himself a wardrobe on Rodeo Drive. He cut his hair and he got some sun at the pool. Standing in front of his hotel room mirror, dressed in a beige suit, he felt giddy and said, "You look better than normal. You look like the big time."

He rented a new brown Mercedes 450 SL and always tried to look as if he was on his way somewhere. He changed wardrobes daily, and wandered the city smiling. Returning to his room, his face would be numb from it, and he would lie on his bed to stare at the ceiling and sweat.

He had begun the first night by bringing a hooker up to his room from the bar. Soon, he'd been with them all, or they'd heard about him and wouldn't do business with him anymore. They said he was a freak. He got to know the right people and called outside for what he needed.

Acting important and busy, he read the paper one noon while waiting for a table at the Brown Derby. A man standing next to him asked to see the financial section while they were waiting. Simon obliged but they talked about things instead: business, finance, the entertainment industry; that Simon was a lawyer but not employed. The man asked Simon's opinion on a couple of points but Simon smiled broadly to decline comment, saying, "Opinions are not relevant, only the law."

After lunch, the man came by Simon's table to leave him his business card and say, "You're right about what you said, about the law. Opinions are only appropriate on Sunday."

Simon grinned and said, "Even if then."

The man laughed and said, "Yes, I wonder if you'd come to see me. I think we're looking for someone like you. The salary is negotiable."

Simon smiled, read the man's card, "Jay Irving Meyer, Chief Counsel, M-G-M Studios, Culver City, CA 90034." and said, "Someone like me—you mean, without opinions?"

Jay Meyer blushed and said, "No . . . yes, well, a man who sticks to the rules . . . the law. Everyone gets emotional about the movie business. That's wrong. It's cut and dried."

Simon said, "I'll come out this afternoon."

As assistant house counsel for M-G-M Studios, Simon fell into it: the best parties and people, the private screenings, invitations to everything, free membership to the clubs. He fell into it the way he fell into a two-hundred-dollar-a-day cocaine habit; with a dirty plop, the way you could slip and fall into a pigpen back at the farm if you didn't watch your step or know what you were doing. His job was keeping the studio clean but they wanted all of every deal and it wasn't always the easiest thing to do. But he tried.

A year turned into two and three years at the studio and Simon was able to keep his face on. One thing he learned back in Chicago, you don't shit where you eat. Don't dip your pen in the company inkwell. Although he had opportunities every day to take advantage of his studio position with women who wanted to get into the business, he was able to keep work and play distinctly separated.

In fact, Simon was the one who wrote and initiated the studio-wide hiring policy. Number one on the list of hiring procedures for M-G-M office personnel: no actresses. An aspiring actress will go to any lengths to get her foot in the door; even learn to type and take shorthand. Simon suggested that lie detector tests be applied to new women coming in, but the studio felt that was too much.

It burned Simon that a woman would look at you innocent and smiling and say she was one thing when she was really something else. He hated a lying woman like that and took time to watch certain ones around the lot. He caught a couple, too, that had other things on their minds but their jobs, and had them fired. He felt a tremendous relief seeing them off the premises; then he didn't have to catch them always checking their makeup.

Simon might have done secret, quirky things at night and in his dreams, but never, ever did he step over the line at the studio. Until he hired Sylvia. She was the first one.

Sylvia was unquestionably the best legal secretary Simon ever had. Highly efficient and businesslike, she made him laugh and think of his mother with the cold abrupt way she treated him, her boss, yet. It was a cinch she didn't want anything from him. She wouldn't even look him in the eye and never stayed in his presence longer than to get what she needed for her work. She was courteous but made it clear she wasn't interested in his type.

Slowly, however, she began to warm up to him. She began to compliment him. How smart he was one day. How well dressed the next. It was a respectful attentiveness that caused Simon to like Sylvia a lot. He trusted her. He had won her over with his charm. It made him feel good to know he could do it. She liked him for fun and for free, wanting nothing in return.

Sylvia sat next to Simon at the studio screenings. Simon would whisper comments that he wanted to go upstairs and Sylvia would take notes, type them and send them on to the studio brass.

Robert Mandell was the head of the studio. Because of the logistics of shooting in Israel, no one had yet seen any of the rushes from the studio's new picture, *Darkwin.* The shoot had been on one week and today, with the stuff just in, Mandell had looked over an editor's shoulder at a Moviola to get crazy. He called an emergency catered lunch in Projection Room One.

A New York actress named Jennifer Peel, a contract player just signed by Universal, on loan-out to M-G-M, was disconcertingly unattractive on film. The second lead in the picture, she was in nearly every shot. No one spoke until the lights came up. Then Robert Mandell came apart.

"Herb," he yelled at his head of production, "Jay, Simon," at his legal staff. "Call Tel Aviv and cancel this turkey. Tell them to hold everything until we get a new girl. It'll all have to be reshot, every scene, although maybe we can cut away on that stuff out on the desert. I only hope—shit, let's see it again."

There was no denying that the dark bags under Jennifer Peel's eyes and her weak chin would ruin the picture.

"Too bad," Mandell yelled in the dark, "that we can't just shoot her tits."

No one laughed. The loss was too great. Because of her stage ability, Jennifer Peel may have been the toast of Broadway, but she was finished before she had begun in pictures. At least until she found herself a good plastic surgeon.

Sylvia was scribbling something on her note pad and when the lights came up she sat on the edge of her chair excitedly to show Simon, "I can do it, I can do this part. PLEASE SUGGEST ME," written boldly across her pad.

Shocked and confused, Simon pretended not to see.

Mandell was screaming, "Recast it. Recast the fucking thing. All right, we're all right on the stuff in front of the desert. We'll cut away and do a voice-over. It's a beautiful sunset, it'll hold their attention for a couple lines, but the rest, everything with that sad, tired looking broad in it, reshoot. Got it, Herb?"

Herb Grossner held up his hand already on the telephone trying to raise the director on the desert location.

Sylvia nudged Simon hard but he wouldn't look until she rudely thrust her note pad in front of his face.

Mandell yelled, "Cheeeerist Almighty, I spend seven hundred for the book and another five plus a piece for the best fucking screenplay ever written in this town, and you guys give me a dog of a broad you can't even look at. That is some shit."

No one spoke up to remind Robert Mandell that he had personally recommended Jennifer Peel for the role; that Jennifer had spent lots of time with him on his boat. But Sylvia had something to say. She was nearly out of her chair, energetically raising her hand.

Simon grabbed her by the knee and crushed it so hard she cried out. He forced her back into her chair and held her there. Everyone looked at first but then went back to their business or lunch and to listen to Robert Mandell's ravings.

With his face on fire, perspiring, Simon continued to hold Sylvia by her knee.

"All right," he whispered. "I'll suggest you, but not here and now. This is the worst time and place. Mandell won't listen. If you want to do it my way, come back to the office and we'll talk. We'll plan the best way."

"Will you tell him, suggest me, today? The iron is hot."

"Yes, as soon as we plan an approach so we don't look like fools."

She relaxed. They went out the side door and back to their office.

He put the "Gone to Lunch" sign out, locked the door behind them and felt remarkably at ease.

Sylvia said, "I could bring such a new, different dimension to the part. It's just exactly the role for me. Only last week in acting class, I did a scene exactly, and I mean, just exactly—"

"I didn't know you went to acting class."

"Well, you know now. I live it and breathe it. It's time the cat was out of the bag because this cat is due."

"Jennifer Peel is the new girl from Universal, Sylvia. Mandell has a deal with Universal on this one. They are co-distributing the film. He is obligated to fill that role with one of their people. It won't be Peel, but it will be one of their people. I know, I wrote the deal. If you'd been a little bit more conscientious about your work, you'd have read it. You typed the entire—"

"Wait. You talk as if . . . you're just placating me, just getting me away so I don't embarrass you. Well, that's not going to stop me. I want this part more than—" She headed for the door, but Simon stood in the way.

"What would everyone think of me? I made the rule about actresses."

"Which was a low-down, slimy rule. But I fooled you, the big lawyer boss himself. Let me pass."

"I suppose you know you're finished with me now. You can't work here."

"Move aside, Mr. Moon. I'm going back to that meeting. You may fire me when I'm done, but—"

"You're fired now."

"Oh, swell. That's just what I'd expect from you."

She turned and walked back to shake her hair out in front of the wall mirror behind her desk. She reached her bag and fixed her makeup. She combed her hair. She reached inside her blouse and undid her bra. Wrestling around, she brought the white elastic thing out of a sleeve and put it in her top desk drawer. She bounced on her heels and watched her bust jiggle.

"Robert Mandell has hit on me a hundred times, Simon, and he'll listen to me now, before he'll listen to you. Now, stand aside."

Simon didn't move.

"I thought you liked me."

"The truth is, Mr. Moon, that I don't like you at all and never have. I used you. There, I said it."

"But what will everyone think of me?" he asked.

"Who gives a damn?" she said, irritated now.

She reached into her blouse and squeezed her nipples to make them stand out hard against her candy-striped silk blouse, and when she reached past him for the door, Simon stopped her with his big hand around her throat. It was the easiest, most natural thing he'd ever done.

Lifting her off her feet, he carried her with one hand in through his office, to his private bathroom. Continuing to hold her that one-handed way, he pushed back the plastic curtain and stood her in the shower stall.

Sylvia could not speak but her bulging eyes held a glistening look of hatred that made Simon smirk and turn away.

"You're fired, Sylvia," he giggled and looked to see her eyes crazier than ever. Blushing, unable to meet her gaze, he put his left hand over her eyes and forehead. He let go with his right, just for the instant it took to get a better grip. Then, pushing the top of her face away with his left, he pulled with his powerful right hand and was totally swept away by the dizzying, euphoric sensation that came with her flailing, blinded desperation, the gasping froth of red over his hands.

Afterward, ignoring the ringing phones, he undressed, laughed and played and saw to it they both had a shower.

Sylvia's nude body was surprisingly beautiful. He could not recall a time when he'd felt so happy, so carefree and gay.

Simon wrapped Sylvia in the plastic shower curtain, answered his own phones and did studio business the rest of the day. When people called for her, he said he hadn't seen her since lunch and although concerned himself, was too busy to try and find her.

He worked late that night and had no problem in the dark carrying Sylvia's body out to the trunk of his car. He cleaned the bathroom with care.

Simon threw Sylvia's body off of a high cliff up on Mulholland Drive. He cleaned the shower curtain at home and brought it back to the studio in his briefcase the next day. Simon reported Sylvia as a no-show to the secretarial pool and she was quickly replaced.

The police finally came but there were no answers. Simon watched the papers but due to the weather, fires, underbrush, wild animals or some other circumstance, the body never was found. Not that it would have mattered. It never would have come back on him. He was a smiling, normal-acting guy, doing a good job for M-G-M Studios.

Simon did not take his killing of Sylvia as a setback but as a great reprieve. Thinking of the deed would pick up his spirits every time. He liked to remember the details before he went to sleep at night and dreamt about it often. He stopped doing cocaine and only kept liquor around for guests. There was a new intoxication in Simon's life; a high that brought an ecstasy way beyond anything he had ever before imagined.

Spending more and more time there, he finally began to live in that secret place in his mind and in the self-centered arrogance that came with it. The men above him at the studio said he was either acting like a know-it-all or a sorehead most of the time. His days at the studio were numbered. Simon laughed to himself. He knew he was too good for them; that it would serve them right to try and run the shithole studio without him. "Lots of luck," he huffed. So he quit, or was fired and the phone call never came for him to go back and save them. He figured the place was going down the toilet. That it was, as rumored, probably up for sale. "Tear the fucking place down and build a cheap housing tract," he screamed.

Simon roamed West Los Angeles and killed three women during that time. Two on the streets and one in a motel room. The Starlight Motel room king-size bed with the whitest, crispest sheets and pillowcases ever, professionally washed, starched and folded, soaked in bright-red blood and jism. She had given him just exactly what he'd wanted and no lip, no female back talk. It had been an incredible, wet lovemaking experience.

Low on funds, Simon opened a small private law practice in the Jupiter Building located at Fourth Street and Santa Monica Boulevard in the city of Santa Monica. His small one-room office was on the third floor where, if he craned his neck out the window and looked west, he could see the grassy knoll and the ocean beyond just four short blocks away. Eventually, that was where he slept too. On a small used mattress in a long closet.

He liked the Santa Monica bars and began to drink again heavier than ever. He was the Santa Monica barroom lawyer. He hung around the grassy knoll. He consciously tried not to, not in his own neighborhood, but he killed women out there. Sometimes, taking an incredible risk, he would carry them somewhere else afterward. Sometimes, he would bring them home with him for a few days.

Two years later, almost to the day, he was totally out of money. He didn't care about the law anymore and had a hard time keeping his smile on. He lost his office, his place to sleep, and did terrible things to women when drinking. Clean things sober, dirty things when half in the bag.

Simon dressed ragged. He blended with the derelicts along Colorado Avenue and on the grassy knoll. He roamed the west end of Los Angeles and the City of Santa Monica at night; down the alleys and back streets. He collected welfare. He sold his blood. He slept under the heavy pine boughs of the big trees along the knoll or in any other shelter he could find.

Constantly possessed, he thought about his next victim a thousand times before he went after her. He'd put it off and put it off and often writhe in paranoia knowing his behavior was insane, far from acting normal. He would sit in the dark corner of an alleyway and wring his aching hands, thinking, worrying about his obsession. He could frighten himself out of it that way, but then he would spot the perfect one and do it again. Just one more time.

The Los Angeles winter of 1979 was unusually chilly and the Santa Monica cops were cleaning up the knoll. Sleeping there could land you in jail.

Simon's only associate from the area was a man called The Miler. He was a tall, thin perpetually suntanned Randolph Scott lookalike. The Miler's brain was wet. Holding an eager, wide-eyed expression, he was constantly running. He would tell anyone who asked that he was running for love. Sharing a bottle of wine, with The Miler anxious to get up and run, Simon would laugh crazily and tell him he had a long way to run to find the thing he was after.

Simon used The Miler as a gopher. He saw what Simon wanted him to see; no more. He was fiercely loyal toward Simon and guarded their "spot," wherever that might be: under a tree, a flop, an alleyway, up underneath the Santa Monica pier, or the unfinished attic of the Westwood Crown movie theater.

The modern, soon-to-be movie theater sat on Westwood Boulevard just up from Wilshire, surrounded by a chain link fence put up by the builder. The fence was easy to get through, next to a telephone pole back in the alley.

The infamous 1979 Los Angeles Teamsters strike kept the unfinished skeletal site at a standstill; without the presence of a single workman for the better part of a year. The theater's stark gray concrete walls were seated in dirt at their foundation and rose two and one half stories to adjoin the wooden, nearly completed roof. Most of the windows were in as were nearly all of the basic internal things made of wood, like the stairways. Work had been stopped with the electrical conduits hanging. The unfinished theater had been a perfect hideout.

Simon and The Miler could even have a small fire in one corner of the basement. There was a liquor store across the street. There were lots of bottles for The Miler to collect and turn in left next to the garages in the surrounding posh neighborhood. The Miler would go through the garbage cans behind the Continental Burger on the corner and provide a decent meal for them anytime.

A German shepherd guard dog was left to roam inside the fenced compound at night. The dog liked The Miler but snarled at Simon until one night Simon used a plank to beat him up good. After that, they tolerated each other. The dog would lie next to the fire or run with The Miler all over town during the night. The dog liked a warm can of Miller Lite beer.

Simon slept between rafters on newly laid insulation in a hidden section underneath one finished corner of roof. He kept his things under the insulation in his spot. His candle and books, his meager belongings, good-smelling things from women. The Miler slept below with the dog.

A guy in a truck would come and collect the dog each morning but never came in until one morning when the dog was gone; as was The Miler. The dog trainer walked around the grounds whistling and went to the truck to bang a food dish, but they had disappeared.

The guy never came back and didn't bring another dog. Simon never saw The Miler or the shepherd again either. It was better too, without them. Simon was alone in the big safe place and loved it. He rarely ate and became emaciated. He brought women there, and when finished with them, had a place for them.

Early one morning, after returning a shovel to the shed, he turned a corner to come face to face with two construction men in hard hats.

"Who are you, mister? What are you doing in here?"

Simon was disappointed but didn't show it. It had to happen. They had to come back sometime. He smiled.

"I wish I had the money to buy this place. It's a nice place."

"How'd you get in?"

"Out by the fence. I wouldn't change a thing, leave it just like it is."

"You'd better get moving, mister, or we'll have to call the cops. We're back to work today."

"Sure, no problem. See you."

Simon could feel them staring at his back while he walked away. Having his secrets on them made his rectum tingle.

Out on the street, in the next block, Simon stopped in the bright morning sunlight to turn and squint back at the place that had been his home. The structure was beginning to swarm with coffee-drinking hard hats who laughed and carried on, glad to be back at work. Redimix concrete trucks lined up on the side street. Diesel engines roared, shooting black clouds from their stacks, churning heavy wet loads.

"Pour that fucking concrete." Simon laughed. "Cover those floors, you hard hat motherfuckers," he shrieked into the noise. "If you only knew."

Some of the men looked down on him from the open second floor.

"If you only knew what's underneath."

He shook his fist at them, waved and ran off down Westwood Boulevard.

FOURTEEN

Simon wasn't stupid. He had moments of perfect clarity and he could certainly read. He read about himself in the papers. They called him The Terror. The reward was fifty thousand and climbing. They wanted him bad.

He knew the punishment for the crime. He understood the code of the habitual, professional criminal. "If you can't do the time, don't do the crime." And he could dream about being put to death in the terrible green room.

But it would never deter him because his situation was absolutely, positively unique. What he did had to be done. He felt if he could prepare properly and lecture on the subject, people would surely understand. There are certain women that must go. They deserve it. How can you make that point?

Or how can you describe the helpless surrender, the falling into your own mind. Down into the dark whirling vortex that sucks at you, that sucks you off. How can you tell somebody how naughty but nice the perfect moment is. How do you make them understand that you are totally out of control until the obsession passes. How do you? You don't. You run.

A black-and-white West Los Angeles sheriff's cruiser had stopped on the opposite side of the street. The two helmeted officers had stared at him and slammed the car for the corner, to make a U and come back.

Frightened worse than ever, Simon ran. He ran back through an alley, through a yard, out across a street, back through another yard, into an open garage and up into the rafters. The incident made him feel weak and disoriented. It made him realize he was in trouble. That evening during rush hour traffic, he walked to the Washington entrance to the San Diego Freeway to hitchhike to Mexico.

It took a long, paranoid time to get a ride, but a truck finally stopped, going all the way to San Diego. Simon tried his damnedest to act normal, to smile and joke with the driver who turned out to be from Kansas.

The truck driver told Simon he'd been on the road himself. He laughed and told Simon stories about the Great Depression in Kansas. Simon did his best to placate the man and laugh when he was supposed to. Simon wasn't sure, he was a bad judge of that sort of thing, but it seemed the man liked him and was happy for the company.

After a couple of hours, Simon was out of energy. He couldn't pretend to laugh any longer and let his head fall when it was too heavy.

"Hey, pardner," the driver asked, "how long since you ate?"

Simon told the truth and the truck driver said, "Well, hell, man, why didn't you say so. This ain't the depression no more. Let's turn off and go up to La Jolla for spaghetti. They got a place there, overlooks the cove, all the spaghet you can eat for a quarter if you buy a pitcher of beer. I think I can spare a buck or two." He laughed good-naturedly.

Simon ate three plates of spaghetti, five meatballs and drank a pitcher of beer. He felt sick but wasn't sure it was from the food. Artie, the truck driver, wouldn't shut up and Simon had promised to play him a game of pool when he returned from the john. Simon put on Artie's heavy insulated coat and walked out the door.

He walked down by the cove in the dark. It was a cold, wet night. He was grateful for the coat. The air made him feel better. He walked down to the Scripps Institute of Oceanography on the far side of the pier. Things were quiet. He slept in the hold of an institute boat that was up on dry dock.

Simon awoke aboard the boat to bright hazy daylight. He was sweating in the insulated coat.

As he crawled on deck to see, the air itself seemed white from the heat. He had to squint to look at things. Sitting up, he had to concentrate his gaze or images wobbled and blurred. "Where in hell am I?" he asked.

He walked a long way down the desolate beach.

A raggedy-looking man appeared, to fall into stride next to him.

"What do you want?" Simon finally asked.

"I'm an astronomer from Scripps," replied the wild-eyed man.

"Sure."

"I am. I'm looking for my wife."

"Well, get away from me and look. There's no women around here."

"Women?" the crazed man said. "The planet is strewn with the corpses left in the wake of those creatures."

Giggling, he ran off down the beach.

When Simon blinked, the man had disappeared. It made him sweat, wondering if there had been a man.

Simon took the tourist stairs up to sit on a bench overlooking the cove.

The fog was in but it was warm and humid. He sat on his insulated coat. He pulled his knees up against him and rocked. He tried to figure things out.

Turning, he saw a jogger come over the lip of the cliffy area above the cove road. Dressed in red shorts and black leotard top, he watched her come his way. A small gray dog ran along down the path beside her.

Over the lip of the hill behind the jogger came a bicyclist dressed in a white tennis outfit, riding hard and fast. He bore down on the jogger and appeared to grab at the back of her head. The dog barked and nipped at the cyclist's feet, who kicked him away.

Simon watched the strongly built man on the bike grab the jogger's ponytail and jerk it back hard. Laughing, continuing to hold her hair, he gave another tremendous yank that shook the flesh over her face.

The girl fought to pull away. She used her hands to try and dislodge his grip. "Stop it," she cried. "Stop it, please." Her screams gave Simon the chills.

The dog barked crazily and jumped to bite the cyclist's feet. When he kicked the dog the girl was able to jerk her hair free.

Flailing, the cyclist grabbed out but his balance was lost. He went down amidst his bicycle into a heap on the pathway.

The girl and her dog were close. They ran in panic, negotiating the last turn before a short straightaway that would bring them out nearly in front of Simon.

Letting the bike lie, the fallen cyclist was up and on the run. Sprinting angrily he quickly caught the jogger not ten feet from Simon.

Grabbing her from behind, he tore the black leotard strap from her right shoulder. Crying out, she clutched at the shiny material where it covered her bust and was barely able to protect her modesty.

"Help me, help me, please," she screamed at Simon. "I'm being attacked."

Watching carefully, Simon saw less the attack than the girl, who interested him immensely. He jogged over. Shaking her, the cyclist screamed that she had skinned his elbows and knees.

"Leave her alone," Simon said calmly.

When the incensed cyclist shifted his weight from foot to foot, Simon saw what a big boy he was. Six foot two, three, maybe with huge hands and feet. His heavy brow was slick with perspiration. His dark eyes were determined.

"Oh, yeah?" he said with a sly grin.

"Yeah," Simon said.

The smile vanished from the big boy's face. His jaw muscles tensed.

"Well, fuck you, pal, leave us alone." He released the girl brusquely.

"Is he your boyfriend?" Simon asked the girl.

"No, no," she begged. "No, I've never seen him before. He's been following me, talking filthy. I don't know him at all."

"I wouldn't stick your nose in this, mister. You're apt to get it bit off."

"I saw the whole thing. I'm a lawyer. You're out of line. Assault, maybe attempted rape. Now, take off."

When the jogger heard "lawyer," her expression changed and she threw herself into Simon's arms. She clung to him. She smelled good. Simon stood staring at the cyclist but he was somewhere else. Her hugging felt glorious. He was aware of his penis.

The big boy moved closer and from where he stood on the pathway just above them, seemed to loom.

He's never been hurt, Simon figured. The kid has the audacity that goes with always having it his way. Of always being the biggest and the toughest. Of never being stopped.

Jamming his fat, strongly boned finger into Simon's chest, he said, "Listen, fuckhead . . ."

The girl hugged him and Simon turned the big boy's finger straight up with a powerful crack that resounded through the foggy day. The cyclist howled but Simon heard only the girl's excitement.

"Oh, good. God, yes, get him."

She stepped out from under Simon's arm to watch. Simon saw her eyes when she urged, "Come on, get him," and his penis jerked.

Raging, the big boy tried to do something with his shoulders and other hand, but Simon was on the make. With a move that was less a sucker punch, more just a punch for a sucker—a young, spoiled, right-side-of-the-tracks, clean-skinned, mama's-boy sucker—Simon moved his left hand to draw attention.

That's where the big boy's eyes went and with the jogger

saying, "Oh, yes, yes," Simon drove his right fist into the big boy's big, thick jaw.

Down he went into a deadened clump before them.

Still on a grade, the unconscious boy began to roll forward until Simon stopped him with his foot against his broken face. Simon moved the sole of his shoe against the boy's nose. Simon tested the bone in the nose by gently pumping at it like a pedal. The big boy's head rolled from side to side under the pressure. The girl smiled.

A queer, sheepish sensation came over Simon that he wasn't sure of, that made him want to use his foot. He gazed at the young woman.

She looked back too, and there was no question who was in charge. And with the powerful feminine look that later had come to mean, "Come on, Simon, we're late bloomers . . . we've got money to make, a life to lead," with the look that sent Simon back into the world to act normal again, like a man; with the look he could easily be made to do anything for, Carol said, "Go ahead," and with an agonizing snap, Simon crushed the big boy's nose.

He couldn't relax and he couldn't read. Anxious, he tried to have some fun with his women, but they seemed stiff and sloppy.

He lay down. He sat up and the irresistible feeling was over him. It caused him to shudder. Saliva squirted into his throat. Putting out the candle, he stood up into the black. His loins ached. His penis hung heavily. He perspired.

Knowing what it was he needed, Simon went across the theater attic to the ventilating shaft. He crawled to the end and peered out through the grillwork into the flamingo-pink hallway below.

No one came or went but the lighting was up. Things were still going on. He waited. He bounced on his haunches like an ape. He'd wait forever if he had to.

Then he saw her. A blonde with a ponytail. A maroon leotard

top like Carol could wear. Bright green shoes against the pink carpet; coming his way.

He began to tremble and gulp breath. She was all alone. Beautiful, blond and dumb like a model. And funny-eyed—soft and blue and myopic or crossed—Siamesed. Her eyes swam in her fair head. She came under him. He craned and squinted and nearly pushed the grill out on top of her looking to make sure she was alone. She was alone and hesitating, looking for the ladies' room.

"Oh, boy, oh, boy," he breathed. He bounced like an excited chimp.

He would go for her. There was not the slightest doubt about it. Even with the theater still open, if it was. Even with the risk, this one was too good to let get away.

There would be danger. It rang in his senses. Exposure, capture, be careful. It's your life. He stared down at her stupid beauty and swore he could smell her pussy.

Just a little more, go on, keep going, go on. Shit, look at those shiny maroon titties. Owwee baby. He wiped his chin, which was wet with saliva. His hands ached and shook frantically.

Fuck the risk. He was past it into wild, reckless abandon. The wonderfully exhilarating chance he took each time.

Come on, blondie, he screamed in his head.

FIFTEEN

The day had turned into a cloudless beauty. The sun shone gloriously pure and hot. With the slight sea breeze, the particularly crisp clean air possessed a salutary inkling of salt. Dwight guessed the temperature of the December day to be 78 degrees.

Returning from lunch, Hero and Dwight met the musclemen just outside the Venice station. The girl and her bandaged boyfriend arrived at the same time on a moped. Gino, the small wrestler, walked timidly, bowlegged, measuring each step. He wouldn't look Hero in the eye.

The girl and the bandaged boyfriend joined the others. They all appeared to be reconciled. The big wrestler said, "That guy you sent over to the hospital, he didn't have no face."

Hero said, "Oh?"

"Yeah, and it didn't happen from no fall either."

"Hmm," Hero said.

"He had cancer, or some horrible disease that ate away his face. There's nothin' there but bones. Jeez." The wrestler shivered.

"So?" Hero said.

"So, I just thought you should know, that's all."

"What happened to him?"

"They just wheeled him away. They seemed to know him. They wheeled him away with the bag off. Everybody at the hospital was shitting their pants looking at him."

"They'll take care of him. You should feel good."

"Me, about what?" the muscleman wanted to know.

"About doing a good deed. You brought him in, maybe even saved his life."

"Oh, yeah. Well, I never thought about that, yeah. I only hope I didn't catch anything."

Hero walked away laughing and yelled back at Dwight, "Give them their ID."

Back in his office, Hero glanced at the stack of new telephone messages on his desk spindle. After reading the first two or three, he tossed them onto his desk. He slapped Dwight on the shoulder on the way to the hot plate, the hot water.

"Do you want a cup of tea?"

"Sure."

"Dwight, sometimes I think I've had enough, as much as I can take. I get fed up with the lowlifes."

"Sure, I know. But—and you probably don't want to hear this—but it's our job."

"Bullshit. It's more than that. That's the problem: leaving it here at five o'clock."

"I know."

"Sometimes I get to agreeing with our jaded friend, Bill Robinson. Burn them all. Every time one of them breaks the law, burn him good. I'll bet it would change."

"Pardon me, Chief," the desk sergeant interrupted from the doorway. "Speaking of Bill Robinson, I got a message for you from him. Robinson wanted me to let you know he picked up that special duty that Dwight phoned in earlier."

Hero wasn't sure what the sergeant meant, until Dwight asked, "The theater?"

The sergeant said, "Right. He said he was going in like a painter, in coveralls. Hang around for a couple of days. He

194

wanted me to tell Hero that it sounded like a good draw. Robinson loves the movies." The sergeant laughed.

"Okay, thanks." Hero waved him away. He looked at Dwight and, after a moment, smiled.

"Can you imagine, fucking Bill Robinson, that tough black son of a bitch, running into The Terror? Oh, goddamn, for a look at that." The thought excited him. He paced. "Of all the guys that might draw that duty, Bill is perfect, just perfect. A tougher son of a bitch there isn't."

"Except you," Dwight said.

"I'm not so sure, Dwight. We're real close, but it doesn't matter. When you're in *that* league it doesn't matter anymore. Imagine him at his best, finding . . . somehow going up against The Terror. Oh shit, what a time."

"But The Terror, The Terror's probably nowhere near the place."

"I know, but there's a chance, and it's fun to imagine. Bill Robinson can put anybody away. It would be slam bam, goodbye Terror."

Hero laughed, said, "Wow," at the thought of it, and feeling better, poured the tea.

Kay was on her way out the door of the houseboat when Hero's phone call stopped her. They made plans for that evening. They were both going to exercise and decided to meet at the Good Earth restaurant for a late dinner at ten o'clock before the movie. Hero would be out of his poetry class at nine forty-five.

"And we can look for Christmas sale windows along the way."

"Sounds great," said Kay. "I'll meet you on the corner outside the restaurant just before ten."

"In that crowd?"

"I'll wear my hair up, my maroon leotard, and green Adidas. You won't be able to miss me, okay?" She laughed.

"Sounds good."

"I love you, Hero."

Hero laughed to himself. "You don't know how good that

sounds, after the bullshit day I've had."

"Goodness, how did you get by before you had me to tell you things and make you feel better?"

"Are you fishing, Kay?"

"You bet. Well?"

"I got by somehow. But I suppose I've got to admit, I don't know how I did it without you."

"I've got something for you, Hero, later on. Something that will make you, well . . ."

"Something that will make me what, Kay?"

"That will make you feel *real* good. Gotta go. Love you."

"Yeah, love you too. Bye."

They hung up and Hero sat for a time thinking how lucky he was.

Late that afternoon, Hero went on a super run. Six miles, down San Vicente, along the knoll and back again. He had recited his poem, "The Heart of Integration," over and over until he thought it was sophomoric and dumb. But that wouldn't stop him. He'd learned not to trust his own judgment past a certain point with his writing. He'd stand in front of the class in a couple of very short hours and recite. He could hold the manuscript too but would try to do it from memory. He knew it well, now. He said it one more time.

He thought about his hands. He would keep the manuscript in front of him on the podium, his hands at his sides. Professor Talmadge said if you don't know what to do with your hands, let them hang at your sides. He had to remember that. He always ended up gesturing to emphasize a point. Talmadge never complained to him; but it felt wrong as he did it and Talmadge had yelled at some of his classmates about their hands.

Driving back to the houseboat to clean up, he thought about Kay. She'd be working out too. Like Hero, Kay loved to sweat. She went to her exercise class at least every other day, sometimes more often.

Kay had left a note saying she would do the rest of the wash another time. That she'd had a run-in with Clyde over the laundry machines. It made Hero's ears burn.

"That asshole," Hero said, throwing Kay's note down. "I don't know why I don't just go down there and kick his ass." But he got cleaned up instead, letting the thing grind him the entire time. That's one of the difficulties that go with living in the city, he rationalized. You've got to put up with people. Share things.

In the tub he thought about the sociopathic study done at Menninger Clinic. The researchers had built an environment just like an urban American neighborhood for laboratory rats. Cushy, too, but close, the way most of us live. The rats lived in modern apartments. They ate well, exercised, reproduced and soon, ate each other. It drove them insane. "Too close," he said, toweling off. Getting dressed, he had a sherry. "Just too fucking close."

Feeling better, Hero dropped the top of the Porsche for the drive over to UCLA. He let the clean night air blow through his hair and thought it was great to see so many stars overhead. He was a bit nervous about reciting but eased his anxiety by thinking how tough some of the others had it. Some of his schoolmates had to drag themselves up before the class. Particularly Rhoda Ollis. She had trouble reciting at all.

Rhoda Ollis was a retestable genius. No matter how her I.Q. was measured, it was forever beyond measurement. From two ordinary parents, her preeminent ability to reason was inexplicable. Rhoda was notorious at the university for ruining the grading curve for the other students. They would see her in a class and transfer. She could play fifty winning games of chess at once but couldn't talk to you directly.

Frail and dark, she dressed in black. She said she had a strong calling, and that she was headed for a doctorate of divinity. She would say those things out loud so you could hear them, but she'd say them, as she said most everything, to herself. She talked back and forth, one side of her personality to the other. One on one, there were always three people in a conversation with Rhoda.

Rhoda was a full-time matriculated student at UCLA. She took Talmadge's poetry class in night extension so she wouldn't have to accept the grade if it were poor. If it would hurt her four-point average. She had taken Poetry I in extension and failed it. She never picked up the grade.

She talked amongst her selves when she recited. Her last poem had been done in sentential calculus. She used rhyming symbols instead of words. It sounded something like Chinese. Afterward she told herself and others that it looked perfect on paper.

"To make symbols rhyme instead of words," Hero laughed, seeing Rhoda in her usual spot in the front of the room.

Hero volunteered to go first. Leaving a copy of his poem with Talmadge for a grade, he went up to the podium and did it. He spoke slowly and easily, enunciating every word with the necessary inflection. His adrenaline raced. The audience was with him. He left his hands at his sides and said it all to their faces without having to look down once.

The applause was loud and made him blush as he took his seat. He looked around and nodded thank you as the clapping continued. Jesus, he thought. What a feeling. To do it with words. My words, my choices. He felt proud.

Hero wasn't crazy about any of the other poems recited that night. The class hour dragged on.

Afterward, outside, Rhoda told Hero, in her way, that she loved his work. Hero said he was anxious to hear her next poem but she was talking to herself and didn't hear. She was telling Hero that she had taken his advice and didn't wander around the campus at night anymore. She still, however, parked in the cheaper parking lots off campus to save money but her father had installed a giant white plastic flower at the top of her car aerial so she could see it right away. She could walk directly to her car deep in any lot, without searching.

Hero said that that was good to hear and told her again not to talk to strangers. He hugged her shoulders and told her she was too special to lose. That the city was an erratic, often dangerous place to live. To be careful.

Breaking away, she stared him quickly in the eye and ran off into the night.

Feeling great, Hero walked briskly across the boulevard to meet Kay at the restaurant. She was dressed as she'd promised, right down to her green Adidas. He looked at her before taking her into his arms. She was beautiful. He held her. She smelled wonderfully distinct. He kissed her soft blond neck. They broke away to stare into each other's eyes and laugh embarrassedly. Hand in hand, they went to eat.

She had taken two exercise classes back to back and felt marvelous. Hero told her how well his poem had gone over in class. He showed her his grade, an "A." She blew him a kiss from across the table. He went over and sat beside her. He played with her left breast for anyone to see until she closed her arm on his hand.

"Hero, people are watching."

"They are so pretty. Pull open the top of your leotard just for a second. Let me see what you've got."

She gave him a look as if he were awful but did it for him anyway.

"Oh, yeah," he said, "pretty nipples."

Sitting back, Kay said, "I'll bet you drove the girls crazy when you were little."

"Who, me? How so?"

"Wanting to see everything. I'll bet you never could see enough."

She laughed and so did he.

Hero licked his fork and then her lips. He kept at it. She let him and he went to her ear. Not moving, they began to breathe heavily. Hero brought her hand to his stiff penis. She squeezed hard but quickly changed the subject by sitting up straight and saying, "Hero, enough, in here . . . honestly." He laughed and moved away to eat.

Kay said, "I hear they use microwave ovens to cook here."

"I heard that too."

"What does it mean?"

"It means that the molecules get changed around in the food."

"Is that healthy?" she asked.

"Who knows? Probably not, but even the best restaurants use them now."

"I don't know. It tastes good. If that means anything."

"It doesn't."

They ate for a while in silence.

"Why," Hero asked, "don't we chuck it in. Sell everything and move away where the air is always clean. Where we can grow our own food?"

Kay said, "Oh, sure. You'd be out of your mind in a week without the city's energy. And what could I do? Model bonnets and milkmaid gowns for the local Sears store?"

"I mean it. Sometimes I can get dead serious about it."

"I know, honey." She touched his leg. "And sometimes you're happy as a lark in the city and a team of horses couldn't drag you away."

"How about two places? Something here, and a farm or ranch someplace. Maybe up north?"

"Let's see what happens," Kay said.

But Hero continued. "Someplace where we could be alone and, speaking for myself, I could do something creative."

"Like?"

"Well, like write."

"Write what? Have you got something in mind?"

"Sort of."

"You do? Tell me, what?"

"A novel."

Kay stopped what she was doing to stare into him. "You're not kidding, are you?"

Hero moved back to his side of the table. He leaned across to her enthusiastically. He took her hands. "I just know I can do it. Professor Talmadge says I've got an instinct for the beginning, the middle and the end of a piece. He tells me I've got it. And you know, I believe him. I want to believe him. It feels so damned good. Working with words."

"Yes, Hero, but a novel is a heck of a lot different than writing a poem, isn't it? Not that I don't think you—"

"I know that," he interrupted. "I can deal with all of that. The desire, the energy. It's just the time that it takes. I'd like to really get into it."

"Well," she said, acting salty, "there's no one stopping you.

But I sure don't know what I'd do out . . . somewhere."

Hero nodded. "I know, but let me tell you this, Kay. As far as priorities go, you and I are right at the top. Up there with God and things holy. It wouldn't be any fun if I couldn't share it with someone . . . with you." "He stroked her hand. "I mean that."

Kay smiled and touched him back. "I know. I know everything that you're saying. We get in a rut."

"Exactly. And I'm not so sure I want to stay in it. If there's an alternative."

"Well, there are alternatives to almost everything."

"Well, Kay, you tell me. Is there a place where we could go? Someplace different, creative, someplace you would be fulfilled . . . happy?"

"Where you could write and I could model?"

"Yes, for now."

"Sure." She smiled like a feline. "But it costs money. . . and takes nerve."

"Where, tell me where?" he asked.

She rolled his thumb in her palms the way she did his penis when she was doing "rolling pin."

"Come on, Kay, where?"

Her eyes twinkled and she said, "Paris."

SIXTEEN

No sooner had they bought tickets and stepped inside the theater lobby than a man was yelling out after Hero, "Fiddleman, hey, Fiddleman."

Hero and Kay turned to see Mike Trainer, chief of West Los Angeles detectives, coming their way.

"Aw shit," Hero said under his breath.

Mike Trainer wore a synthetic blue suit and visored hat with a red feather in the brim. His shirt was wrinkled. He wore black referee's shoes that helped absorb the shake from his big belly as he came toward them. A burning cigarette was between the fingers of his outstretched hand. Mike Trainer chain-smoked.

"Well, lookee here," Trainer declared. "Hero Fiddleman and one pretty blonde."

"Do I know you," Hero asked, "or just your type?"

Mike Trainer laughed and said, "Very funny. What brings you into this neck of the woods, Hero, and don't tell me it's to see a movie."

"That's why, Mike. What's it to you?"

"You mean you expect me to believe that old Chief Fiddleman just happened to decide to bring the pretty girl *here* tonight? What a coincidence. I don't believe it."

"That's your problem, Mike. Come on, Kay."

"Hey, Hero." Trainer stopped them. "Why can't you leave this one to me, just me and my guys, just once?"

"I don't know what you're talking about, Mike."

"Bullshit. Sorry lady. But don't bullshit me, Hero. I know why you're here. Same reason I'm here. I suppose Gates has got you crossing lines again. Is that it? Doesn't he think I can handle it?"

"Mike , I don't want to hear about your insecurities. I've got problems of my own. We're here to see a film and relax. See you around." Hero escorted Kay into the theater.

When they entered, Mike Trainer held the door. Light flooded in down the aisle around them. There was almost no one to irritate, the place was dead.

Mike yelled, "If it means anything to you, I've been through this store with a fine-toothed comb. The theater isn't the key, Hero, believe me."

Hero said, "Thanks, Mike, see you," and they took seats in approximately the middle of the theater.

Hero was glad he'd missed the titles. The film was a yawn. But Kay enjoyed it. She laughed and carried on and talked about the actors and actresses. She either knew them or private things about them. She said the movie was shot at Benji Turkel's mansion. And sure enough, pretty Helen Parker, Benji's girl friend, was in the movie, which meant a trade to Kay. She laughed and enjoyed her insightfulness.

On two different occasions during the movie Hero excused himself to walk around. Mike Trainer was gone, the lobby quiet. He looked the entire place over from stem to stern, upstairs and down, back and forth, and found nothing. The second time around, he found Bill Robinson, out in the lobby having a smoke.

Glad to see each other, they shook hands enthusiastically.

Hero laughed and kidded Bill about his outfit: white painter's coveralls, white shirt and hat, black face.

"The manager busted me," Bill said, "so I showed him my shield. He showed me around, nice enough guy... even gave me an extra set of house keys." Bill Robinson dangled the keys in front of Hero who took them and pocketed them without an explanation.

"Did you see Mike Trainer?" Hero wanted to know, but Robinson didn't know him, which was fine. "So, nothing, huh?" Hero asked.

"Zero. Grilled the manager too. He's seen nothing."

"Are you sure... not a single thing?"

"Nothing unusual to him. Everyday stuff. A broken phone. Puke on the carpet. The change drawer short by a dime or twenty cents, every day lately. Kids steal the candy, popcorn. Nothing. The place is pretty neat too. They keep it clean." Hero stared off across the pink lobby, thinking.

"I don't think there's anything here, Chief. You still want me to...?"

"Yes." Hero came back abruptly. Yes, definitely. Stay here until you're relieved or you can't stand it any more." They laughed. "But lay low. Stay low in a seat and do rounds every so often."

"Okay. You're the boss." Robinson put out his cigarette and asked, "Do you know what we're looking for?"

"Vaguely," Hero replied.

"And it's got to do with The Terror?"

"Sure."

"Is that who or what I'm looking for?"

"Sure."

"Well, how will I know him, I mean—"

Hero's eyes stopped him. They looked at each other until Hero said, "You'll know it. If you find something you'll know it. I'm sure of that. And, Bill..."

"Yes?"

"Don't be so casual about this thing. I want you to be careful. Are you armed?"

Robinson smiled his perfect white-toothed smile, patted his front right pocket, and said, "Do the bad-assed nigger ever go without?" They laughed and Robinson crossed the pink lobby to go back into the theater.

Hero sat perfectly still for a while, thinking. Then he broke his train of thought to go back inside, into the darkness, to sit next to Kay and hold her hand.

When the film was over, the lights came up to show Hero only a handful of people in the theater, all getting up to leave. Hero laughed to himself when he saw the toe of a lone white shoe showing over a seat up near the front. Kay said she had to use the toilet. They walked out to the lobby. Hero waited and scouted the candy counter while Kay went upstairs.

He watched her from behind and thought her ass looked fabulous. A couple of beautiful handfuls. Kay disappeared from view.

Suddenly, he chased up the stairs behind her. "Kay," he yelled. She stopped where she was, two-thirds of the way down the pink hallway, and turned to smile. "Come here," Hero said.

She hesitated.

"Come here, honey."

Kay came back to join him at the head of the staircase. "I've got to go, too. Let's run across Wilshire and go to the top of the Kirkeby. They've got a wishing well in the bar and black onyx johns. Might as well go in a snazzy one. Then we'll get a table, a cappuccino, and look out over the city. And we can make a wish. Toss a coin into the wishing well. What say you, princess?"

Kay looked behind her down the pink hallway and back at Hero. "Okay," she said finally, "but let's get going. I've really got to go bad. And honey?"

"Yes?"

They were down the stairs and out the front door of the theater, having fun.

"You'd better have an extra special wish in mind, because I have. And I'm warning you, this is my lucky night."

SEVENTEEN

When she disappeared from view, Simon whinnied out, "No...no...no...please," and raged around his tin cage like a crazed rat in a trap.

In angry frustration, he went to his haunches, held his breath, and looked again. He craned his neck but there was nothing but a forsaken, pink emptiness.

Shit. Fuck. He abused himself. He punched his legs until he went down flat onto his back. He heard the dizzy blonde, with her head thrown back, laughing. He cringed and curled his toes while they turned their backs and laughed. Suddenly, everyone was laughing. The chamber echoed with it. The universe resounded. He was nauseous. He gritted his teeth to close his ears.

Gratefully, a quick thought of Carol came to the rescue. Carol could do him some good. Tell him what he needed to hear. Give him some of her good relief. Suckle him. Stop him from falling.

Drifting, tumbling, he sat up with a metallic slam. He wiped the slop from his face. He waited for the lights to go down. Then he waited some more.

In the lobby, headed for a dime, the smell of popcorn stopped him. His senses flared. He was starving.

Ravenously, he ate a box of chocolate bonbons, a large buttered popcorn, and drank a Coke. Outdoors it was black.

With a dime from the cash drawer, Simon went to the telephone. His hands were shaking but he made the call. A busy signal barked back loudly in his ear. He hung up and tried again with the same result.

Clutching the dime, he roamed the theater. He went upstairs to the men's room and urinated. Back in the lobby he ate popcorn by the handful from the machine. He ate the dime. He felt it go down. More Coke. To the telephone with a new dime. Still busy. Back to the lobby to pace.

Sitting on the staircase, fingering the wrought-iron railing, he looked up to find an illusion. A man. A white, black and pink man at the foot of the stairs: motionless, staring.

Wait, he told himself. Get sharp, this is real. This is tangible. There is movement. But he held there gawking as though madness had totally extorted objectivity from him. Somewhere in his mind there was the screech: normal, act normal, be normal. But Simon couldn't comply. He was all normaled out. "Shoo . . . shoo," he said, waving his hands as he would at a disgusting white-and-black larvaed fly.

His pulse began to race. The white-and-black man was coming. He would shut his eyes and when he opened them, the apparition would be gone. That didn't happen. A shining black revolver and unmistakable policeman's badge appeared, suddenly making the illusion very, very authentic.

The fact made Simon growl then scream out in his head not to be taken to the sickeningly sweet green room. Then he laughed to himself, intense now, watching every move.

"Bring me a matron," Simon demanded with a grin. The obstinate-expressioned white-and-black man hesitated. Simon could easily see the man hated him and was disgusted by him and wanted to take him to the room of sweet cider. That his sole purpose was to bring Simon down. To kill him.

Putting on his best face, Simon said, "If you can pull the trigger, boy, I'll show you how to die." But using the moment, Simon lunged and kicked the gun from his hand. At least two toes broke out loud. The gun flew behind the candy counter and Simon took an instant from his laughter to straighten his toes through his sock.

Now they stood on the pink carpet across from each other. The man moved funny. He waved his hands before him in a swimming gesticulation as though casting a spell and moved ever so carefully to his left, orbiting Simon.

For a while, it seemed like a circus with Simon grabbing and lunging awkwardly at an animated white-and-black clown. Simon laughed while he moved around within his circle. Then the very strong man was somehow into Simon's legs and Simon was down, flat on his back onto the pink carpet.

Simon moved. But the policeman, definitely a professional, fighting policeman, moved first and flipped Simon over onto his face. A hard numbing blow came twice to the back of his neck. Stars flew past him. He may have blacked out.

The pain in his shoulder brought him back and the jangling sensation of cold metal handcuffs being thrust around his wrist.

The mean gang of Kansas City kids used to hold Simon down and tie his wrists. His father could tie him up too. He despised it. The older kids would poke him with sticks or bounce balls off him and make fun of his skin. They would point and say, "Yuk . . . ugh," but then pile onto him while the giggling sluts would cheer and direct their brave young cocks to beat up the big ugly clod.

The last year that happened, he had been eleven. After that, his muscle tone and bulk came along and even a gang was no match for him. No matter, it was never what they did to him that hurt anyway. It was the snickering whispers and laughter that caused the unbearable pain.

"Try this, boy," Simon growled and through sheer brute strength, forced his arm down until the hold was broken. He rolled over under the cop to face him. The quick black man tried to blind him with what seemed a karate chop to the eyes, but Simon got his hand in the way, and bucked him off onto the floor.

Standing, panting, they faced each other. Simon's toes throbbed. The white-and-black cop moved like greased lightning to the attack. Simon spit in his face as he came. He had had enough.

Sidestepping, Simon got ahold of the back of his slippery black neck and drove him to the carpet onto his face. Improving the neck hold with one hand, Simon grabbed one of the man's ankles with the other. With a "Hup," Simon clean-jerked the man straight up above his head. He brought him down hard, back first, over his outstretched knee.

So agile and strong was the policeman that no serious injury occurred, nothing to deter him. He struggled but Simon wouldn't let go. Simon assumed a kneeling and knee-up position on the floor, and exerting all of his strength, bent the black man over his knee.

Simon laughed, "Aha," when he knew he had him positioned properly and pushed both powerful hands down toward the pink floor.

The white-and-black policeman screamed out, "Oh, Christ, nooooooo," as his back exploded loudly over Simon's knee.

With much of the whiteness fast becoming red, Simon bundled the man up and ran with him down through the theater.

Leaving a white shoe jammed in the exit door, he carried him out into the cool night. The area was quiet. The parking lots across the alley were completely empty but for one lone compact car that sat in the middle of the north lot, a huge white flower atop its aerial.

Simon selected the large green iron garbage can behind the drapery shop next door. The broken man was easily swathed in discarded material, and buried near the bottom of the can.

Just before he turned to leave, he saw her. A lone female entering the north parking lot across the alley.

Dressed in dark clothing, she appeared to be humming or singing to herself. Dumb little twit. He hated her. He looked around and they were suddenly, exquisitely alone. She was giggling. His breath came hard and irregular. It would be a spell. The world flowed together to swirl. The fever was through him. Exhilarated, he ran for her.

She was not startled when he approached her from behind and touched her shoulder. She turned around, pale in the oblique lighting. A peculiar smile across her face, she said, "Hello," and asked herself, "What have we here?"

"Guess, cunt," Simon said, touching her neck. She closed her eyes but continued to smile and jabber nonsense. With his hand on her frail shoulder for support, Simon pulled her to him. He put his hand around her sweet neck to feel the soft thing. He stroked it gently up and down like a giant penis and trembled. He closed his hand.

Her eyes popped open wide. Somehow, her words continued, as did her perfectly secure demeanor. She held his eyes and he looked in. He heard her conversation. It deciphered loud and clear in his senses. He was in reality. He saw his hand on her throat. It looked wrong, ugly. It felt frozen. He shook his head to clear it. Then he really heard what was going on and let go of her as though she were on fire. He broke and ran.

Halfway back across the lot, he turned and, shaking, pointing an accusing finger, said, "I heard you, you're talking with . . ." Oh, no, he told himself without continuing. You're completely out of your mind. It's all over for you. But he yelled, "You're talking with . . . with . . ."

"God," the frail girl answered directly, smiling. "Of course, you silly nut. She's my mother. She wouldn't let anything happen to me."

Back inside the theater, with the heavy doors slammed behind him, Simon wondered wildly if that had really happened. He cracked the door and took a peek. The lot was empty. "Holy shit," he said. "Holy shit." He ran up onto the stage and did pushups.

Afterward, he hated himself for missing her.

Behind the huge movie screen, Simon discovered a small red lightbulb burning next to another exit door. Beneath the light was a wall telephone. An old davenport sat against the firebrick wall under the phone.

Simon slumped into the sofa and got comfortable. He arranged himself so he could see the telephone. He sat up and tested the line. There was a dial tone. It worked. He hung the receiver back up.

He lay there for what seemed a long time. He slept hard and dreamt of calling. In an incredibly powerful wet nightmare that left him shaken with its substantiality, Simon made obedient love to Carol.

Later, he sat up and made the call. His heart jumped into his throat. The telephone was ringing. The line was clear.

EIGHTEEN

Kay went somewhere early with a girl friend and Hero slept late. Yawning, he plugged the phone in and scratched his scalp, saying, "Goddamn, did I need that."

Half dressed and brushing his teeth, he was on the way out the door to walk Stretch when he stepped over the newspaper. The headline caused him to freeze. "Terror on Prowl Again." Hero said, "Damn," and knelt as he felt something go out of him, to read the story.

Shaking his head, he figured that somebody near the top had leaked it, because the paper had the entire picture. They knew everything he knew, from the torn-up redhead on down. They were guessing too; as they were so good at doing. About the reverend's daughter and Jean Pilgrim and anybody else that fit.

"What a drag," Hero said, standing. To have to work with the world in on it. "Shit." And he thought about the awful fear it would bring the women.

Dwight yelled at him and waved from the top of the quay. Hero waved back and Dwight jumped the fence to come running down the gangplank and out onto the dock.

Clyde came out from the far side of his boat to yell at Dwight for being so loud until he saw Hero glaring. He went back where he'd been. To his Bloody Mary, Hero figured.

"Hero," Dwight said anxiously. "What's with your phone?"

"I slept in."

"They got Bill, Chief," Dwight blurted.

"They?" Hero questioned. "Bill?"

Dwight nodded and swallowed hard. "They . . . he . . . it-. . . The Terror, who the hell knows. Bill Robinson is dead. His back broken in two."

Hero felt a coldness creep up his spine and over his scalp. He swallowed the mouthful of toothpaste, sensing that would be it for breakfast.

"Tell me," Hero said. They went inside.

"They found him at the garbage dump. Wrapped in drapery material. He was still warm when they found him. Coroner said . . ." Dwight checked his watch. "Well, right now he's only been dead approximately five, six, seven hours."

"I just saw him last night," Hero said solemnly.

"Yeah?"

"Yeah, in the theater. Dwight, where did the garbage can come from that . . ."

"Westwood," Dwight interjected. "Where else? They pick up early every morning."

Hero yelled "Shit," and punched the wall. "It's my fucking fault, shit on a shingle. I sent him into it. Fuck."

"Hey, come on, Hero, come on. You know better than that."

"I do?" Hero confronted him.

He was getting dressed, faster, more inside out than ever, saying, "That motherfucker."

"I've already been by the theater, Chief. If that's what you're thinking. Locked up tight as a drum. Dark inside. I looked in all the windows. But—"

"But?" Hero stopped.

214

"But there's a drapery shop right next door."

"Jesus Christ." Hero tied his last shoelace and strapped on his gun.

"Who knows?"

"About Robinson?"

"Yeah, does the press know?"

"Sure. The garbage people found him."

"Shit."

"But nobody knows where he was working."

"So, nobody knows he was at the theater?"

"Probably not . . . not yet. But I think it's the drapery shop, somebody from the drapery shop, that's the key. But it's all closed up, tight too. Probably open by now. The theater won't open until late this afternoon. We could call the manager at home, if—"

Hero was out the door. "Dwight, go back to the station and sit tight."

"Oh, come on—"

"No, that's the way I want it. I'll want you there if I need you. Besides, it's no big deal. I've got to do something for myself, that's all. I'm not expecting to close this thing yet."

"But—"

"Dwight, just do what I'm asking, okay? Go in and stay by the phones. See what comes in. There may be something on Bill."

Leaving Dwight in the doorway, Hero ran up the gangplank and jumped the fence. The top was still down on The Tub. He saw Stretch taking a leak up near the end of the lot. "Shoot, I forgot all about him. Sneaked under the fence, the fucker."

Squeezing the theater keys in his wet palm, Hero looked back down at the boat and back at Stretch. He thought for a minute and yelled, "Come on, Stretch," and held open the car door. Stretch was on the run, his long sausage body racing an inch from the ground.

"If you want to come with me, hurry up," Hero yelled, and the dog was into the car, panting happily.

Feeling enraged and guilty about Bill Robinson, Hero was

across town in record time. He'd have been stopped too, but the black-and-white that turned and chased him finally saw who it was.

"I'm not so sure about this," he told Stretch angrily, "but if it'll make me feel any better, I've got to have a look. I've got to do *something*. I think Dwight's full of shit about the drapery shop. It's the theater. Something about that fucking theater."

He patted Stretch's coat that shined in the sun.

"Nice, half-assed day," he said sarcastically. "Too bad Bill Robinson won't be around to enjoy it." Shaking his head hard, he screamed, "Goddamn it" at the sun.

He parked in front of the theater on Westwood Boulevard in the passenger loading zone. Stretch urinated on a parking meter a few yards away. Feeling irritable, Hero scolded him not to piss or shit in the theater. Stretch wagged his tail. Hero used two keys to quietly let them inside and whispered, "Shhh" to Stretch past his finger while he locked the plate-glass doors behind them.

But for the daylight that came in through the doors, a dimly lit chandelier above the staircase and tiny emergency lights here and there, the theater was dark. He felt a tinge of claustrophobia.

"Gloomy-assed, weird place," he said angrily. He pulled his police special from his shoulder holster and held it ready. "I'm not scared but I'm not stupid either. Let's go." They walked cautiously into the darkness.

Inside the doors of the auditorium, at the top of the aisle, they stopped and stared. Nothing unusual. Row after row of shaded empty seating. The movie screen, silver beads, gathered what little illumination there was. He shrugged. A dark empty theater.

He wouldn't turn up the house lights, not yet, and wished he'd brought a flashlight.

Back in the lobby, more at ease, he holstered his gun. He paced. He sipped from the fountain and leaned against the staircase looking out into the day. How, he asked himself, aggravated, could this damn thing have happened? How the hell could anybody get that close? Break his fucking back. How does anybody break the back of that tough son of a bitch? He rubbed his unshaven beard and tried to figure it.

Upstairs to take a leak, he told Stretch to "stay" in the hallway. The men's room was totally black until he found the light. He felt frustrated. How? he asked himself in the mirror. Unless they jumped him. Ambushed him. Sure, shit, that's got to be it. Nobody, I can't imagine anybody, beating him in a fair fight.

But who the hell? Maybe, he flashed, the personnel? The manager, or a guy, a couple guys that work here. But that's no good. The cops on the West Side have lie-detected everybody they could get their mitts on; twice. No, it's not an employee. Then who, goddamn it? Bill Robinson was locked in here last night. Just as sure as shit. He punched the palm of his hand in angry frustration.

Washing his hands, he thought he heard a bell, a telephone ringing. He quickly shut the tap and listened. No, splashing water can make that sound. But wait, wait a minute. How about the telephones? I wonder, he asked himself, drying his hands. I wonder if they've checked that. A simple little thing like that. Those morons.

Stretch was interested in something along the hallway wall and didn't want to leave. "Don't," Hero said. "Come on." They ran down the stairs and to the pay phones.

Dwight hadn't come in yet but Hero recited the theater pay phone numbers to the desk sergeant and listened to them read back as he did his explicit instructions for Dwight. "Check out *all* the calls that have been made on these lines since Christmas, all hours. Call me back here." He hung up, optimistic about the idea.

Stretch was gone. He felt a quick chill run through him but knew that was silly.

He found him with his tail wagging, looking down from the head of the pink staircase. When Stretch saw Hero, he turned and disappeared back into the dark hallway.

Hero ran upstairs to find Stretch in front of the men's room door, his tail stiff as a rail, his nose pointed across the hall.

"What the hell are you doing?" Hero asked.

Stretch stopped to wag his tail furiously and resumed pointing.

Up close, Hero took the point and, irritated, said, "There's nothing there, a wall. Kay must be feeding you health food again. Come on." But the dog held the point.

"You fucker, what the hell . . ." Then he saw it. A large, nearly square ventilating shaft halfway up the far, shadowy pink wall. He stopped and stared at the metal grillwork that covered the opening. His eyes dropped to the heavy standing ashtray below. The sight startled him and glared. The possibilities.

"You're not trying to—what are you trying to tell me?" He was aware of his heartbeat. "I wonder," he whispered. "if they've checked that thing out.

"Preposterous," he said, but directly underneath the shaft he tested the weight and balance of the ashtray, realizing it could easily support a man. "Jesus," he said, looking up at the vent. A trickle of perspiration ran down between his buttocks.

Up onto the ashtray, Hero tugged at the grillwork cover. It came off easily into his hands. Too easily. He closed his eyes for dust but there was none. Peering in, there was nothing to see but hollow darkness.

Quickly, he got down, leaned the grill cover against the wall and was into the men's room. He turned the light back on and opened the door. A long yellow cut of lighting went across the hallway to perfectly illuminate the ventilated wall from floor to ceiling. He wedged a paper towel under the door to keep it open.

Back up on the ashtray, the light came over him to fill up the shaft. He saw the large motionless fan at the end.

"So?" he said, "a fan."

His adrenaline ebbed. But a closer scrutiny revealed an area back next to the fan's housing that seemed to have depth. And the more he stood staring, the more it seemed there was a strange, immaculate pathway through the dust at the bottom of the cannister.

Part of him said, this is nuts, but the policeman, Bill Robinson's friend said, "Fuck it . . . go for it."

Jumping, he pulled himself up into the hole. It was easy, very easy. He was quickly able to distinguish that the corner next to the fan wasn't a corner at all but an opening of some kind. And there was something else. Something in the air that made him feel anxious; sweaty.

Wagging his finger at Stretch to "stay," Hero jerked out his .38, crawled to the far end of the shaft and put his head through the top of the opening.

There were rafters where the light fell and beams cut of raw wood, and insulation. Nothing out of the ordinary. Nothing to make him venture farther. It's an attic. A goddamned attic, that's all. But there was definitely something in the air. A somehow familiar sweet taste or smell that provoked his senses.

Standing there, gawking, in the midst of all that uninhabited architecture, Hero was taken with the sensation of being utterly alone. Alone in the middle of nowhere. A place where people never ever go. Isolated. Buried alive.

He shook the claustrophobic feeling off and without much thought, slipped through the space into the attic. He moved aside to admit a broad stab of illumination that had no periphery, no margin of gradation. There was total blackness and there was light. A precise golden hole through the dark that went straight back to a slanted wooden wall. He reached out into it to assure himself of his weapon.

The odor was conspicuous now and something caught his eye down near the corner of the attic. One lone piece of cloth sticking up into the light. He paused in the stagnant silence to analyze the smell. He shook his head. It wasn't wood or insulation. Perhaps worn grease from the machinery, or heat from electrical wiring against asbestos. A dead animal. No, but he knew it. It would come.

Balancing on two rafters, he made his way into the attic.

Soon, he reached down into the light and touched the innocuous piece of material. A piece of nothing rag left by workmen years before. The cloth hung onto something heavy at its base. Kneeling, he put his hand down into the darkness.

Suddenly, the smell came to him. It retched through him as his fingertips fell onto the unmistakable tacky wetness of decaying human flesh.

His heart leapt into his throat to beat like a sledge. His senses jammed. Snatching his hand away, he jumped up like a jack out of a box.

Straining his eyes into the blackness where his hand had been, he tried to think. "Jesus Christ Almighty. . ." Dust particles swam through the silent stream of light before him.

Then suddenly, incredibly, the men's room door slammed shut loudly below and the attic was plunged into total pitch blackness.

Hero gasped. A bolt of fear shot through him that made his scalp tingle, his ears ring. He strained his eyes to see. His mind raced. He flashed on Stretch, his long, hot dog body tied into a broken knot. A powerful perfumed whiff of putrification came. He lost track of space. Groping into the black, he fell back onto his buttocks.

"Good God," he exclaimed, attempting to get it together. He grasped his .38. He bounced to test where he sat, on a human rib cage; and no amount of masculinity or cool could constrain his abrupt groaning outcry.

He shot up to freeze. His trigger finger went crazy to blast away but he stopped. Hold on, he screamed in his head. Hold on. Don't panic. Be cool. He stood there swaying in the dark trying desperately to find some common sense.

He stared in back of him for a sign of movement; anything to fill full of lead.

He listened. Nothing. Total silence. The nauseating odor of decomposing flesh seemed everywhere now. He wondered. The door, the wadded-up paper door stop.

Whistling loudly, he yelled, "Stretch . . . Stretch . . . speak boy, speak." He whistled again. The attic contained the sounds with a thud but Stretch began to bark and run around in the hallway below.

"Son of a bitch," he sighed.

Feeling silly about certain things, relieved, angry, but composed and definitely back in business, Hero stooped in the dark to feel what was what.

The body he had sat on was bloated and nude, a female. Her neck was torn out. His adrenaline surged. The Terror. This is it. His heart skipped a beat when he felt an empty eye socket.

The ruffled blouse was the only clothing on another distended, completely rigor-mortised female. There seemed to be just the two bodies. Both corpses were slimy. Not blood, either, the composition was wrong. But leaking bodily fluids, or perhaps semen. Disgusted, he wiped his hands on his pants cuffs.

"Fuck the theater's ceiling," he said, and ran from the place over the plaster.

When he stuck his head back out into the hallway, a telephone was ringing. Dropping to the carpet, he ran to answer it, saying, "Good dog . . . good boy," to a bouncing Stretch along the way.

Beside himself with excitement, Hero must have babbled when he got on the phone because Dwight kept saying, "Settle down . . . settle down."

Finally, Hero took a deep breath and said, "Whew, you ain't gonna fucking believe . . . Dwight, there are at least two bodies in the attic here. Women . . . The Terror . . . it's a lead pipe cinch he—"

"Are you alone?" Dwight broke in.

A tinge of fear gripped him when he said, "I think so. Stretch is with me. He's doing a lot of sniffing but doesn't act like there's anybody around. The place seems secure, whatever the fuck that means. The phones—anything?"

"Plenty. I've got it all checked out, and there's a call that's been made from those numbers you left. Sometimes one, sometimes the other, five times since Christmas. And listen to this. The calls were made at strange hours, three, four, five in the morning. There's not supposed to be anybody in there then, is there?"

"Hell, no. Who is it?"

"Well, the telephone company computer has it plain as day, 555-0317, and I checked it out."

"And the name?"

"Simon Moon."

"Simon Moon?"

"Yep, he's a lawyer up the street in the Kirkeby Building. Fourteenth floor. The 555 number is his home."

"Boy, you don't fuck around, do you?"

"Nope. I try and do what you tell me. And, are you ready for this?"

"Shoot."

"I checked his office and they haven't seen him since Christmas . . . their Christmas party. He played Santa Claus, gave away the presents. A big brooding guy. Shit, do you suppose . . . ?"

"The Terror?"

"Yeah."

"Yeah, I more than suppose."

"Jesus. I tried the 555 number and it's busy. And speaking of busy phones, who have you been talking to?"

"What do you mean. I've been in the attic, remember. I just came—" A coldness came. "Why, Dwight?"

Dwight was silent. Hero could feel his anxiety through the line. "Dwight?"

"Yeah."

"What's going on?"

"Well, then, who in hell . . . Are you positive, absolutely positive that you're all alone in there? How about the manager?"

"No, I'm almost certain. The place is black, why?"

"Because that other number you gave me has been busy . . . right along."

Hero's mind began chasing the theater down. The places where another phone might be. The manager's office, for sure, but locked and dark. He had just passed it again. Probably, positively, a private line anyway. The projection booth? Backstage? A pay phone extension? He rubbed his chin. Unless someone had been here, where he was now standing.

"Chief, if it wasn't you on the line, then who . . . Hold on a second." A moment later, Dwight said, "Hey, ah, Chief—"

"What?"

"It's still busy. I just called it."

Hero looked at the other pay phone. He picked it up and listened. Air. He put in a dime but the phone wouldn't accept it. Air, loud, close.

"Shit," he said, hanging the phone back up carefully. The hair on the nape of his neck felt wet.

He looked up to find Stretch before him, wagging his tail. In his mouth was a small black leather case from which a shining gold detective shield hung.

"Chief, come on, Chief, what's going on with that other phone? Are you sure you're all right?"

Hero squeezed the twin hatched wooden grips of his .38 police special. His palm was wet. He looked at Stretch holding Bill Robinson's shield. His voice wavered as he tried to speak calmly. "No, Dwight, I'm not okay. All of a sudden, I think something is very wrong. Get your ass over here. And Dwight?"

"Chief?"

"Bring a fucking army."

NINETEEN

The telephone rang in Simon's ear but he wasn't sure where he was. He was unable to claim any distinct image of himself. He knew he was a man of the shadows, nothing else. Carol answered the phone. She seemed a million miles away, her voice vague, unsympathetic. He needed her. He screamed.

"I love you, Carol . . . I need you. You are the one—"

"Simon . . . Simon."

The abrupt tone in her voice brought him back closer to himself. He sat on the arm of the sofa. He stared into the red exit bulb and wouldn't blink.

"Simon." She spoke just his name in her condescending saccharine tone as if speaking to Charlotte, their child.

"Simon, I don't know where you are, or where you've been, and I don't want to know."

His eyes blazed painfully into the red hue. Perspiration ran off his chin. A scolding. A wonderful scolding.

"Simon, I want you to have courage when I tell you this."

His stomach went into a knot. "I don't live here anymore, Simon. This is no longer my home."

Air, air, he screamed in his brain. His breath came out of him in a gush, bringing forth a guttural utterance that sounded like, "Ma—Ma." He produced a cotton-mouthed laugh. "Oh, no, Carol. Don't say that. It makes me go boomo in my pants." He laughed.

She didn't laugh. She said, "I've had strong reservations, Simon, wondering, always asking myself if I was secure. If you were going to stay on the ball. I made a mistake when I married you, Simon. A big mistake, but I blame no one but myself. I thought you were sad, even pathetic, and I thought I could help you, fix you. And after all, you are a lawyer, you've got certain skills. You should be able to help me too. Earn a decent living and get me the things I should have.

"But you're too confused, too preoccupied, and since the baby, since I've felt myself again, I've allowed myself to talk to other men—and it happened. I want to tell you before someone else does. I am in a relationship with another man, Simon, and I'm going to try like the devil—I'm *going* to make it work."

Simon's mind flew to Carol getting set to run a race. Warming up, she would say, "I may not win, but I'm going to finish—I'm going to try like the devil to finish." She always finished what she set out to do.

He went to a strange faceless man but saw his penis; that was easy to see. The image burned red and lucid, and tenacious Carol took hold of the big stiff thing, smiling, saying, "Blow it over me, new man. Blow it over my face. It's all for you."

A sickening sensation rolled down his intestines as though his belt were too tight and squeezing tighter, tighter, until the new man ejaculated over Carol's beautiful puckered mouth. She tongued it off, slowly, seductively, and Simon's stomach came up onto the backstage floor.

He retched from the awful taste, and knowing that the man would be good to her. His eyes burned and he knew he would know a good thing when he saw one and treat it with kid gloves.

Simon lost track of time but moaned, "Oh, no," and somewhere, off on the red planet, Carol said, "Oh, yes, and Simon, most everything important is gone from here. It's only coincidence you're catching me here now. I'm only back for a few things. I don't live here anymore.

"Dwayne is here, that's his name. He is outside waiting right now. And Simon, if it makes you feel any better, I want you to know, Dwayne is a good man. You know my judgment is good and that I never lie. He's a real good person, very good to me. Very successful. Let's face it, Simon. You never did know how to make money.

"And I want you to know he absolutely loves and adores Charlotte. She even coos and calls him Daddy sometimes, which I consider very lucky, extraordinary timing. At any rate, he's a good man and Charlotte likes him too."

Flashing, synapsing crazily, Simon wondered if guys named Dwayne had big cocks. He mumbled, "Do you love him?"

Pausing before she replied, Carol spoke carefully. "I care for him a great deal, Simon, and I'm going to make it work."

"Does he fuck her good?" he cried, wondering out loud, "Does her pussy get wet for him?" In the silence, Simon imagined Carol's reply.

"Fuck me good? Why, Simon. Of course not."

He went "Whew" with relief.

"No one fucks my hot lips but you, you know that. That's special private property, just for you. I may be going away to live with him up on his hill, to be his woman, to marry him, but no, honey. Don't be silly. Dwayne and I don't have sex. No one touches that soft brown pussy but you. It only gets wet for you. You're the only one that can flush me. So, if you don't mind, I'll be back for that. You big, well-hung stud."

But that was all bullshit, and Simon heard sharp Andy laughing and saying, "Don't be a schmuck, man, some of those guys with dough fuck okay, too."

Simon was going to be sick again and he could tell by the quality of the air coming through the telephone receiver that Carol was going to hang up. She would not address herself to his vulgar immaturity.

He knew what it was all about now anyway. It ain't your pussy no more, Simon. Now it belongs to Big Dwayne.

"Goodbye, Simon."

"Wait . . . wait," he shouted.

"I'll leave you a note—or be in touch. You'll come through this, and in a year, you'll probably thank me. Goodbye, Simon. Good luck."

The phone went dead. He let it slide from his hand to bang and then hang against the brick wall.

He began to tremble. He laughed out loud like a madman, saying, "I'll thank her. In a year, I'll thank her," to try and minimize the situation, but there was a shriek mounting inside him; like a live lobster dropped into boiling water.

He stood still, and it overwhelmed him until he screamed out just once, a wounded beast, and stopped to snarl, "I'll kill her. I'll kill the fucking cunt."

Feeling remarkably cogent, he slammed out the theater exit into the bright day. Down the alley he ran, past the bin where he had stuffed the black-and-white man. He looked twice to see that it now stood empty.

He crossed Wilshire Boulevard against the light and was nearly hit by a station wagon that careened and sideswiped another car to avoid him. As he ran up the front steps of his office building, someone from the collision yelled, "Wait, you son of a bitch," but Simon kept going.

In the elevator, people stared. His breathing was heavy. He kept his eyes down. He was sure they could hear his heart beating. He glanced up. They were made of wax with melting features. Sweat poured off him.

He ran through the outer office of the law firm and down the long hall to his office. He passed the secretarial nook where Slam should have been, but her chair was empty.

Into his office, he found Slam seated at his desk, rocking back on his big chair, her legs over a pulled-out drawer. She was talking on the telephone. Her mouth fell open when she saw him.

"Is it Carol . . . is it Carol?" he demanded, frothing, hoping. He reached for the receiver.

Slam held the phone out to him. "My . . . my mother . . . Mr. Moon . . . Simon, where . . . ?"

Simon drove the palm of his hand into her face. Slam and the chair both went over backward. The coasters spun around and around on the upside-down chair. Slam lay on her face unmoving.

"Stupid bitch."

He opened his desk drawer and the small ring box that held Carol's diamond ring. He put the ring into his pocket.

With his keys in his hand, he fled the building.

When the battery was dead on his car, he slammed the windshield with his fist and shattered it.

He left the car door open and ran from the subterranean garage out onto the side street. The police were in front, at the scene of the accident, so he ran in the other direction, into Westwood Village.

"I'll kill her... I swear, I'll kill her..."

He spotted a Beverly Hills cab in front of Swensen's Ice Cream and got in. The burly cigar-smoking cabbie had a head of black hair and tattoos over both forearms.

Simon gave the address and vacated his nostrils between his fingers onto the rear floor of the cab. The cabbie slowed the cab to say, "Aw, come on, fella, not in my—" He stopped midsentence when he saw Simon in his rearview mirror and drove on, saying, "Jesus, mister, what's wrong? Where have you been?"

"Away," Simon moaned. "Away, away, long enough for my wife to fuck another guy, to go away with him. I'll kill her. I'll fucking—"

"Oh, well," the cabbie said, flicking the ash from his cigar and laughing. "So that's it. Shit, why didn't you say so. What else is new? They'll do it every time."

"Cocksuckers," Simon screamed. The anger helped bring him into focus. He tried to hang onto it.

"So, is it finished between you and her?" the cabbie asked in the rearview.

"Don't look at me," Simon screamed, slamming the seat back next to the cab driver's shoulder.

"All right, all right, already." He turned the rearview mirror away and said, "Don't punch me, pal. I've been where you are. Just trying to help ya, cheer ya up. I suppose the guy's got dough, huh? My old lady went off for the money. You can never trust them, ever. Jack and Jill went up the hill to fetch a pail of water. Jill came down with a five-dollar bill, do you think she went up for water?" He laughed.

Simon said, "Just drive," and closed his eyes.

The cabbie told Simon about his new girl who wanted everything fifty-fifty; equal. Except when *he* took her out to dinner it was the Ritz. When she treated it was McDonald's. "Equal my ass."

But Simon didn't hear much of it. His brain was on fire.

The cabbie was saying something about women running the world, and probably doing a good job if we'd let them— something about the power of the pussy, pussy power—when they pulled into the driveway. Simon's stomach went to a new low.

The curtains were gone. He could see the house was dark and vacant. The garage door was open. Boxes and green-bagged junk were out for the garbage collector. A pathetic dying Christmas tree stood amidst the garbage cans.

The front lawn was littered with paper. The grass was crushed flat in paths where the movers had trod.

"Looks like she's gone, all right, man. Sorry."

The voice brought him back. He gave the cabbie a big bill and got out.

"Jesus, thanks, buddy. Is there anything . . . ?"

"Go away."

The cab disappeared and Simon ached from being alone.

Numb, he went into the garage. He pushed the paint cans off the top of his tool chest with one powerful sweep and rummaged in the chest until he found his gun; an old .45-caliber Colt western revolver. Scrounging, he found one live round of ammunition in the bottom corner of the chest.

He loaded the single shell into the cylinder and clicked it up until the next action would bring it under the pistol's hammer. He thought about what Coco used to say back in the Kansas whorehouse. "Suicide, Simon, it kills two people. That's what it's for."

He put the gun in his waistband and peed in the corner of the garage. His penis was so shrunken he could hardly get a hold of it. Shivering, he wondered what Carol would do if he shot himself.

He saw her mouth fall open and scream, "Oh, my God, no." She fainted and had to be carried away. She screamed to Dwayne, "I loved him—I loved him. I only loved him. Get away, Dwayne—don't touch me. My life is lost without my precious Simon."

But another idea wiped the smirk from his brain. Carol was just finished reading a bright yellow telegram and looked up to say, "Loser, what a loser. I surely did the right thing." And Dwayne was there in the shadows. "What is it, special Carol?" Carol smiled at Dwayne lovingly. "Nothing, darling, believe me when I tell you, *nothing* at all." She threw the telegram into the fireplace and when it had disappeared into crisp blackness, she laughed and walked away holding hands with Dwayne.

The illusion couldn't have been more real. Simon stood there frozen until a fluttering piece of garbage out on the lawn stole his attention. He ran out of the garage and up to the front of the house.

Inside, the air was stale and there was the smell of garbage. The house was a mess. He walked through to the bedroom and stared at the impressions left in the carpet by the feet of their big bed. He lay down on the floor where the bed had been.

He stared up at the crack in the stuccoed ceiling that needed repair. The same crack he had concentrated on a thousand times so as not to ejaculate prematurely when Carol sat atop him during sex. A powerful black feeling of doom settled over him. He tried to stand but couldn't. He crawled.

Soaked with perspiration, he crawled around the house until dust from the carpet sent him into a sneezing jag. He crawled past the sliding doors into the hall closet and curled into a ball. He lay in a semiconscious state until someone was rocking him, pushing his shoulder with a foot.

He looked up to find Carol standing above him. She stood in the closet's entrance dressed in red running shorts and a black leotard. She carried her portable hair dryer in her hand.

"Are you all right?" she asked.

He rubbed his eyes to make sure. He didn't speak but reached excitedly into his pocket to produce the diamond ring. He got onto his knees and held it up as close as he could to her face.

She said, "All right, Simon, I see. It's a diamond ring."

Looking at her, Simon thought she was beautiful. His mind stuttered but he fought for propriety, for normalcy. He made what he felt was his most important case. "It may be a ring to you, Carol, but it represents an attitude to me . . . my new attitude."

"It's too late, Simon." She stepped back to turn and he was onto his feet. He dropped the ring in his pocket and grabbed her arm.

"You piece of shit," he screamed. "You picked me."

Carol said, "No, I did not. I most certainly did not . . . pick you." She withdrew her arm from his grip.

He froze. His head swam searching for the truth. She had picked him. He knew it. But she looked him cold in the eye and lied. He thought about Andy. How he said all women play a game. Lying comes naturally.

"You fuck," he said, pulling out the .45. He jammed it against her breast. "I'll kill you, you—"

"Ouch, Simon, don't do that. You hurt me. And don't act so immature. I'm not afraid of you, and that silly old gun."

"Suck my cock, or I'll kill you."

She laughed. "You've got to be kidding. Don't you understand, Simon, it's done. I am not on your side anymore."

Disgusted, Carol turned and walked away. She walked out of the house.

Simon felt the blood drain from his face as he went to the window to watch her. Her nose was in the air. She jogged down to a waiting car, a new Mercedes sedan.

Simon aimed the gun at them but couldn't find the nerve to fire. His hand ached so badly holding the gun up he finally let it hang at his side, which was worse. He tucked the gun into his pants.

The Mercedes pulled away. Simon reached out after it. The car disappeared up the street.

The shrieking was back, worse than before. He stood in the

same spot until he couldn't take any more, and ran out the door down to the garage.

He brought a handful of red safety flares out from behind a set of tires. He tore the tops off them while he walked out into the driveway. He lit them all and threw the first one through the glass window of the bedroom.

He threw the second one there too and the rest into any of the other windows that would break. The big bay window wouldn't shatter and bounced the flare back onto the lawn. He threw the last one into the junk, the paint cans, at the rear of the garage. He sat down on the lawn to watch.

Shortly, smoke began to ooze, then billow from the broken windows of the house. The rear of the garage was in flames.

Someone, a neighbor, came running. She screamed, "My God, Simon, what are you doing?" He shot her in the face.

He walked slowly up the street. At the top of the rise, he turned and watched the roof of the house catch on fire. Then the entire house seemed to burn. A heavy cloud of black smoke began to rise and fill the sky.

The neighbor woman was up onto her hands and knees, crawling in circles.

Simon walked and walked and never did hear sirens.

After what seemed an hour or more he found himself in Beverly Hills on Wilshire Boulevard across from a large modern sporting goods store. He went in. He brought a box of .45-caliber ammunition up to the checkout counter.

The clerk asked where his shoes were and looking more closely, paled to see his feet were bleeding. He saw the gun in his waistband and when he looked into Simon's eyes, swallowed hard to say, "That's okay. . . take them . . . forget about it, just don't . . ."

When Simon walked away, the clerk scampered out from behind the counter to run to the rear of the store.

Simon walked to the corner and sat on a bus bench in the sun. A young blond female in a white dress sat at the other end of the bench. He loaded the .45 and put it into his lap. The girl watched and didn't seem affected at all. He held the diamond ring out to her. She smiled and offered him a puff of a joint.

TWENTY

Hero turned up the theater house lights and went all through the place with Stretch. He opened the exit doors, let the day in and, moving fast but conscientiously, had a decent look around.

He checked the office and projection booth and left them both unlocked. Backstage, he found the phone off the hook, hanging against the wall, and a fresh puddle of vomit. He secured the phone. Stretch found Bill Robinson's white shoe outside the rear southerly exit door. Hero cursed out loud and swore he'd get this guy. If it was the last thing he did.

Hero met Dwight in front of the theater excited and convinced that The Terror had just left the place a short time before.

Dwight had four good men with him. Hero hurriedly explained what he knew and gave them the set of theater keys. He told the men to get into the theater and dig, but mostly to set up security and to pass it to the West Side team when they arrived.

"Don't let anybody up into the attic but Forensics . . . nobody. We don't need any heavy hands to screw this one up."

The men dispersed into the theater and Hero brought Dwight with him, running to the telephones.

"Call Simon Moon's office and check it out. I'll call Mike Trainer."

Mike Trainer, West Los Angeles chief of detectives, had worked all night and was at home sleeping, but his office put Hero through. As he quickly told Mike what he'd found, Dwight began to talk excitedly into his pay phone.

"What, he did what . . . ?"

Hero hung up and anxiously waited.

Dwight hung up to exclaim, "Holy mackerel, the guy, Simon Moon, just damn near killed his secretary. Punched her or something. Gave her a concussion and ran out of the office."

"When?"

"Just now, fifteen, twenty minutes ago."

"Jesus, do we know where he lives?"

"Sure, it's right here, on my pad. Here it is."

"Let's go. Stretch, come on. Let's get this son of a bitch, Dwight, once and for all."

Outside, Hero scooped up Stretch and threw him into the back seat of Dwight's police Plymouth.

Dwight drove fast. Two perfect hands weaving them in and out of traffic. Hero turned on the siren and lights.

"Won't we scare him off?" Dwight asked.

"I hope so," Hero said. "Maybe save somebody's life. But we'll get him. Don't worry about that. We'll get him." Hero rubbed his hands together and could hardly wait.

Traffic pulled over or stopped for them and they opened their radio for all calls. Stretch was loving the ride. Back and forth, back and forth he ran across the slippery back seat as the police Plymouth careened through West Los Angeles.

Hero and Dwight didn't speak but sat in stiff anticipation, their adrenaline coursing, their minds to themselves.

As many times as Hero had been through this end of the city, things today seemed different, more distinct. Everywhere there appeared to be high-rise construction. Powerful concrete and steel-faced modern architecture that went forever up into the sun. There was excitement, vitality in the city's growth.

A fire call came over the radio. Then the shooting.

"Holy Toledo," Dwight said, "that's the place. That's Moon's house that's on fire."

"Yeah. Jesus Christ. And now somebody's got a gun."

A minute later they saw the smoke; thick and black, filling the sky. Dwight took the last corner with a two-wheeled screech and roared up in front of the house; the first authority to arrive.

The house was almost totally ablaze. A group of neighbors gathered around someone who was down on the front lawn.

A woman with curlers in her hair ran down to the car screaming hysterically, "She's been shot, she's been shot, she's been shot in the head."

"Get some more help," Hero said, handing Dwight the radio microphone. He ran up the front lawn to see. The yard was hot from the fire.

He broke through the crowd yelling, "Back, back, stand back—Police."

The woman lay on her back. Her eyes were glazed from shock but she was conscious. When Hero got close, she whispered, "Will I live? Am I going to die?"

Hero took her pulse, which seemed strong. He examined the wound. A deep gully of a wound that ran from the front of her hairline straight back into her scalp. There was not a lot of bleeding. Hero felt the wound. Her skull seemed intact, not torn apart as it would have been had the shot been fired an inch lower.

"Yes, I think you are going to live. You've been grazed. You're lucky. Now tell me, who did this to you?"

She licked her dry lips, blinked and spoke in a high-toned English accent. "Oh dear, Simon did it. Simon shot me."

"Where is he?" Hero asked.

"Oh," she singsonged, "I wouldn't know that."

Hero grasped her shoulders and wanted to shake her but asked her firmly instead, "Try to remember. Did he have a car? Which way did he go . . . anything. Try and think."

237

"Oh, he walked. He was walking, all right. He shot me and walked away up the rise. He was burning his own house. He looked quite insane. Quite mad."

Standing, Hero yelled for Dwight. Then he stood glaring up the street in the direction Simon Moon had gone.

"Dwight, stay here with her until an ambulance comes. She seems all right but you never know."

"But—"

"I'm taking your car. Get another one as soon as you can. Stay in touch by radio. He's on foot, and he's got a gun."

Dwight went to work on the injured woman with a couple of blankets, and Hero ran for the car.

With the light and siren off, Hero scoured the area. He zoomed the streets, stopping to look up and down alleys and in backyards. "Slow down," he told himself, "you'll run somebody over." But he couldn't. If anything, as the minutes dragged on, he drove even faster.

Jumping a curb, he roared down Manning Avenue. He double-checked the radio to make sure all channels were open.

Starting, stopping, searching, a half hour went by. But Hero wasn't concentrating on time. He was gripping the wheel and sweating, thinking about the women Simon Moon had butchered with his bare hands. He pictured the corpses. He thought about Bill Robinson. He kept his mind there, his ire up to pursue.

Beyond the obvious relief to society, he didn't want to consider the significance of concluding this case. After all this time. To get The Terror. What it would mean to him, to his future. He thought about Kay. Forty-five minutes were gone.

Dwight came over the radio. He was alone in a black-and-white a few blocks north of Hero.

They worked the area together and got out an all-points bulletin. An hour was gone.

As he was beginning to lose all hope of finding the killer, a general police alert came. A big insane-looking man had just walked out of Abercrombie and Fitch, a high-class Beverly Hills sporting goods store, with a box of .45-caliber ammunition.

"Abercrombie and Fitch, that's below Beverly Drive, isn't it, Dwight?" he asked into the mike.

"Yes, I know the place exactly. Buy my wool socks there. It's right at Canon Drive and Wilshire Boulevard. It's on Wilshire though, not Canon."

"Let's go. I'm two minutes away."

"Me too. I'm right behind you."

"Go in from the side, Dwight, down Canon or up Canon. I'll go straight in Wilshire. We'll meet in the middle of the block from two directions." Hero floored it.

"Hero," the radio squawked, "this is Banyon in Beverly Hills. What's up?"

"We're in pursuit of a man we believe to be the Los Angeles Terror. He's armed and *extremely* dangerous. We think he's the guy that just grabbed that .45-caliber ammunition at Abercrombie's. We're crossing over, coming into Beverly Hills. I want this guy bad."

"Okay, he's yours, but we're moving on it too."

"That's okay, that's good. Come in from the east but—"

"Hero, wait. Wait a minute."

Hero turned the radio up and crossed into Beverly Hills next to the Hilton Hotel. He gunned it.

"Hero, this is Banyon. One of our motors has got a visual on the guy. He's sitting on a bus bench at Wilshire and Reeves next to a girl. He's—wait a minute." He clicked off and back. "He's armed. Holding a Colt western which looks like a .45 in his lap. Waving the damned thing around. He's laughing and talking to the girl."

"Shit," Hero said angrily. "Keep the motor back. I'm almost there."

"Me too, Chief," from Dwight.

"Banyon, what's he doing now?"

"Same thing. Sitting there talking to the dame."

"Okay, close off Wilshire. Hold the traffic from the east. I'm going in. I can see the area now."

Banyon said, "You got it. I'm coming over myself." He cut out and when Hero swerved around a city bus, he saw them.

The big-shouldered man, with the Colt .45 in his lap, that he knew to be Simon Moon, The Terror; and the blond girl. They sat next to each other on the bus bench. There were plenty of other pedestrians too but no one on top of them, or immediately close. Hero's heart pounded.

Because of his speed and excitement, Hero was very close, fast. Not wanting to pass them, he hit the brakes. The Plymouth screeched and slid sideways into the middle of Wilshire Boulevard to stop.

Traffic immediately began to pile up behind him. Simon Moon had to see him. Hero held onto the steering wheel in an absurd crouch and watched. Stretch jumped up front next to him.

Sure, absolutely. The Terror, Simon Moon, could see him. It was a cinch. The girl too, but they sat there in the sun talking as though oblivious.

Then, with a sudden roar and slam, Dwight was there too. Up onto the sidewalk across the street and out quickly to kneel behind the trunk of his car.

The streets began to crawl with cops. They were down the block by the original motor who had first made contact, holding back Wilshire traffic, blocking off Canon and then Reeves. They were in back of Hero diverting everything. No one ventured in front of Hero and Dwight. They were the point men.

"Jesus," Hero sighed, his heart beating wildly. "It looks like we've got him boxed in. Finally. But why in the hell doesn't he move? Get up and run. Does he want to be taken? What's he going to do with that fucking .45? And the girl, what's her story? Are they blind? Goddamn, what a time to sit in the sun talking."

Hero couldn't stop staring at Simon Moon. His hugeness, his positively psychotic demeanor. The gun in his lap or hand, back and forth.

He waited for the men to get in place, impressed with the Beverly Hills police; famous for a two-minute response. Anywhere in the city in two minutes.

Now the area was almost entirely cordoned off, secure. A few more seconds. Hero gripped the steering wheel, his mind racing with decisions.

When he smelled it, he sniffed again, but reacted too late. Stretch's instincts were quicker than Hero's.

In the time it took to smell the aroma, register the word marijuana and shout, "No, Stretch," the dog, the marijuana sniffer, was out the car's window and gone. "Shit, no," Hero yelled. "Holy shit, no."

Then the dog was up onto the bench between Simon Moon and the girl. He began to bark. Exasperated, Hero kicked the dash and jumped out to crouch behind the vehicle.

Simon Moon waved his gun as he talked.

A bright reflection over at Dwight's car caught Hero's eye. There was no question. The reflection was of nickel plating.

Dwight had his cannon out, his Magnum. Hero saw him aiming with not one but both of his perfect hands. The best shot in the world.

"No, Dwight, no," Hero yelled. "Jesus, watch out for Stretch."

The weiner dog surprised Simon. His yapping threw a discord into the day; Simon's sense of well-being with the blond girl who looked nice wearing the diamond ring.

The girl petted the dog and blew a puff of dope into his face. He quit barking which was a good thing because Simon would have killed him. He thought he could kill lots of things right now. Anything that got in his way. He had the inkling.

The girl gave the dog another hit and he sat down between them to wag his tail.

"They want *me,*" the girl said, gesturing with her bejeweled hand to the police who were acting frantic in the streets around them.

She nudged Simon to show she had a rumpled-up new dress with the price tag still on, in her purse. "I stole it," she said. "They are after me to put me back in. Fuck 'em, let 'em come, the pigs. Want another hit?"

Simon took another puff and looked up into the sun. It was a splendid white sun with a blazing indistinguishable periphery.

He sighed and wanted to relax but something caught his eye; a reflection. The bright reflection of a silver gun across the street. It snapped him back to a certain reality, to survival. To panic.

Simon grabbed the girl by her frail neck and yanked her over in front of him. He jumped to his feet, knocking the dog to the ground.

Using the screaming girl as a shield he hurried across Wilshire Boulevard toward the reflecting gun, to the closest vehicle. The dog tore at his pants leg.

Straining to aim but unable to make a clear shot, Hero watched in helpless frustration.

Screaming, "Back...back," The Terror made it to Dwight's car. He was wrestling the girl, kicking Stretch and getting into the car when Dwight attempted a shot.

Hero thought it was a crazy time to try it with all of the movement. But a single loud explosion from Dwight's Magnum and a metallic twang echoed out across the city. Everyone seemed to stop and hold to see except Simon Moon who was into the car in a flash and away with a screeching roar. Someone else tried a shot, shattering the rear window of the car.

Two motors went down with a crashing slam as the police car rammed through the barricade and sped off north through Beverly Hills.

Hero ran to the scene yelling, "Wait...wait...hold everything just a minute. He won't get far."

The blond girl sat dazed where she had been dropped onto the street. She rubbed at a ring on her finger. Stretch sat next to her wagging his tail. Next to Stretch lay Simon Moon's Colt .45, the chamber blown away by Dwight's shot.

Police were running everywhere. Sirens were up. Tires screeched. Picking up Stretch, Hero motioned for Dwight to come along.

They drove fast, south out of Beverly Hills and west up Olympic Boulevard.

"What's up, Chief? Where are we going?"

Hero didn't feel like talking. He drove with his jaw clenched, praying that he was right.

Coming down Westwood Boulevard they saw it at the same time. The black-and-white police car, the rear window shattered, parked in front of the theater.

Adrenaline screamed through Hero's veins. His ears burned.

"Jeesus, Hero, it's the car. How in heck did you . . ?"

"Where else, Dwight? Where else would he go to feel safe—to hide?"

Moving fast, fighting to control his excitement, Hero scolded Stretch to "stay" but on second thought paused to lock him in the car.

Surprisingly, the theater was open for afternoon business. The front doors were open wide but unattended, as was the ticket booth. Two pedestrians stood inside next to the candy counter looking befuddled.

Then two uniformed ticket people appeared walking fast through the lobby with the manager. They were headed up the pink staircase. Guns drawn, Hero and Dwight fell in step.

A man lay motionless down the hallway beneath the ventilating shaft. The grill cover lay against the wall next to a stepladder. Another man Hero recognized from Forensics knelt, attending the unconscious man. A flash camera lay broken and scattered around them over the floor.

When the kneeling man saw Hero, he jumped excitedly to his feet to point into the black hole in the wall above them. "He threw him right out of there. Pushed me aside, climbed in and threw Jim out bodily. Christ, the guy must be strong as a horse, and crazy as a—"

"Where is everybody?" Hero demanded.

"Gone, cleaned up. The bodies are on their way in. Everything is done except for shooting, photographing the place—all the angles. It was just me and Jim . . ."

"Is Jim . . . ?

"Alive? Yeah, just knocked out, I think. He's breathing."

After sending one of the theater employees to call the paramedics and West Side police, Hero stood with the others, in a silent group, staring up at the square black hole in the wall.

Suddenly, Hero broke away to move quickly to the stepladder. He climbed and was nearly into the hole before Dwight yelled, "No, no," and grabbed him from below. "No, Hero, are you nuts? Come on down, wait. He's cornered. Wait and we'll get help and shoot some tear gas up there and—"

"Dwight, let go of my leg."

"Don't do it, Chief. Please wait. Come on, I'm asking you to please wait . . ."

But Hero shook his leg free and was gone into the darkness.

Hero crawled through the metallic-sounding blackness until he reached the fan housing and the opening into the theater attic. He put his head in.

Holding perfectly still, straining to listen, he heard only the pounding of his heart in his ears. Shit, he said to himself. Completely black.

Wet with perspiration, he tried to use his head, to qualify this thing, but it was no use. Good judgment wouldn't come. Only emotion. The desire to win. This was it anyway. The final test. His most important good deed. What he had brought himself to. The flourish. The culmination.

Poised before the attic opening, he screamed in his head, All right, Simon Moon, I'm coming in, and this ain't Bill Robinson or some helpless woman either. Fire your best shot, you sick son of a bitch. Here comes Hero Fiddleman.

Placing his gun onto the tin behind him, with elbows out, Hero took a deep breath and dove into the attic.

Ten feet in he stopped to stand and gape into the darkness that surrounded him. Nothing. He wouldn't breathe. He hung in the black, hands outstretched, taut with readiness; his hair on end. Where is he? Where?

Suddenly someone, probably Dwight, was behind him with a flashlight to illuminate the attic in the most insane, probing way imaginable, and in that first dimly lit instant, from off to his immediate right, came The Terror, raging, "You're in my place."

There was a click from Dwight's Magnum and Hero yelled, "No." Simon grabbed Hero by the head.

God, Hero flashed with a chill. What power, vise grips. But he unloaded, too.

Muscling into position, Hero threw five staccato punches as hard as he knew how into Simon's left side. The brute's ribs cracked out loud. He screamed but had Hero by the hair trying to do something to his eyes.

Move, Hero urged himself. Next, instinct. He kicked hard and accurately into Simon's testicles with a thunk.

Simon let go to hold his stomach and stare. Close, they hesitated to look into each other's eyes in the crazy light. There was a stifling closeness, perspiration, a breathlessness.

"Come on, Bad Ass," Hero said, panting. "Show me what you've got. Show me how you do it to the women."

Simon's eyes went dark. He screamed and pretended to swing with his left but suckered to drive a right into Hero's ear and send him sprawling.

Hero must have lost consciousness because Simon was somehow over him forcing a huge, incredibly powerful hand over his air supply. A tingling fear raced up Hero's spine as he tried in vain for a desperate breath. Perspiration fell onto him from the growling beast above.

Frantic, Hero found a finger and bit until it cracked.

Simon howled and let up enough for Hero to gulp a breath and sit up, driving his forehead into Simon's face. Simon's nose broke loud and wet.

Hero was up to kick, but Simon closed his arms around his legs and shimmied up Hero's body to try for a crushing bear hug.

Face to face now, grappling, fighting for position, for life, they twisted and turned and suddenly, the floor was gone beneath them.

They slammed past rafters as they crashed for the stage. Engulfed by abrupt amplified sounds, they fell through an eerie kind of hallucinogenic atmosphere illuminated by colorful, momentarily blinding images.

In midair, Hero did his thing. Mustering in that split second every bit of training he'd ever had, every bit of tenacity, he went to his advantage: his fast mind.

Writhing, he upended to get one foot under The Terror's jaw as they hit the stage. And he made sure that's just how they landed. Onto Simon's head with a loud snap. "You son of a bitch."

There was the theater, and the loudness of his own breathing, but he heard it: a murmur.

Bending, kneeling, Hero strained to listen. It was a last dying gasp.

Simon Moon whispered, "Thank you."

"Jesus," Hero said.

The audience was not large but they made a loud fuss until the lights came up. Then the motion picture stopped as did the sound track.

Hero stood above Simon Moon, The Terror, and as he did, thought that he perceived an incredible look of peace come over the man, a look of normalcy now. It made Hero sigh.

Dwight's voice was there above the confusion. "Hero, are you all right? Chief, talk to me."

When Hero put his hand out to quiet Dwight, the theater became still.

With his head hung, Hero walked slowly down the stage, then stopped to turn around and stare back at Simon. As though to make sure.

Standing there in the silence, a feeling of pride came, accompanied by an overwhelming, exhaustive relief at seeing The Terror dead, the women in the city safe.

But there was a melancholy too. Relinquishing something that had held his interest, kept him going, better, obsessed him for so long. Victor Hugo's dogged Javert. Plodding and plodding, to what end? It had ended. The reasons were suddenly unimportant.

Dwight was up close, speaking in a confidential tone. "What's wrong? Hero. What's the matter?"

Hero smiled and said, "Nothing, old friend. You're a good man, that's all. Good for the job, my job... to preserve and to protect. It's all yours, Dwight. Eat it, sleep it, swing with it. Good luck."

Flabbergasted, Dwight tried to speak but Hero shushed him to walk away.

Feeling better than he could remember in a long time, Hero walked through the lobby and out into the bright afternoon. He brought an exuberant Stretch out of the car to hold and pet. Stretch slopped him on the chin.

Standing in the warm sun, he squinted to check the Santa Monica Mountains to the northwest. The air was cleaning up fine. He thought about a good long run and his beautiful Kay, all he had to share with her later on.

Those who are smart
don't pretend about art
there's no rhyme
for the time that is spent
Hasten to say
there must be a way
So let's pray our cranial rent
To learn all the stuff
is not quite enough
for the juices must curdle within
So open your heart
and you'll have a part
safely away from the din
Please seize a place
away from the pace
where creation
at ease you can nibble
and lo with good luck
and omission of shuck
down with the plebiscite's dribble
Ruler of all
whether short whether tall
deep pleasures
your reward will be
And the time that's been lost
without knowing the cost
new person
will not even see.

                                    The beginning.